THEIR
WICKED
GAMES

BOOKS BY D.K. HOOD

DETECTIVES KANE AND ALTON PREQUELS

Lose Your Breath

Don't Look Back

DETECTIVES KANE AND ALTON SERIES

Don't Tell a Soul

Bring Me Flowers

Follow Me Home

The Crying Season

Where Angels Fear

Whisper in the Night

Break the Silence

Her Broken Wings

Her Shallow Grave

Promises in the Dark

Be Mine Forever

Cross My Heart

Fallen Angel

Pray for Mercy

Kiss Her Goodnight

Her Bleeding Heart

Chase Her Shadow

Now You See Me

D.K. HOOD

THEIR WICKED GAMES

bookouture

Published by Bookouture in 2023

An imprint of Storyfire Ltd.
Carmelite House
50 Victoria Embankment
London EC4Y 0DZ

www.bookouture.com

ISBN: 978-1-83790-312-2
eBook ISBN: 978-1-83790-311-5

To Michelle. If there's an example of how to be strong and resilient, it's you. You're titanium.

PROLOGUE

SUNDAY MORNING

Spring break had been a long time coming, and excited to be free from school at last, Leo Kelly and his best friends Ash Rogers and Zoe Ward headed into Stanton Forest for a day of fishing. They'd chosen the Devil's Punchbowl waterhole, a favorite spot and not one discovered by the tourists. Being some ways from the hiking trails, it offered a secluded and bountiful day's fishing. A stream running from one of the many lakes below Black Rock Falls fed the waterhole and replenished the fish at a rapid rate. As they moved higher up the mountainside, a chill seeped through Leo's clothes, raising goosebumps on his flesh. He hadn't expected the morning to be so cold. As they moved deeper into the dense forest, he led his friends along the trail at a good pace. The way ahead narrowed to little more than an animal track and they dropped into single file, negotiating their fishing rods and backpacks through the vegetation. Scanning the forest for bears and other wildlife, he slowed when something moved ahead. A crack of a branch pierced the silence. The hairs on the back of his neck prickled and warning bells clanged in his head. Stopping abruptly, he peered through the gloom. "Did you see that?"

"Didn't see a thing." Zoe flicked her long blonde hair over one shoulder. "You imagining things again, Leo?"

"Whoa." Ash adjusted his backpack and stared into the forest. "I figured it was my imagination, but yeah, I thought I saw someone moving through the trees a ways back."

Concerned, Leo turned to look at him. "I thought I saw someone in camouflage, moving ahead and to the left." Nervous, he glanced over his shoulder. "Do you figure someone is following us?"

"There." Ash pointed into the trees, his face creased with concern. "That can't be the same person. If they'd crossed the trail, we'd have seen them. Maybe it's just hunters."

"Not in this part of the forest, and they'd be wearing orange vests, not hiding behind camouflage." Zoe moved closer to Leo. "It's too far to go back. We should push on to the fishing hole. There might be other people there."

"We should spread out." Ash scanned the forest in all directions. "We don't know who is out there and we make an easy target bunched up like this."

Heart racing, Leo nodded. "Okay, we run from tree to tree, stopping and then moving on. If they're still following us by the time we get to the fishing hole, I'll call the sheriff."

"You can't do that." Ash indicated to Zoe with his chin. "We don't have fishing permits and you know the first thing that she'll do is ask us to produce them."

Rubbing the back of his neck, Leo looked from one to the other. "You just tell her you're watching me fish. We can hide your fishing rods in the trees and come back for them later."

A rustle close by and a shadow moving silenced them. Someone was stalking them. Panic gripped Leo. He must get his friends to safety. Using hand gestures to indicate he planned to go ahead, he took off, moving swiftly from tree to tree. He glanced behind him, scanned the forest, and then motioned for them to follow. Crunching footsteps came from his right and something whizzed past his head. He gaped in horror as a crossbow bolt thwacked into a nearby trunk. Fear had him by the throat as he ducked low and ran to the next tree. Midstride, a rush of searing pain sliced into the back of his leg. He hung on to a tree and stared in horror at the bolt protruding out of his flesh. "I've been hit. Go back." He waved frantically at the others. "Call the sheriff."

Ten yards behind him, Zoe was on the move. She dashed toward him and opened her mouth to say something, but in a sickening thud, a bolt pierced her neck. Frozen with fear, Leo stared in disbelief as her eyes widened, and her hands flapped wildly at her throat before she crumpled to the ground. Trembling with terror and fighting back waves of nausea, Leo dragged his injured leg toward her. Panic gripped him at the sight of her wide vacant eyes. Unable to make his mouth form words, he stared around the slight bend in the trail. Slumped on his side, Ash lifted his gaze to him and made a gurgling sound. Blood bubbled from his open mouth, his eyes rolled back, and he fell sideways, eyes fixed and staring.

Terrified, Leo looked all around. He wanted to scream and tear someone apart. "Why are you doing this?"

An arrow hit him like a cannonball to the chest. Stunned, he fell hard on his side unable to take a breath and grasped the bolt protruding from his chest. Running footsteps thundered toward him, but the last thing he heard was whoops of joy before the forest spun and darkness rushed up to swallow him.

ONE

SUNDAY AFTERNOON

Eyes squeezed tight, Sheriff Jenna Alton pressed her cheek into the back of her husband's leather jacket as the motorcycle accelerated along the highway. Exhilarated, she tightened her grip around his waist as they flew past vehicles so fast she could hardly take a breath. When the smell of pine trees and fresh mountain air hit her in the face, she opened her eyes, but the forest was just a flash of green. She trusted Kane's driving but it had taken him some time to convince her to ride with him. Knowing his love of speed, she'd been hesitant. As they whipped past more vehicles, she peeked over his shoulder. Ahead the highway was clear and she relaxed a little. Soothed by the purring sound of the engine, the wind slamming into her, but still the feeling of vulnerability scared her. One small mistake at high speed and it was them against the blacktop and anything else in their way.

Off the grid, ex-special forces sniper and Secret Service agent, with ties right up to the Oval Office, David Kane had come into her life almost five years ago, after she'd arrived in Black Rock Falls, and he'd become her deputy sheriff. His story was similar to her own. After taking down and giving evidence against underworld kingpin Viktor Carlos, Jenna had left the FBI, and her life as DEA agent Avril Parker, far behind. Under witness protection but living in plain sight, with a new face and name, she'd fought her way to become sheriff in the backwoods town of Black Rock Falls.

During her time as sheriff, she had gathered a superior team around her. She had trained Deputy Jake Rowley and hired Zac Rio, a gold shield detective from LA. Rio had a retentive memory, apart from other gifts, and was able to recall crime scenes and make evaluations on the fly. Dr. Shane Wolfe, the medical examiner also doubled as Kane's handler, having been the voice in his ear during his tours of duty. Together they made up a superior crime-fighting team, which was just as well because Black Rock Falls had become known as Serial Killer Central. A series of novels covering the cases had become best-sellers and made the town a tourist destination. Although, why people flocked to possibly one of the most dangerous towns in the state confused her.

The motorcycle slowed and Kane turned off the highway and onto a narrow dirt road leading into the forest. They drove through dense pines for about half a mile before turning into a side road, posted with a sign warning that trespassers would be shot on sight, but Kane ignored the sign and they bounced over tire ruts along a dirt road weaving in and out of trees. The sound of water running in the distance came over the purr of the engine. As the road opened up into a clearing beside the river, she turned to see a neat cabin with smoke coming out of the chimney. Smiling at the sight, she relaxed the grip on Kane, her fingers numb from the effort of holding on so tightly. The motorcycle stopped in front of the stoop and she unfastened the strap on her helmet and let out a long breath. "Wow! You drive so fast. I don't figure I took a breath from the time we left till just now."

"Oh, sorry." Kane's brow wrinkled into a frown. "I should

have taken it easy for your first time on the Harley, but I figured you'd be fine as it's not your first ride on a motorcycle with me."

Shaking her head, Jenna smiled. "No need for an apology. I enjoyed the thrill and it's my fault for not riding with you sooner."

Kane had built the classic Harley, spending months locating parts and creating his dream machine. This along with a bullet-proof, bombproof missile of a black tricked-out truck affectionately known as the Beast were his pride and joy. The pressure of work meant that weekends like this one were few and far between, but they had struck gold when Special Agent Ty Carter and his partner, Jo Wells, arrived in town earlier in the week. Jenna had offered them the cottage on her ranch as a base while they investigated a local case. They were good friends, and she trusted them, so when Carter offered to care for their animals and give them the use of his fishing cabin for the weekend, they'd jumped at the chance.

Jenna's cat, Pumpkin, was self-sufficient, but Duke, Kane's bloodhound tracker dog, was very dependent on Kane and they rarely left him behind. After being found close to death, Kane had rescued the neurotic dog, who was so frightened of storms he hid, and words like *bath* and *vet* had to be spelled to avoid a meltdown. Duke trusted few people, but one of them was Carter, mainly because he'd bonded with Carter's Doberman and bomb-disposal dog, Zorro.

Scanning the area, Jenna grinned at Kane. "So, this is Carter's secret hideaway when he's in town." She ran her gaze over the log cabin. Although small, it backed up to the mountain and, surrounded by trees, it was safe and solid. A porch swing sat on the front stoop. Wisps of curled wood overflowed from a bucket beside a few sticks for whittling. It was just how she'd imagined it. "Why doesn't he stay here with Jo when he's on a case?"

"Oh, maybe because there's only one bedroom." Kane smiled at her. "When I went fishing with him, I slept in front of the fire. It's not a place to bring Jo. She'd be uncomfortable. She likes her own space." He pulled her close. "I don't intend to go fishing. Some nice walks and toasting marshmallows in front of an open fire sounds good to me."

Giggling, Jenna kissed him. "Okay, now I know why you wanted me to bring linen. I'm guessing Carter likes sleeping rough?"

"Nope, I just didn't want to leave him a pile of laundry." Kane shrugged. "I know he hauls his laundry to town to be washed." He gave a reluctant sigh and let her go. "I'll get the bags inside and go and start the generator." He pulled the saddlebags from the motorcycle and waved her ahead. "The key is above the door."

Jenna collected their helmets and led the way onto the stoop. She found the key and opened the door. To her surprise the inside was spotless, floors swept clean, and a fire was burning in the hearth. It was a small cabin, with a stuffed sofa before the fire, a small kitchen with table and chairs, and one dark bedroom with no window. "Is there a bathroom?"

"Outside, and a shower, but it's cold. The water is pumped straight from the river." Kane grinned at her. "It's only for one night. I'll heat some water and you can wash in the kitchen sink if it's too cold for you."

Shaking her head, Jenna laughed. "I'll be fine." She dived into the saddlebags and pulled out linen. I'll make up the bed. You get the generator working, it's as dark as a cave in that room."

"Sure." Kane disappeared outside.

Jenna walked around the cabin and checked out the small kitchen. The cabinets were packed with tinned goods, cans of coffee, milk powder, and dogfood. Everything was there for

Carter to survive on for a week or so with his dog. She blinked as lights flooded the cabin and took the linen into the bedroom. By the time Kane had chopped more wood and built up the fire, she'd finished making the bed and walked into the other room. "How come the fire was alight?"

"Carter dropped by to restock the kitchen. He'd already asked me if we wanted a night in the cabin and set the fire to make it cozy for us." Kane replaced the guard around the fire and straightened. "Grab my backpack and we'll go for a walk along the riverbank." He sighed. "It's strange not having Duke with us. I should have driven the Beast."

Jenna handed him his backpack, wondering why it weighed so much, and shook her head. "He loves to play with Zorro. It's like a vacation for him, but I do miss him. He's part of our family." She took his hand and they walked out of the door, locking it behind them. Her mind went to Kane's visit to their close friend Atohi Blackhawk, a Native American tracker, who owned Duke's mother and a number of bloodhounds. "Talking about family, it's been ages since Atohi took him to the res to put over his bitch. Did it take, do you know? Is Duke going to be a daddy?"

"He's been a daddy quite a few times and she had seven this time, so it's a lucky litter." Kane chuckled. "It's not something Blackhawk discusses with you, is all. Why?"

The thought of seeing a litter of puppies warmed Jenna's heart. "Can we have one of Duke's pups?"

"Blackhawk always offers me the pick of the litter, but I have Duke." He gave her a long look. "A puppy is a lot of work and a lifetime of care. They grow up real fast. Are you sure we have time to raise a puppy?"

Snorting, Jenna looked at him. "I sure hope so, because if a baby comes along, we won't have a choice." Her stomach dropped and a deep sadness engulfed her. "It's never going to happen, is it?"

"The doctor said we were both fine and stressing over it will only make things worse." Kane sighed and squeezed her hand as they headed toward the riverbank. "We've only been married for nine months, Jenna. Relax, enjoy our alone time together, because once we have a baby, life is going to become hectic, especially if you insist on continuing as sheriff." He stopped by the river and turned to her. "Whatever you decide, I'll support your decision."

Leaning into him, Jenna sighed. "Well, I guess it's a good thing because it's taking forever for the mayor to build the kindergarten." She looked at Kane. "How will we deal with security while the new cottage is being built?"

They'd discussed a cottage for a nanny, drawn up plans, and gotten approval. Jenna had made the suggestion and Kane had planned and organized it. Although, as both of them carried secrets, bringing a stranger into their lives would be dangerous, but if she decided to remain as sheriff, having a reliable trained person her baby knew would be an advantage if they were on a case.

"Wolfe is organizing it." Kane shrugged. As his handler and contact to the powers that be, Wolfe would make sure they were safe. "When the time comes, he'll organize a nanny."

Staring at the crystal-clear water, a chill slid over Jenna as the reminder that being married to Kane, a valuable asset to the government, had far-reaching complications. With a bounty on his head, Kane had already lost his previous wife in a car bombing. Even with a new name and face, his retinal scan, fingerprints, and DNA would never change and there was always a chance of discovery. She had the same problem, but Kane's enemies came from across the globe. The simple selection of a nanny could compromise him. She looked at him. "A puppy suddenly sounds easy. When can we go and look at them?"

"Soon." Kane smiled at her. "I'll call Blackhawk and ask him when they're ready to leave home. There is one proviso."

Frowning, Jenna looked at him. "And that is?"

"Duke has to like him." Kane scanned the forest ahead of them. "Or, he'll never come out from under our bed."

Jenna laughed. "Deal."

TWO

MONDAY

Sighing, Deputy Zac Rio pushed his chair away from his desk
and stared at the ceiling. He had two cases and neither of them
had offered up any leads. He had received a notification from
the Blackwater sheriff's department about a possible meth-
amphetamine lab setting up in their county. The group, under
surveillance by the Blackwater sheriff for some time, had disappeared along with the snow during the melt. Kane and Jenna
had hunted them down and discovered they'd stored equipment
and supplies in an abandoned warehouse on the outskirts of
town. They'd arrested a young man guarding the place, but
after going with Rowley to secure the scene, Rio had found the
warehouse empty and wiped clean. The two vans on site had
vanished. The only explanation was that the perpetrators had
been close by and moved their apparatus fast, which suggested a
large competent team. BOLOs on the vans had come up empty.
The man in custody wasn't talking and remained locked up in
county.

It was obvious the meth lab had moved to another base.
There were plenty of abandoned buildings all over. Black Rock

Falls spread across a wide area and it was impossible to search every inch, although he and Deputy Rowley had sent up the drones and completed a grid search daily over suspicious areas. They'd being comparing the images for the last week but no suspicious movements had been noted. He hoped that whoever was running the drug kitchen had moved on to another county, but Jenna had insisted they keep due diligence.

The next case involved Native American tracker Atohi Blackhawk. He was a good friend of Jenna and Kane. Last week he had come to the office with a list of suspected gravesites he'd discovered during his time in the forest. Rio and Rowley had taken the horses and escorted him back to the sites. They'd marked them all with crime scene tape and taken GPS coordinates. None of the graves appeared to be fresh, so they'd notified the ME. As Wolfe had Norrell Larson, a forensic anthropologist, on his team, she would head up the investigation. In the meantime, without a time frame to go on, Rio had little to do. Rowley had just returned from patrol and dropped into the seat at his desk. "Anything interesting happening out there?"

"Nope." Rowley added notes to his daybook. "I issued a few speeding fines. Booked three people for jaywalking and one person for allowing his dog to foul the sidewalk." He glanced over at him and smiled. "That's the most action I've had for a month."

Yawning, Rio pushed to his feet and went through the office to the kitchenette. He looked at Rowley over one shoulder. "We have takeout from Aunt Betty's Café and fresh coffee. We might as well take a break now. Just in case the sky falls in anytime soon." He chuckled.

They were halfway through their lunch, when Maggie, the receptionist on the front counter, came to his desk waving a piece of paper. Rio swallowed his coffee and looked up at her. "Is there a problem?"

"There sure is." Maggie slapped the paper down in front of him. "The forest warden found three bodies on one of the hiking trails. He just called it in. Here are his details and the coordinates."

"Did he give any other details?" Rowley was on his feet, pulling on his jacket.

"Nope. Only that you should get there ASAP." Maggie looked from one to the other. "Do you want me to contact the sheriff?"

Confused why the forest warden hadn't provided more details, Rio shook his head. "Not yet. We'll go and take a look. It might be a hunting accident. If it is, there's no need to disturb them."

"Okay." Maggie gave them a stern look. "Don't you forget to call in and give me your position. If you don't and get yourself into trouble out there, I won't be able to send you backup."

After being a gold shield detective in LA for two years prior to arriving in Black Rock Falls, Rio knew the deal, but he also understood Maggie felt she was responsible for them during Jenna and Kane's absence. He nodded and turned to grab survival packs out of the closet. "I'll call in when we get to the location, Maggie." He tossed a pack to Rowley, grabbed his jacket, and followed him out the door.

As Rowley headed for the location, Rio called the forest warden to get more information. "This is Deputy Zac Rio. We're on our way to your location. Can you give me an update on the bodies you found on the hiking trail?"

"We have three victims, all Caucasian, approximately sixteen to eighteen years old, two male and one female. All have sustained kill shots from, I suspect, an arrow. I doubt if this is a hunting accident, as this isn't a designated area for archers. It is a specifically marked hiking trail. I am convinced this is a homicide." The forest warden let out a shuddering sigh. *"I have one of my colleagues on horseback guarding the entrance to this trail,*

I'm approximately twenty yards from the crime scene. I haven't seen anyone in this area since I arrived, approximately ten minutes ago. We were following up reports of a mountain lion in the area, and managed to move it on, but other wildlife are moving in. We need to move these bodies before dark."

Running the protocol through his mind, Rio cleared his throat. "Okay, I'll notify the medical examiner and we'll be there shortly." He disconnected and then called Wolfe to explain the situation.

Fortunately, Rowley had been raised in the area and knew all the trails to the local fishing holes. After perusing the map, he'd taken advantage of the fire roads to get as close as possible, to the trail. Rio stepped out of the cruiser, and a cool breeze from the mountains, still carrying the frosty aroma of snow, brushed his cheeks. He inhaled deeply, knowing that the pine-scented fresh air wouldn't last long. He turned to Rowley. "Can you find your way from here?"

"Yeah, I used to come here all the time as a kid." Rowley collected his things from the back seat. "It's the worst-kept secret in town. I'll send Wolfe the directions to get here the way we came. If he follows his GPS, he'll be walking about an extra mile. I figure we're only about three or four hundred yards from the crime scene." He hung his backpack over one shoulder and took out his phone. He indicated to a trail on the left. "That way."

Slowly scanning the lush dense forest, Rio placed one hand on his arm. "We need to proceed with caution, there's possibly a killer on the loose in the forest. He could be considering us as his next victims right now. Make sure you inform Wolfe to be on his guard."

"Sure." Rowley turned slowly, looking all around. "Our Kevlar vests are in the back of my truck." He pulled open the back door and dragged them out. He handed one to Rio. "Better safe than sorry. These will stop a bullet or an arrow. I figure if he's attacking with a knife, he won't be game enough to take on both of us."

Rio removed his jacket and pulled on the vest. "Okay, but no talking once we're on the trail. I don't want to alert anyone of our presence until we get on-scene." He shrugged into his jacket and grabbed his rifle from the back of Rowley's truck. "Move out."

Stanton Forest surrounded Black Rock Falls from the lowlands to the foot of the mountains spreading west. At this time of year, after the melt when new growth was in abundance, the forest became dense and formidable. Walking the trails could be a beautiful or terrifying experience. As they walked, sunlight filtered through the trees, dappling the way ahead with constantly moving shadows and small patches of bright sunlight. As they went deeper, the sunlight was obscured by the dense canopy above, making small tunnels of darkness along the way. In fact, it was the perfect place for an ambush and many people intent on murder had used it to their advantage.

These facts were in the back of Rio's mind as they continued along the trail. With the wind from the mountain at their back, the stench of death didn't reach them until he spotted the crime scene tape flapping in the breeze. He pulled out his phone and called the forest warden to alert him to their presence. He pushed the phone back into his pocket and turned to Rowley. "The forest warden is on the other side of the victims." He pulled booties from his backpack and handed a pair to Rowley. "Suit up. We don't want to contaminate the scene." He understood that Rowley was squeamish. "Are you going to be okay, viewing the corpses?"

"Yeah, from here they don't look so bad." Rowley was staring down the pathway. "Although I figure the wildlife has chewed on them some."

Keeping to the perimeter of the trail, Rio led the way, constantly scanning all around for any sign of movement. The birds had been quite noisy on their way to the scene but had fallen silent on their arrival, which made Rio believe that the killer had left the immediate area. As they approached the first prone figure, he pulled out his phone and recorded the scene. "First victim is a male, Caucasian. He has one wound between the shoulder blades and another in his right thigh." He bent to lift the victim's arm. "Rigor has already set in." He swept his phone camera slowly around the body, taking in the immediate area.

"Those wounds have been made by a crossbow bolt." Rowley crouched down and peered at the victim's back. "I'd say his shirt was torn open like that when they removed the bolt. The wound is a typical shape, and I've seen it many times before." He pointed back up the trail. "The first spots of blood are there, and by the disturbance of the pine needles, he would have received the leg injury first and dragged himself here, before receiving the kill shot."

Impressed, Rio kept the camera running as they moved to the next body. "This is the body of a young woman, Caucasian, approximately sixteen years old. She has a through-and-through injury on the neck. He swung his camera back to Rowley. "What do you think?"

"Crossbow again, and with that injury, she might have staggered a few steps and then fell, but what is puzzling me is the trajectory of the bolt." Rowley turned slowly, peering into the trees. "Do you know how difficult it is to get a clean shot like this one, in a dense forest? There would be only one, maybe two, possible lines of sight. We need to get Kane here. He is the best person to track the trajectory of the bolts."

Nodding, Rio continued down the trail and discovered the third victim, another young Caucasian male with similar injuries to the young woman. He made out the forest warden sitting on his horse, surveying the area intently. He waved to him, and the man turned his horse toward him and stopped ten yards from the bodies. After recording the scene with care, Rio made the call to Jenna. "I'm so sorry to disturb you, but we have a triple homicide."

THREE

Concerned by Rio's call, Jenna leaned back on the porch swing, coffee in one hand, and stared at Kane. She'd put her phone on speaker the moment Rio had mentioned the word *homicide*. "Why is it the moment we leave town someone decides to start killing people?"

"From what Rowley was saying, we may be looking at an initial hunting accident." Kane stood and pulled her to her feet. "We need to be on scene. If he is correct, we're not talking about serial killers. It could be an opportunistic thrill kill or an accident and they panicked and killed everyone." He frowned and scratched his cheek. "I just hope it isn't some type of initiation. With all the strange cults emerging of late, anything is possible."

Staring at him in disbelief, Jenna swallowed the last mouthful of coffee and headed inside. She'd already stripped the bed and packed the linen for the trip home. They'd planned to hike farther up the mountain, and return home in time for lunch, stopping by Aunt Betty's Café on the way for takeout. She took one last glance over her shoulder at the beautiful scenery. The cabin was set in one of the most tranquil settings she'd ever seen. It was no wonder Carter had purchased this cabin to get away from the pressures of his job. The few hours she'd had here alone with Kane had been wonderful. The phone chimed again and from the caller ID it was Wolfe. "Morning. If you are calling about the three bodies in Stanton Forest, Rio and Rowley called just before. We're heading in that direction now. I have the coordinates and Rowley's directions to get there, but we don't have the Beast."

"Then I suggest you swing by home and get it, and maybe bring along Carter and Jo. I figure we're dealing with more than one killer, and they could still be in the immediate area. I would advise caution." Wolfe lowered his voice and she could hear him moving away from the low conversation around him. *"Is Dave listening in?"*

"Yeah, I'm here." Kane moved closer to her side.

"I'm seeing multiple shooters. Rowley insists the injuries have been inflicted by crossbow bolts. I figured this was an ambush. I need you on scene ASAP to assist me in determining the trajectory of the shots." Wolfe took a deep breath and let it out with a sigh. *"Dave, this homicide is very familiar. It resembles a cleanup team."*

"That involves teenagers?" Kane scratched his chin. "What could they possibly know to trigger such a reaction and why leave the bodies in the forest? Nah, it makes no sense whatsoever. There has to be another explanation."

"I'm just telling you what I'm seeing here." Wolfe's agitation came through the speaker. *"Think about it, Dave. When did you ever clean up the bodies?"*

"Well, my targets were usually a long distance away and surrounded by the enemy." Kane shrugged. "Mine were hit-and-run missions. This is different."

"This is an extermination." Wolfe cleared his throat. *"These kids didn't stand a chance."*

Horrified, Jenna stared at Kane. She understood what his work as a sniper involved, but what Wolfe was intimating chilled her to the bone. She handed Kane her phone, went to the sink to wash the cups, and then collected her things and pushed them into the saddlebags. Behind her, Kane was speaking in hushed tones to Wolfe. When he disconnected, she handed him the saddlebags and his helmet. "We need to get on scene as soon as possible. You can fill me in with the gory details when we get back to the ranch."

"Are you mad at me?" Kane turned her to face him.

Trying to keep the concern from her voice, Jenna shook her head. "No, it's just when you speak about your missions, you're so cold. Targets, not people. Were they ever people to you?"

"I thought you were okay with what I did before I came to Black Rock Falls." Kane examined her face, his eyes troubled. "Once we became involved, I never hid the fact that I was a government assassin and killed enemies who threatened the freedom of the USA. I'll never apologize for what I did, nor am I sorry. For me it was just a job and, yeah, I would do it again, and will do it again if I'm ever called upon to protect my country." He cupped her cheek. "We live in freedom because soldiers like me lay down their lives for the good of all."

Shaking her head slowly, Jenna stared into his eyes. She knew and loved this man, and seeing him doubt her cut deep. "I know what you did. You've never hidden anything from me, well, apart from your actual missions. I believe we're at cross purposes here. Do you honestly believe what you did during your time in service matters to me? What disturbed me about Wolfe's call was what I'm sure is worrying him too: the evidence points to a pack of killers roaming the forest, which means any one of us could be next, or they might target the entire team."

"I seriously doubt that they would still be there." Kane headed outside and secured the saddlebags onto the Harley.

Jenna followed and climbed onto the motorcycle behind him. "I sure hope not."

. . .

After arriving at the ranch, Jenna dashed inside to change, while Kane brought Carter and Jo up to speed. Jo Wells' specialty as a behavioral analyst took profiling to a whole new level. Her take on the crime scene would be crucial, and having her as a friend Jenna could go to for advice was priceless. Jo's work and current series of books on the workings of serial killers' minds often had her away from the Snakeskin Gully field office speaking at FBI seminars. It was fortunate their last case had brought them to Black Rock Falls.

Pulling her Kevlar vest over her head, she headed out the front door. Kane and the others were suited up and ready to leave. Duke came bounding over to her, tail waving like a windmill. She bent to rub his ears before she headed for the Beast. She smiled at Jo and Carter. "Thanks for taking care of everything for us."

"Anytime." Carter smiled. "How did you like my little slice of Shangri-la?"

Jenna glanced at Kane. "Perfect. It's so peaceful there and the moonlight on the river at night is mesmerizing." She pulled open the truck door. "It took a murder to drag us away. I'm glad you're both here. Wolfe is very concerned about this one."

"I'm not surprised." Carter climbed into the back seat and wedged himself between the door and both dogs. Jo squeezed in the other side. "It sounds complicated, and if the killers are still hanging around, a show of force is a good thing. They won't be expecting the FBI on scene as well."

They headed along the highway through town and took Stanton to the forest. The forest looked just the same, and was green and fragrant with a hint of snow from the mountains, but the beauty Jenna had come to love hid dark secrets. The fresh murders, and now the possibility of unsolved cold cases, weighed on her shoulders the deeper they went into the dim interior. After negotiating the fire road, they found the team's vehicles and made their way along the narrow trail in single file.

Jenna notified Wolfe they were on scene as Kane led the way with Carter coming up behind, both men scanning the forest with every step toward the crime scene. Jenna moved up closer to Kane. Ahead of him, Duke ambled along, his nose on the ground, no doubt recognizing the scents of the other members of the team. "This has to be a random thrill kill. I find it hard to believe anyone planned to ambush a group of kids. Most teenagers are unpredictable and don't know what they are doing from one hour to the next during spring break. It would be diffi-cult to plan a hit, if this is what Wolfe suggested."

"I guess we will have to make that determination when we get there." Kane waved a hand in front of his nose and snorted in disgust. He pulled a face mask out of his pocket. "The crime scene can't be far away. I can smell it." He pulled on the mask and turned to look at Jenna. "As first responders, did Rio and Rowley do a recon of the immediate area for evidence?"

Running the phone call through her mind, Jenna shrugged. "Rio didn't mention it specifically, but he's experienced enough to have followed procedure."

In apprehension of what lay ahead of them, Jenna's stomach tightened. The stink of death was seeping through her mask like an entity, thick and pungent. The sound of voices came from just ahead, and Duke's tail wagged and he gave a short bark in greeting.

"By me, Duke." Kane patted his leg. "Come here, boy." He turned and looked back at the others. "Stay over to the right. We should be able to circle around the bodies through the trees."

Inquisitive, Jenna peered around him and swallowed hard. The first victim, a male teenager, his head toward them, lay expressionless, as if time had stopped with his death. Ants swarmed over his face and above a murder of crows argued, waiting for their turn to feast. Suddenly nauseous, she turned away and followed Kane through the trees. She hated this part of her job. Seeing young lives wasted kept her awake at night.

FOUR

The atmosphere in the forest was somber. The team was moving around in almost complete silence, taking photographs and hunting for evidence surrounding the bodies. Fishing gear lay near the victims, and it was obvious they'd been heading for the Devil's Punchbowl fishing hole, when they'd been attacked. Kane shook his head. "Why attack a bunch of kids going fishing? It makes no sense. They weren't a threat to anyone."

"Murder never makes sense, Dave." Jenna sighed. "I've seen enough here. I'll leave Wolfe to do his thing and go and speak to the forest warden. Wolfe will need you to determine the trajectory of the arrows or whatever." She indicated through the pines to where the pale and obviously stressed forest warden stood leaning against a trunk. "Call me if you find anything significant." She walked away through the trees.

"I'll get an update from Rio and Rowley." Carter headed off in their direction.

"I think I'll tag along with you, Dave." Jo stared at the bodies. "This looks like it's going to be an interesting case."

Kane ordered Duke to stay beside Zorro, gloved up, and went to Wolfe's side. "The victims are spread out. Somehow I figured they'd be in a bunch." He scanned the forest for the fiftieth time that day and then moved his attention back to the position of the first victim, a young male approximately sixteen to eighteen years old. The teenager was lying face down with his head turned to one side.

"The ground is soft, and we found no footprints past the blood spatter, just up there." Wolfe indicated to the end of the trail in the direction they had arrived from. "I figure he was hit in the thigh and staggered back this way to warn the others. The second shot came from behind, and he dropped where he stood, falling flat on his face." He looked at Kane. "With the trees and all, there wouldn't be too many clear shots available."

Summing up the dynamics of the area, Kane nodded. "If the shooter used a crossbow, we have to assume he took both shots from the same position. It would be difficult to maneuver the bow when the trees are this dense." He looked at sprawled figure of a female about the same age farther down the trail. "And her?"

Keeping to the tree line on the edge of the trail, they went to examine the second victim. Confused by the angles of the shots, Kane shook his head slowly, taking in the entry and exit wounds in the girl's throat. The ground around her had been disturbed and hastily brushed over with a tree branch to disguise the footprints in the damp soil. "They took the time to remove the bolts and sanitize the scene."

"Yeah, that's what sent up a red flag for me." Wolfe gave him a direct stare. "This isn't an opportunistic thrill kill, is it?" He cleared his throat. "This looks way too organized. I wonder what these kids witnessed. Someone wanted them dead, that's for darn sure."

Unconvinced, Kane walked along the trail to the third body and crouched down beside it. He examined the face of the young man and then flicked his attention back and forth from one victim to the other. He looked at Wolfe. "Don't you think it's a little unusual that the three victims all have their eyes closed? Most people who die suddenly always seem to have their eyes open." He bent closer and brushed ants from the young man's face. "I figure there's something under the eyelids."

"Let me take a look." Wolfe lifted an eyelid to reveal a one-cent piece. "Well, I'll be." He pulled an evidence bag from his kit, removed the coin with tweezers, and examining the second eye, found another. "Two for two."

After examining the other two bodies, they discovered all had coins under their eyelids. Kane turned to look at Jo, who had been following their progress while sticking to the trees. "This is a calling card. Does anyone come to mind, Jo?"

"Oh yeah, they sure do." Jo moved a few steps closer. "Are the coins pennies?"

"Yeah." Wolfe held up an evidence bag. "The same on every victim."

"It's the same MO as James Earl Stafford, known as Jimmy Two Cents out of Clear Spring, North Dakota." Jo walked along the tree line and peered at the bodies. "There is a small problem. James Earl Stafford is currently doing time and his weapon of choice was a knife."

As she was speaking, Kane was examining the variation in the trajectory of the wounds on the bodies. "We have a copycat, well, a bunch of them. These victims were shot by three different people." He turned to Wolfe. "I'll scope out the area. It shouldn't take too long to discover where each of them was standing at the time." He pulled out his phone to call Carter and then asked Rowley to come over. "Rowley is our go-to guy for anything to do with archery. He hunts with a crossbow and will be able to give us the optimum distance for the shooters from the targets."

"How long will you need me to leave the bodies in situ?" Wolfe gave him a concerned stare. "They're decomposing in front of my eyes. We need to get them back to the morgue ASAP."

Kane pulled out his hunting knife and removed four branches from the trees around him. He stripped off the side branches to produce four stakes. He dropped two beside the first body and one beside each of the others. "If we measure the height of each victim and point of entry on the stake, we should be able to determine the trajectory of each bolt. One thing I do need to know is the direction of the wounds."

"That's easy enough." Wolfe went through his kit for a tape measure. "All the wounds are in a very slight downward slope."

"A crossbow shoots in a straight line." Rowley came out of the trees and stood beside Kane. "The shooters must have been in a slightly elevated position to achieve a wound like that and, as accuracy was necessary, they would have been shooting from approximately thirty yards or less."

"What have you found?" Jenna stood on the edge of the trail flanked by Rio and Carter.

Kane explained about the coins and the link to Jimmy Two Cents as he prepared the stakes. "The stakes are used as markers to determine the trajectory of each wound."

"Do you think we are dealing with a copycat killer?" Jenna stared at Jo.

"I doubt it." Jo shook her head. "The information about the coins was never released."

When Wolfe's team had the victims in body bags and on their way to the morgue, Kane set the stakes in the ground and used his sniper rifle scope to determine the trajectory. The shooters had been positioned in an arc and each had chosen a direct line of sight to the trail. He sent Rio and Rowley to the first shooter's position, using his phone to keep them in the right direction. It didn't take long before they found the trampled ground where the shooter had waited for his prey. He waited for them to photograph and mark the area, but as with the crime scene, the killers had taken precautions to sanitize the area. After repeating the procedure, they had collected enough data to prove beyond reasonable doubt that three shooters were involved.

"I think we should walk the forest in the general area of the shooters." Jenna stood hands on hips and looked from one to the other. "People make mistakes, they must have left a partial footprint or something behind. Search the area again. Look for cigarette butts, candy wrappers, the smell of pee. If they were holed up and waiting a time for these kids to walk along the trail, they would have brought something with them to eat and drink." She looked directly at Kane. "I'm finding it hard to believe this is an opportunistic thrill kill. From what I'm seeing here, it would take recon of the immediate area to discover the few direct lines of sight to the trail."

Impressed, Kane nodded. "My thoughts exactly." He swung his attention to Jo. "When we get back to the office, we'll need to find out more about Jimmy Two Cents."

They spent the next hour or so searching the forest but didn't find anything they could use until Jenna let out a shout of triumph and waived a small scrap of material in the air. Kane moved to her side. "What did you find?"

"A piece of army surplus camo and it looks fresh." Jenna held up an evidence bag. "It was caught on that broken branch back there. Another thing I've noticed: indents in the forest floor. Places where my footprints are evident, someone has walked there without leaving a trace. I figure they were wearing something over their boots to disguise their footprints and camouflage gear. They would have been a group of silent assassins. Now we just have to figure out why they killed these kids."

FIVE

Jenna's approach to investigations was never the same. She used gut instinct most of the time. Although, she followed procedure by correlating her deputies' information in a case file and always had a visual on the whiteboard, so that anybody entering the room could see firsthand where the investigation was going. As Carter and Jo had unofficially joined the team, she decided to set up a base in the conference room on the same floor as her office. The room filled with the refreshing smell of freshly brewed coffee, as everyone consumed the takeout from Aunt Betty's Café. Grabbing bites to eat, she updated the whiteboard with all the information they'd gathered to date. She attached the photographs of the victims and then turned to Rowley. "Do we still have the college and high school yearbooks?"

"Yeah, I'll go down and get them from the office." Rowley stuffed the last piece of a pulled-pork roll into his mouth and headed for the door.

She looked at the others all waiting expectantly for her to continue. "The first priority is identifying the victims, and I would imagine, going on the small amount of supplies they carried in their backpacks, they live locally. We have a few copies of the yearbooks from the local schools and college. I think that would be a good place to start."

"Well, sure as heck, the missing persons calls will be coming into the office soon." Carter sipped a soda. "Wolfe figures those kids have been there since early this morning. I'm surprised they haven't been completely consumed by critters. The bodies were only nibbled on. If a mountain lion or bear had wandered by, we wouldn't have found much more than the backpacks. I'd say they're likely due home for supper." He let out a long sigh. "That's the worst part of this job, having to break it to the parents that their kids aren't coming home."

Sorrow washed over Jenna, but she pushed it to one side. It was her job to bring these murderers to justice. This case was so different to the others they had faced. She would have to look at it from every angle and think outside the box. She took her seat beside Kane and nodded. "It sure is." Her phone chimed a message. She opened it and lifted her head. "That was Wolfe. The autopsy is at ten and as it's a homicide he doesn't need permission from the parents to proceed. I hope we've discovered their IDs by then."

"The pennies forced under the eyelids are significant." Kane looked at Jo. "If this is the trademark for Jimmy Two Cents, as he's been away for at least ten years, the likelihood of anyone copying his MO would be remote."

During the long winter Jenna had spent a good deal of her downtime researching old serial killer cases. Discovering the different types of trophies that most of them kept intrigued her. She'd researched the backgrounds of each one in an effort to discover what had triggered them. Over the last four years she had developed an understanding of how a psychopath's mind worked, and understood that although most of them were born with the condition, not all of them evolved into a killer. Having read everything that Jo Wells had written on the subject, and being beside her during interviews in prison with psychopathic killers, had given her an insight into their behavior. Somehow things didn't add up with the current case, and she believed that attributing the murders to a psychopath or psychopaths would be an error of judgment.

She looked at Jo. "Would you classify Jimmy Two Cents as a psychopathic serial killer?"

"Yeah, he was unstoppable and had convinced himself he would die in a hail of bullets." Jo leaned back in her chair, twiddling her pen between her fingers. "It took a SWAT team to take him down, and before you ask, he was living with a woman at the time. She became suspicious and went to the cops. Up to that time, the investigators on the case had little evidence. The coins were the only indication that the cases were linked."

Intrigued, Jenna leaned forward on the table. "Was it usual for him to kill more than one victim at a time?"

"Not that I'm aware." Jo opened her laptop and scrolled through the files. "I'll send everyone a copy of the case files. I requested them before Christmas. I had planned to interview James Earl Stafford sometime this year for my next book." She glanced up from the screen. "There you go. That's all the information I have on him."

Incoming email signals chimed around the room as the files dropped into inboxes. Jenna opened the file and scanned it. "Although he favored a knife, it seems he used a variety of different weapons and killed victims of all ages. All were Caucasian but there is one thing that stands out."

"Yeah, they're messy." Kane looked up from his laptop. "Jimmy was a slasher and our murders are clean. He enjoyed his kills and each was overkill. What I witnessed today was as close to an execution as you could get. Minimal hits with deadly precision. If I didn't know better, I would have considered it was professionally organized." He cleared his throat. "I know kids get into a ton of trouble these days, but I can't imagine something they did or witnessed was on such a high scale it attracted this type of a reaction."

"Yeah." Carter moved a toothpick across his lips. "I agree. There are far easier ways of dealing with kids of this age." He looked at Jenna. "I figure we're gonna have to look outside the box on this one, Jenna. We've received no intel that any known hit teams have moved into Black Rock Falls and, trust me, after this town became Serial Killer Central, our IT whiz kid, Bobby Kalo, installed facial recognition software at the airport arrivals. Anyone who gets off a flight is scanned, and if a known criminal arrives, an alert is sent to our office. This type of hit would take a professional team from out of town."

"Sorry, folks, but I don't agree." Rowley walked back into the office carrying a pile of yearbooks. He dumped them on the desk and stood hands on hips looking at Carter. "There are archery and crossbow clubs all over, and many of them compete in teams. Many of them are teenagers." He looked at Jo. "I've been reading your books too, and from what I understand, it doesn't take a group of psychopaths to become a lethal team."

"It would only take one charismatic leader who had influence over the others." Jo pushed her laptop to one side and met his gaze. "In groups there are always leaders and followers. If the leader of one group is particularly influential over the others, it wouldn't be too difficult to convince them that it would be exciting to go out on a people hunt. This could be a psychopathic killer's first hit. Of course, he'd blame the others for making him do it, but once the dynamite's fuse is lit..."

"How could he possibly encourage normal kids to kill each other?" Rio looked unconvinced. "I have trouble getting the twins to take out the trash."

"Remember just how smart these people are." Jo smiled at him. "He would arrange something suitably annoying against his group to encourage them to get revenge. He would add incidents as he went along until he had his group agreeing with him. It's another form of grooming, like the ones pedophiles use."

Clearing her throat to get everyone's attention, Jenna leaned forward in her seat. "Okay, once we've identified the victims, we have a starting place to look for suspects. We'll assume they moved in the same circles as their killers. As Rowley said there are groups of teenagers in archery clubs in town. We start there. Grab a book and start looking."

SIX

Unable to discover the victims in the yearbook he'd been given, Kane moved his attention to viewing Jimmy Two Cents crime scene images and looking for any parallel to the current case. There was no distinguishing pattern whatsoever. All the murders appeared to be random thrill kills. One thing for darn sure, Jimmy Two Cents wasn't an organized serial killer. This alone convinced him that James Earl Stafford wasn't the instigator of these crimes. He understood how prisoners had far-reaching contacts on the outside, many who would do anything they asked. *Hybristophilia* came to mind, the psychological term used for women who were romantically attracted to criminals, but unfortunately hero worship wasn't restricted to women. He looked up from his laptop and caught Jo's attention. "Do you have any idea if Stafford has access to the outside world?"

"He has pen pals, restricted access to the internet, and visitors." Jo raised one eyebrow. "Where is this going, Dave?"

Shrugging, Kane smiled. "Gut feeling. The facts tell me he isn't involved but my gut is trying to convince me otherwise." He drummed his fingers on the desk, thinking for a beat. "How could he exert his influence over a bunch of kids?"

"Hmm, well unless they're family members, I doubt he would be able to correspond with anyone under the age of twenty-one. I'm sure the system wouldn't risk any of the prisoners having contact with young people or kids. I know there's a death row pen pal webpage, where prisoners can post. You do realize that murderers usually receive more mail than anyone else, even in this day and age. Prisoners still write letters. I guess they have plenty of time to waste." She stared into space and then returned her gaze to him. "Right now, we only know that the victims are teenagers. The killers could be any age. We're only surmising that they're part of an archery team and around the same age. Your idea could work but I figure you're limiting the possibilities. Murderers are admired by a wide range of people. It would be difficult to estimate Stafford's capabilities. I haven't met the man, and he might be as charismatic as Ted Bundy."

Kane reflected on the apparently stable and well-liked serial killer who brutally murdered at least twenty-eight women between 1974 and '78 across five states. "Yeah, I believe that he was the one who destroyed the myth that a killer was a dirty old man."

"He certainly changed how we look at psychopathic serial killers." Jo stood and went to the counter to refill the coffee machines. "You wouldn't believe how many really nice guys and women I've met during my research and interviews for my books. Some of them are scary at times. I've seen them change in a split second, from a friendly old grandpa figure to a mass murderer. Sometimes when I question them, it triggers a memory, and in that instant the cold-blooded killer is exposed. I'm now aware it lies just under the surface of all of them but is very carefully disguised by a false persona." She leaned against the counter. "You must realize that these people have carried the dark side with them since childhood and are very proficient at hiding it behind a mask of nice."

"Found them." Rio stood and carried the yearbook to Jenna. "Leo Kelly, Zoe Ward, and Ash Rogers, in the order we found them on the trail."

"Okay, we'll take Leo Kelly; Jo and Carter, Zoe Ward; and Rio and Rowley, Ash Rogers." Jenna stood and added names to the whiteboard. "Hunt down everything you can find on these kids. Obviously, their details, any friends, and if they were involved in an archery or crossbow club. Once you've established their details, I'm afraid it will be your responsibility to notify the parents and make arrangements with Wolfe for them to view the body. We'll need a positive ID ASAP." She looked at Carter. "Take Rio's cruiser. He'll be with Rowley." She took a breath. "Ask the parents for their media devices. We already have their phones. Once Wolfe has processed them, you'll need Kalo to unlock them for you, and then follow up with any contacts. We need to know if these kids had enemies or any recent disagreements or problems with anyone. Kids talk, so their friends would know the answers to these questions." She sighed. "I doubt you'll get information from the parents after they've received such a shock, so work on the friends." She swung her attention to Rowley. "If you can make up a list of all the archery or crossbow clubs that you know about around town, I'd appreciate it. We've received cooperation in the past with archery clubs. They usually can supply the list of their best members, especially those who compete."

"Sure." Rowley nodded. "There are two that specialize in crossbows. I figure we start there because to obtain the shots that these killers achieved took skill. We examined the trees around the murder scene and didn't find any recent bolt holes. Those kids were taken down by clean shots. That takes some doing at that range. We are looking at proficient marksmen and they shouldn't be too hard to find."

"Okay, get at it." Jenna looked at the team. "Let's get these crazies before they hurt anyone else."

Kane's head was still filled with Jo's take on the Ted Bundy case. Her valuable insight into serial killers had revolutionized how law enforcement hunted them down. As if on autopilot he added Leo Kelly's name into the DMV database and waited for a hit. He looked up at Jenna. "Okay, I have an address. He lives out at Lilac Way." He checked the map app on his phone. "It's out by the college. He'd be a freshman. They all graduated from high school the same year."

"Okay, let's go." Jenna stood and grabbed her jacket. "I'll call Wolfe on the way and bring him up to date."

Kane whistled to Duke and the dog bounded out of Jenna's office, ears flapping, tail windmilling. He grinned at him. "I guess this means you'd like to come with us?"

"He loved walking in the forest this morning. You should take him with you next time you go fishing." Jenna smiled at him. "Look at him, doing his happy dance. After being left behind on Sunday, he isn't planning on missing out again."

Shrugging into his jacket, Kane nodded. "Well, he always came with me before we were married, but now he likes to stay home with you. He really does what he pleases. Maybe he figures you need protecting while I'm away." He followed Jenna downstairs and waited while she explained to Maggie where they were all heading.

He'd had the unfortunate task of notifying relatives of the death of a loved one many a time and it never got easier. As he headed for the Beast, he slid one arm around Jenna's shoulder. "I never know what to say to the parents." He took a deep breath of clean mountain air and let it out slowly. "'I'm sorry for your loss' doesn't come close, does it?"

"Nope." Jenna pushed on her hat and leaned into him. "At least they didn't see the murder scene. Not that it takes away the pain, but at least Wolfe will make sure they look as if they're asleep... well, Emily will." She was referring to Wolfe's daughter and ME in training.

Kane removed his arm to allow Jenna to walk around the hood and opened the back door for Duke. As he bent inside to attach Duke's harness, a roar of a powerful engine and squeal of brakes broke the silence. He lifted his head as a truck mounted the sidewalk. In a split second, the back door opened and someone dragged Jenna kicking and squealing inside. "What the...?"

The vehicle took off at high speed, shedding rubber across the blacktop and fishtailing toward the forest. They sped away, driving up the wrong side of the road to avoid traffic. Moving on remote control, Kane slid behind the wheel, backed out of the parking slot, and followed. He flicked on lights and sirens before calling it in. "I'm in pursuit of a silver GMC heading toward Stanton. They've kidnapped Jenna."

"*Oh, my God.*" Maggie's voice crackled through the radio. "*I'll tell the others.*"

In the background Kane heard her speaking on the phone and then footsteps running. He stared at the disappearing truck and cursed under his breath. Someone had a death wish that was for darn sure. Anger slid over him like an ice-cold cloak as he floored the Beast. Hearing the satisfying roar of the finely tuned speed demon, he'd catch them in no time. Without warning, a cattle truck shot out from a side street and stalled, blocking Main. He slammed on his brakes, sliding sideways and missing the truck by inches. Inside the cab, the driver froze at the sight of him. Was the cattle truck part of the kidnapping team? Sounding his horn to move the traffic behind him, he reversed and spun the Beast around. "Maggie, you there?"

"*Yes, I'm here.*"

Kane searched the sidewalk for pedestrians, but everyone had scattered anticipating his next move. "Get Rowley to pick up the driver of a cattle truck blocking Main. He has to be involved."

"Copy. I'm, right behind you." Rowley's voice came over the radio. *"Carter is following me."*

Kane mounted the sidewalk to pass the truck and accelerated along Stanton, but the GMC was moving away in the distance at a reckless speed. Concerned for Jenna's safety, he ground his teeth. Panicking wouldn't solve the problem and he allowed his mind to drop into combat mode. Calmness surrounded him and time slowed as the killing machine slid into place. "Don't worry. I've got this."

"Don't do anything stupid, Dave." Carter's serious voice broke through the speaker. *"We'll be right behind you."*

Kane snorted. He'd deal with this Kane style. "They have my wife, and you won't be able to catch me. They have some tricked-out truck and they're driving like lunatics, but I'll catch them. Nobody touches Jenna." He switched off the radio and activated Jenna's tracker, seeing the screen light up with a steady throbbing light on the map. He stared into the distance as the silver GMC slipped in front of an eighteen-wheeler and vanished. "You can run but you can't hide."

SEVEN

The hood had dropped over Jenna's face so fast she hadn't seen it coming. Grabbed from behind, someone had slipped a zip tie around her wrists before she had time to call out to Kane. Someone lifted her off her feet, and male voices surrounded her speaking in hushed urgent tones. She kicked out, screaming, and threw her head backward to strike the person behind her. When they cursed, and punched her in the side of the head, her vision filled with white spots, but she struck out again, aiming to do more damage. The smell of sweat oozed through the thin black material covering her face but she could also smell books. Had they used a kid's library bag as a hood? A steel grip grabbed her ankles and wrapped them with tape. On her back with her hands tied behind her, she was defenseless. She moved her hands, and balling one into a fist was able to depress her tracker ring with the fingers of her other hand. Kane would already be tracking her but now he'd be able to hear everything that was happening. "Let me go. Are you crazy?"

"I like your handgun." A cool voice came from above her. It was the man she'd headbutted and now lay against in the back seat of a truck. "An M18, nice choice. I like the tan color as well. Have you tried it with the night-vision option?"

The sound of her handgun being stripped down and reassembled made her blood run cold. Her weapon was military issue and this guy knew it well. "Why don't you take my hood off, so I can breathe and we'll discuss why you kidnapped me." Jenna fought to keep her voice calm. If this was a psychopath, negotiation would be off the table. She must not show fear. "What do you want?"

"Nothing from you." He chuckled. "You're my hostage. Act nice and I won't hurt you. Fight and scream and I'll give you to my boys. What's it to be, Sheriff?"

Confused, Jenna tried to ease the ties cutting into her wrists. "You want me as a bargaining chip? For what?"

"I'll discuss that with someone in charge later." He barked a laugh. "I don't negotiate with women."

If she was valuable to them, they wouldn't risk hitting her again. "Who do you intend to negotiate with, the mayor?"

"Does the mayor have my kid brother in custody, for doing nothing?" The man's voice grew angry. "You can't charge someone for just sitting outside a building and there ain't no law in this state that says you can't carry a weapon." He pushed her into a sitting position. "You took one of mine, so I'm taking one of yours. Like I said before, there's no negotiation of terms. Your deputy sheriff gets one chance, and then I give you to my boys. When they've finished with you, trust me, you won't be worth nothing."

The vehicle made a sudden turn off the highway and tree branches scratched the side of the truck. They went straight for a short while before turning left again and bouncing over rough ground. They traveled for some minutes and then stopped. Doors opened and Jenna was roughly dragged from the back seat. With her ankles secured, she couldn't stand up and fell forward. Somebody caught her and she was tossed into the air and over a man's shoulder. The scent of stale sweat seeped through her hood and memories of being kidnapped four years ago slammed into her mind. Her heart thundered in her chest as the PTSD she'd suffered after the incident suddenly surfaced. Sweat coated her skin and panic gripped her. At that time, she'd been trapped inside a bunker with a serial killer intent on raping and murdering her. If it hadn't been for Kane, she would have died a terrible death. Would he be in time to save her again?

Trying to reason with her tortured memories, she dragged in long steady breaths and concentrated on something pleasant. She pictured a litter of bloodhound puppies and the joy of owning one of Duke's sons. Her heart rate slowed. Kane would be coming and he would be as mad as hell. Bouncing over the man's shoulder as he climbed the steps and walked into a building, she could hear hushed voices. It had been the same as inside the vehicle. She sensed the other men and smelled them, but they had kept silent during the trip. Only the man carrying her had spoken and he sounded like a local. Concern gripped her. If these men had seen Kane around town, they would know his reputation. Although none of them could possibly know what they were up against. A few rumors had arisen after he had disarmed a biker gang the previous year, taking six men down alone, but when anyone asked her for details, she just laughed it off. Drawing attention to him could be problematic. She breathed through her nose considering how she could get information to him. He'd need to know how many men he was up against. When the man lowered her into a straight-back chair, she lifted her head. "Can you remove this hood? I need a drink of water. Any mistreatment of me will have serious repercussions."

She moved her head trying to make out the directions of the footsteps as people filed into the room. She could hear boots on a wooden floor and assumed they were in a cabin in the forest. It was the same voice who answered her.

"I'll lift it up so you can have some water, but it's not getting removed."

Listening intently, Jenna counted four distinct movements around her. Counting the man standing directly in front of her, she had five to contend with. She needed to get the information to Kane without them realizing he could hear every word they said. "Does it take five of you to kidnap one female sheriff?"

"Maybe it's just me, maybe a whole crew." The hood was lifted above her nose and a cup of water pressed to her mouth. "But it only takes one of us to kill you. I could dump your body out here, and by morning there'd be nothing left. What with the bears and all." He laughed. "When you've finished drinking, I need the number of your deputy sheriff. I figure I should give him a call, as he didn't bother to pursue us. That guy must be some kind of chicken to leave you to fend for yourself."

The water tasted like it came from a well and was tainted with dead leaves. Thirsty, Jenna sipped cautiously, aware the drink might be drugged. She turned her face away from the cup and it was removed. "Thank you." She cleared her throat. "His number is in my phone and my phone is in the truck. I'm sorry. Maybe call the office or 911?"

Before the hood was dropped back down, she caught sight of two sets of boots to her right, men leaning against the wall, with rifles resting beside them. A breeze brushed her face, and what felt like cotton drapes brushed her cheek. "Am I sitting beside a window?"

"Yeah, it's kinda stuffy in here." The man walked away.

In the distance, the distinct roar of the Beast reached her like a calming balm. Kane was coming and she needed to get him as much information as possible. "You seem to know your way around weapons. I prefer a rifle. I have two. I'm not sure how many pistols I've owned over the years. It's hard to keep count." She hoped that Kane would get her coded message.

The sound of the engine became softer and Jenna's heart sank. Had Kane lost her tracker signal? Surely, he would be close behind and have her on his phone but what if he had no bars? Panic gripped her as the man paced up and down as if deciding what to do with her. Agitation came off him in waves, and the next moment, footsteps came again as the men shuffled outside. Soft conversation came through the window, but Jenna couldn't understand what they were saying. She couldn't stand but she could move around on the seat and bent forward to shake off the hood. She looked around to get her bearings and stared out of the window. "Dave, I'm inside a cabin. It's at the end of a dirt road partially obscured by trees. I see five men, outside. All are wearing sidearms and knives. Two are carrying rifles. I don't see body armor but they're all wearing camouflage gear and look like survivalists. All the cammies are different and old style. I'm tied, hand and foot, so will be no use to you in a fight." She blew out a long breath. "I figure they're the owners of the meth lab. The guy we arrested, he's one of their crew and they want to negotiate a swap. I hope you've brought backup." She scanned the forest, searching for any signs of her team. "Now I've seen their faces, if this all goes to hell, they'll kill me for sure."

Jenna stared into the forest and didn't see any movement or hear a sound. The men were standing in a semicircle facing the trees, speaking in fast hushed tones. Kane was out there, somewhere, she could almost feel him close by.

"Sheriff's department. On your knees. Hands on your heads." Kane stepped out of the trees, his expression like granite, weapon drawn. He stood in the open, legs apart, and glared at them. "Drop your weapons."

One of them men laughed, and Jenna gasped in horror as the men went for their guns. A rapid burst of gunshots rang out, echoing through the quiet forest and sending birds flying en masse into the air. When Kane jerked, the sickening knowledge that he'd been hit strangled the cry in her throat. He was still on his feet and firing rapidly. In seconds, the five men fell to the ground—some cried out, others fell silently—and lay in crumpled humps. She stared at Kane, and gasped with relief when he unzipped his jacket to reveal a Kevlar vest. He shook his head and poked one finger through the hole in his jacket and then, as if he were on a Sunday walk, whistled to Duke, who came bounding out of the trees. He looked up, searching for her, and their eyes met. Tears stung the backs of Jenna's eyes. "Are you okay?"

"I'll do." Kane narrowed his gaze. "You?"

Jenna sighed with relief. "I'm just peachy."

She couldn't prevent the tears running down her cheeks as she watched Kane check each of the men for life signs. A shiver went through her. He'd killed them all without hesitation. Moments later, Carter came running out of the forest, weapon drawn. He stopped to survey the carnage with a look of incredulity on his face.

"I heard the shots and you identifying yourself. You faced these guys alone? Are you crazy? Are they all dead?" Carter was shaking his head. "What happened here and why did you allow them to get off a shot?"

"Yes, no, yes. You know what happened, Ty. These men kidnapped my wife." Kane shrugged. "I chased them down and identified myself. I told them to get on their knees, but they all decided to draw down on me. Yeah, they got off a few rounds before I fired. I don't kill unless my life is in danger." He indicated to his vest. "They were aiming to kill. I caught one in the jacket, but most went past my ears." He stared at him. "Thanks for caring. I'll be bruised is all. They weren't so lucky."

"It was self-defense." Carter walked around the bodies. "They're all still holding their firearms and I'm a witness. I saw them fire first. You had no choice." Carter pulled out his phone. "I'll process the scene. Where's Jenna?"

"In the cabin." Kane glanced up at her. "I need to go to her now." He turned back to Carter. "Call Wolfe and Rio. I can't be involved in the investigation."

"It's a righteous shoot. Wait up. I'll need a shot of the bullet hole in your vest. I'll leave Wolfe to pry it out and bag it." Carter snapped away with his phone. "How many shots did you fire?"

"Five." Kane gave him a long stare. "I don't waste ammo." He handed him his weapon and then walked away and headed for the cabin.

Fighting back tears, Jenna looked up at Kane as he walked through the door rubbing his chest. He'd walked alone into a gunfight to save her. If one head shot had connected, he'd be dead. "Are you hurt?"

"Nah, the vest caught the one bullet that got close. I'll be bruised, is all. Don't worry about it." Kane took out his knife to cut through the zip ties and then the tape around her ankles. He examined her face and gently touched her cheek. "They hit you, didn't they? Which one?"

Jenna stood and wrapped her arms around him. "I don't know. He put a hood over my head, but he has my M18. He was skilled, military maybe. He stripped it down and reassembled it in seconds." She shook her head. "I didn't hear them until it was too late. All the training you've given me, and they still managed to grab me."

"You were attacked from behind, and you couldn't see. You fought them but they were too strong. We all have our limits, Jenna. You did everything possible to stay alive and give me clear concise information." Kane stared into her eyes. "I'm proud of you. You did everything by the book." He shook his head. "I threw the rulebook out of the window. I should have waited for backup and would have been right on their tail but for a darn cattle truck blocking the road. Those precious minutes it took me to get through the pedestrians on the sidewalk meant I lost sight of them. I figure the driver of the cattle truck was a plant to delay me. Rowley picked him up I hope. He was right behind me."

Jenna nodded. "Once again the tracker ring saved my butt."

"Yeah, it's a lifesaver." Kane stared out of the window. "Those guys, I figure they're the group running the meth lab. It looks like we have them all: one lookout, the guy in the truck, and those outside."

Nodding, Jenna touched her sore face with her fingertips. "That will be one case solved, if either of the two left alive talk for a deal."

"They'll deal to save their own skins." Kane sighed. "I'd take you home now, but we'll need to stay for a time." Kane slid off his backpack, opened it, and handed her a bottle of water and an energy bar. "Rio will take our statements and Wolfe is on his way." He led her back to the chair. "I'm guessing the press will have a field day when they discover I killed five men." He narrowed his gaze at her. "You should suspend me pending an investigation. Wolfe won't be happy about all the publicity."

Shaking her head, Jenna sighed. "Okay, you're suspended until Carter, Rio, and Wolfe have examined the scene and taken statements, but I need you to assist me with a murder case. We'll keep the incident under wraps. I really don't want the fact I was kidnapped all over the media either. I'll speak to the DA."

"It won't go away that easy, Jenna." Kane's expression was serious. "These men have families and might cause trouble. It was a righteous shoot and Carter is a witness. He heard me identify myself. You must do this by the book or it will come back and bite me in the butt."

Of course, Kane was right, and Jenna nodded. "Fine. Rio will follow procedure. He always does. Right now, I'm not worried. We've survived another incident and all that matters is that we're okay."

EIGHT

It wasn't the first time Carter had seen Kane in action. Everything about the man impressed him. He'd walked into a seemingly impossible situation with calm deliberation. The security of liquid Kevlar vest notwithstanding, it took a ton of guts to take down a group of armed men intent on killing him. He walked the crime scene with Wolfe and Rio, giving them as much detail as he could remember.

"What distance were you away from Kane when he fired the first shot?" Rio's pen hovered above the statement book.

Carter scratched his cheek, trying to estimate the distance. "Not far, fifteen yards maybe. I had to take cover behind a tree because bullets were whizzing past my head. When the shooters were down, I ran to the scene to offer assistance, but they were all deceased." He gave him a long look. "Kane didn't fire the first shot. I saw him get hit in the chest, then he opened fire. It was so fast I didn't have time to react."

"Yeah, the M18 is a semiautomatic, and I've never known him to miss." Rio shrugged. "Your account of what happened matches Kane's and Jenna's statements. In my opinion, we don't need to pursue further investigation." He held out the statement book for Carter to sign.

Wanting to be sure there would be no blowback for Kane, Carter signed his statement and then took the top copies of all the statements from the book. "I'll take these to the DA personally and run it past him. He needs to make a determination, but from the facts and what I witnessed personally, Kane is in the clear."

A gunshot rang out and Carter instinctively drew his weapon. "Is that Wolfe?"

"Yeah, he discovered a ton of sawdust out back, and he's doing a ballistic test on Kane's weapon." Rio smiled. "He just shot into the sawdust. He'll use the bullet to match the ones Kane shot into the bodies. He needs a bullet so he can return Kane's weapon, but Jenna suspended him, pending an investigation."

Carter shrugged. "That's all we need in the middle of a murder case. I'm sure it's unnecessary. We've finished our investigation on scene, and Wolfe has confirmed that each man has one gunshot wound." He walked over to Wolfe. "If you don't need me, I'm going to head back into town to speak to the DA. We need Jenna and Kane back on the homicide case ASAP. We have parents out there who don't know their kids have been murdered."

"We just need to bag and tag." Wolfe looked over at the bodies still sprawled on the grass. "They're all carrying ID, which I find a little difficult to believe considering they're supposed to be cooking crystal meth." He shrugged. "I'll run their prints when I get back to the office and see if it matches their IDs. I noticed a few tattoos that looked familiar. I figure some of these men served in the military. What the heck were they doing involved in a crystal meth lab?"

Perplexed, Carter shook his head. "I guess not all of us go

into law enforcement. My concern is we might have found only the tip of the iceberg. Rio will need to look a little deeper into the associates of these men. We have the driver of the cattle truck in custody. He might be able to shed some light on who was involved, but I doubt the guy we arrested outside the meth lab is going to talk."

"Okay." Wolfe handed Carter Kane's M18. "I'm done with this and I'm sure you agree with me that there's no valid reason to relieve Kane of his weapon."

Carter nodded. "None that comes to mind." He turned toward the cabin. "I'll go and tell Kane and Jenna we're done here."

He headed up the steps and found Kane seated with Jenna on his lap. Her head rested on his shoulder and an imprint of knuckles shone red on her cheek. He frowned. "You should have mentioned you were injured, Jenna. Do you need to go to the ER?"

"Me? No, I'm good." Jenna slid off Kane's lap and stood. "Dave's probably got a cracked rib and I'm not seeing any duty of care for him, if he's considered a suspect." She pushed hair from her face. "Have you finished the investigation?"

Shaking his head, Carter smiled and tossed a toothpick into his mouth. "Yeah, we're done and he's never been a suspect, Jenna. I witnessed a righteous shoot. They fired first, as you witnessed, and Kane was acting in self-defense. In fact, the moment they drew their weapons, as a law enforcement officer and within Montana law, he was well within his rights to take them down." He handed Kane his gun. "I'll run the statements past the DA and when he clears you, Rio can put out a carefully worded media release, saying something like, the Black Rock Falls Sheriff's Department and the Snakeskin Gully FBI raided a meth lab on the outskirts of town. During the ensuing gunfight, all the perpetrators received fatal gunshot wounds."

He moved the toothpick across his lips. "No names, no worries." He indicated to the door with his thumb. "I'm heading back to town now. I'll see you back at the office." He turned on his heel and went out the door. *Those two sure need some alone time.*

NINE

Troubled by Jenna's silence, Kane waited for the bodies to be bagged and loaded into Wolfe's van before he led Jenna outside. Her M18 had been fingerprinted and photographed, and Wolfe handed it to her.

"You were lucky those guys weren't sampling their own product or you might have suffered more serious injuries. Let me take a look at you." Wolfe examined Jenna's face and pressed his fingers gently over the marks. "Bruising but no damage. Is the inside of your mouth okay?"

"Yeah, I'm fine. Just a headache, is all." She looked at Kane. "Dave is bruised as well. How do you know he hasn't cracked a rib?"

"He'd know." Wolfe smiled at her. "He has had enough of them to know." He turned to Kane. "If you get any shortness of breath, call me."

"How far away is the Beast?" Jenna peered at the dirt road leading from the cabin.

Kane lifted her chin and looked into her eyes. "It's a few hundred yards away. Do you want me to go get it?"

"No, I'd rather walk." She bent to rub Duke's ears. "Duke loves a walk in the forest and I could do with the fresh air."

It took only a few minutes to reach the Beast, and Jenna was silent on the ride back to the office. She usually discussed her worries with him, and the lack of communication was just not like her. Maybe it was because it was the first time she'd seen him take down a group of men. He'd killed in the line of duty in her presence but never in a showdown like before. Concerned she might be seeing him in a different light, when he parked out front he turned to her. "Is there something on your mind? Something you need to discuss with me?"

"Yeah, there is." Jenna turned in her seat to look at him. "I'll leave the interview of the man Rowley took into custody to him and Rio, but we need to go and see the parents of the kids murdered in the forest. I guess with Rio and Rowley tied up, we'll have to take their victim's parents as well. I figure Carter and Jo can manage the third one... well, I hope so. We can't leave it any longer, but I need to go inside and try to cover these marks on my face. Do you mind waiting?"

Shaking his head in disbelief, Kane stared at her. "They can wait another half an hour. You need to sit down and have a cup of coffee and something to eat before you do anything." He cleared his throat. "I sure need to take some pain meds and unwind a little before we plunge into another stressful situation, that's for darn sure."

"I didn't think, I'm sorry." Jenna squeezed his arm. "You always seem to take everything in your stride. I know you were worried about me, but taking down those men didn't concern you, did it?"

Taking lives did concern him, but he didn't dwell on it. He sighed. "I don't kill someone and feel nothing, Jenna. The fact is, it was them or me. They wanted to kill me, and I gave them the option to walk away. They chose to draw down on me, so honestly, I won't lose any sleep over what happened, but seeing you kidnapped is another matter." He glanced at her. "Are you sure you'll cope with talking to the parents? You've just been kidnapped. I don't want you to experience another PTSD episode."

"I said we should keep going today because when I had PTSD the shrink told me to follow the day's plan, because it would help. I didn't suffer an attack but thought if we just carried on as normal, it would take the edge off. The truth is, what happened has shaken me up more than I had imagined. It wasn't being kidnapped so much, because I knew that you would come and find me, it was seeing you take the shot in the chest." Her eyes filled with tears. "I thought for a moment I'd lost you."

Kane cupped her cheek and kissed her. "I'm hard to kill, Jenna. It took only a minute or so to put on the liquid Kevlar vest. I was banking on taking them by surprise. I might be a big target, but when people panic, they tend to shoot wide. I was confident I could take them down before they got me. The big guy, the one I figure pulled you into the truck, is the one who fired the shot that hit me. He'd obviously been trained to hit center mass, and this was what I was banking on. I knew the vest would take the hit." He smiled. "If it had gotten nasty, I had plenty of trees to hide behind and Carter was on my tail. I've faced down more men than that alone, but I didn't like you seeing me in action. It's a part of me you didn't need to witness."

"It wasn't the killing, Dave. I've seen enough in my time but seeing them shoot at you was terrifying." Jenna shook her head. "Don't look at me like that. I know telling you I worry about you is a bad thing. Wolfe told me one time not to become your Achilles heel or I'd get you killed. Today, I messed up and put you in danger. I get that."

Exasperated, Kane snorted. "Like it was your fault some gorilla dragged you into their truck? Honestly, Jenna, that's not what's worrying me. Out there, I was in the zone and oblivious to anything but the target. I wasn't angry by the time I faced them, but when the first bullet hit me I went into survival mode. Seeing me like that isn't pretty and not something I ever wanted to reveal to you. It's something I'd rather forget but it's programmed into me. It's not going away anytime soon."

"I understand and next time I'll close my eyes." Jenna let out a long sigh. "If you're feeling okay, how about dropping by Aunt Betty's? We can grab a meal and you can take some pain meds. I'll ask if Susie Hartwig will fix up my face for me. She's great at makeup."

Duke barked his approval and Jenna laughed. "That makes it two against one."

Kane grinned at her. "Okay, you twisted my arm." He started the Beast and headed to the diner. They hurried inside and waited at the counter.

After placing their order, Susie Hartwig, the manager, whisked Jenna away into a back room and Kane took Duke to their usual table at the back corner of the diner. As a service dog, Duke was allowed to go anywhere and was well known throughout town. Apart from the sheriff's department logo on his coat, he carried a deputy's badge on his collar. Aunt Betty's Café was one of his favorite places as Susie always had leftover meat for him. Kane sat down and Wendy, the assistant manager, came right along with a pot of fresh coffee, cups, and the fixings.

"Jenna looks as if someone punched her in the head." Wendy gave him a long look and raised one eyebrow.

Abashed that the thought that he'd do such a thing could enter her mind, he stared at her. "Someone did, but they won't be laying hands again on a woman or anyone else anytime soon." He swallowed the need to tell her he'd killed the man responsible. If he let that slip, it would be all over town by suppertime.

"That's good to know." Wendy smiled at him. "I'll make

sure your slice of cherry pie is extra wide. You look like you've had a rough day and it's only lunchtime."

You have no idea. Amused, Kane nodded. "Thank you kindly."

The meals arrived soon after Jenna sat at the table. Kane smiled at her. "Good as new." He'd made up his mind to keep her occupied with the homicide, in the hope it would stop a slide into a PTSD episode. "We'll need to concentrate on gathering a list of suspects. Whoever killed those kids practice regularly, so our first port of call should be the crossbow ranges. Do you want to go there after we visit the parents?"

"That sounds like a plan." Jenna sipped her coffee and eyed him over the rim. "When we've eaten, I'll give Rowley a call to give us an update."

When she made the call, Kane listened with interest on one of Jenna's wireless earbuds.

"Have you interviewed the driver of the cattle truck?"

"Yeah, he insisted that stalling his truck in front of Kane was an accident." Rowley sounded amused. *"The problem with this is, one of the men who Kane shot and the watchout we arrested out front of the meth lab are brothers. When I mentioned this to him, he clammed up and asked for a lawyer. Right now, he's in interview room one with Sam Cross. Rio is going to interview him once we get the go-ahead from his lawyer."* He let out a long sigh. *"I've just returned from visiting Ash Roger's mother and giving her the bad news. I'll never get used to doing that. She mentioned the kids were just going fishing, is all, and can't believe what's happened. I told her Wolfe would be contacting her about a viewing ASAP. I called Father Derry also and he'll visit the families to offer his support. Carter dropped by before. He said the DA is reading over the statements on the shooting and will make a decision shortly. Apparently, he considered it a clean shoot, but Carter said he was just being thorough. Carter's*

left already. He headed out with Jo to speak to Zoe Ward's parents."

"Okay, thanks, Jake. I knew I could count on you." Jenna blew out a long sigh. "We're heading out to Lilac Way to hopefully speak to Leo Kelly's parents."

"His mother should be home. She's a stay-at-home mom. The three families are friends. I'll keep you updated when we hear back from the DA." He disconnected.

Kane squeezed her hand. "You've trained him well. He's very reliable and so is Rio. The office runs like a well-oiled machine."

"You're not worried about the DA's findings, are you?" Jenna pushed away her plate and reached for her refilled cup.

Shrugging, he met her gaze. "There's always an inquiry. It's part of the process, as you well know. He might ask for psych tests, but I figure he'll speak to Wolfe first and you know what he'll say. So no, I'm not overly worried. Taking them out has probably saved the county a fortune in legal and prison costs and taken millions of dollars' worth of drugs off the street." He took a forkful of the delicious pie, chewed, and swallowed. "It's not like I had a choice."

"I've seen you wound armed guys rather than kill them. Why was this different?" Jenna leaned forward in her chair. "Was it because they kidnapped me?"

It was a question he'd been expecting, and he shook his head. "Nope, if you're referring to the bikers who attacked you some time ago, they were going for their guns, so I had time to wound their shooting arms to prevent them drawing down on me. The guys in the forest were already shooting at me and posed a deadly threat. I didn't have the time to place my shots to give them a chance to try again. I had to take them down. It was me or them, like I said. What happened to you had nothing to do with my reasoning. I don't like killing people, Jenna. I'd have rather taken them in for questioning and followed up on their drug distribution. Now that's going to be difficult unless the DA cuts a deal with the truckdriver and he gives up information to save his hide."

"Okay, I understand. It's all good, Dave. With Rio on their tails, we'll get the information and hand it off to the DEA." Jenna emptied her cup. "When you're done here, we'd better get at it. This sure has been a long day. I can't believe it's only ten after one."

TEN

Devastated, Jenna sat in the Beast staring blankly into nothingness. Mrs. Kelly had clung to her, sobbing at the news of her son's death. Her deep penetrating grief had overwhelmed Jenna and she had not been able to untangle herself from the weeping woman until her husband had arrived with Father Derry, the latter having visited Mr. Kelly at his office to break the tragic news. Although Father Derry had a calming effect on the poor woman, her grief at losing her only son was palpable. When Kane started the engine, the small flame that had ignited in her to find justice for the young victims burst into an inferno. She looked at Kane. "I'm never giving up until we find the men who killed those kids."

"The first range isn't far from here." Kane regarded her closely. "Do you need a break? It was pretty intense back there."

Mentally giving herself a shake, Jenna fastened her seatbelt. "No breaks. I'm not stopping until I have a list of suspects. I'm going to hunt these men down like they did those kids." She turned to look at him. "No mercy."

"Okay." Kane turned the truck around and headed down Lilac.

At the end of the road, he turned into Stanton and accelerated. They drove past the Triple Z Roadhouse and took a sharp left into the Bullseye Archery Center and followed the blacktop to the store. Jenna pushed open her door and headed inside. She went straight to the front counter. The salesman turned from filling one of the displays and stared at her, mouth open. "I need some information and I need it now. Which of your members hang around in a group of three and are seriously good marksmen?"

The young man behind the counter just stared at her, wide eyed, his mouth opening and shutting like a landed trout. Anger rising, Jenna leaned on the counter. "Don't just stand there gaping at me. Three crossbow shooters murdered three teenagers in the forest this morning. I need to speak to anyone who could be involved and I need this information yesterday."

"I'm not sure I'm allowed to give you that type of information, Sheriff." The man took a step backward and crossed his arms over his chest. "Don't you need a warrant or something?"

Resting one hand on the handle of her M18, Jenna stared him down. "If you're withholding information from me, I'll charge you with obstruction of justice. You have five seconds to give me some names."

"Well, most of them come here in twos or alone." He rubbed his chin thinking. "There are only three who hunt together that I can recall, who are marksmen."

"We need their names and any other information you can give us." Kane stepped beside her, his notebook open in his hand. "Where they work for instance or their address, even a suburb would be helpful."

Geoff Bannister is a bartender at the Cattleman's Hotel. I believe he lives out at Alpine Ridge." The young man's hands shook as he looked up at Kane and make furtive glances toward Jenna. "Carl Harper, he works at the lumberyard, and Lonnie Barlow, he works at the general store and lives on Maple."

Satisfied, Jenna nodded. "Is that everyone you can think of?"

"Yeah, like I said, not many hunt in threes, but they've hung around together for a time." The young man swallowed hard. "That's all I can think of right now."

Jenna nodded and pulled out a card. "If you think of anyone else, call me, because if I discover you're withholding evidence, I'll be back with a warrant for your arrest."

"Yes, ma'am." The young man pushed the card into his top pocket with a shaky hand.

Anger still simmering, Jenna headed back to the Beast. Determined to find more suspects, she scrolled through her phone looking for other archery ranges. "I've found another crossbow range. Would you believe it's out back of our regular shooting range?"

"Yeah, I was heading that way." Kane fell into step beside her. "I figure that kid will be needing some fresh underwear after the grilling you gave him. You need to ease up some, Jenna. Most people will cooperate if you give them the right reason."

Jenna climbed into the Beast and waited for him to slide behind the wheel. "I haven't got time to be nice to people right now. Before we know it, this group of killers will strike again. You know the deal as well as I do. Once they start doing something like this, they don't give up until we stop them."

Ten minutes later, they arrived at the shooting club and followed the road until they came to the crossbow range. It was the same setup as the other place, with a small store that sold supplies and took the fees for the use of the range. An old man sat behind the counter, with receding gray hair and deep lines around his eyes from years of smiling. He greeted them both as if they were old friends. Jenna explained the situation. "Do you know three people who hunt together? As it's an unusual combination, they would surely be noticed. Can you think of anyone at all?"

"Three men who hunt together and are marksmen?" The old man thought for a beat. "We have many marksmen who frequent this club and many hunters. A good deal of them go out in groups. The only three people I can recall who come here together and use the range are two men and one woman." He opened a large book on the counter. "I'm old-school. I keep all the bookings in this ledger. When the other shift takes over from me, they upload them into the computer, but I insist they include a copy in here."

"Can you give us names?" Kane opened his notebook. "Any other information you might have would be very useful: ages, where they live, occupations, and the like."

"Okay, let me see now." The salesman ran his finger down the pages one at a time. "Here we go. Alicia Palmer, she works for my dentist. She's young, maybe twenty. She comes here with Bill Ripley. He's a freshman at college. The other one is older maybe mid-twenties. Jesse Davis took over Mustang Creek Ranch when his father died. I recall these three won their divisions in the last championship round we held. It was a tough field, so they're all excellent marksmen." He swung his gaze to Jenna. "I've seen Jesse talking with your deputy, Jake Rowley. Seems they go way back to grade school."

Relieved, Jenna smiled at him and handed him her card. "That's very helpful, thank you. If anyone else comes to mind, call me. Do you know of any other crossbow ranges in town?"

"There were three, but one closed after the floods last year and never reopened. There's just me and Bullseye open now."

Jenna smiled. "Okay, thanks for your time." She led the way back to the truck, and while Duke ran around sniffing, she stopped in the parking lot to stare at the forest and mountains. Under a clear blue sky, the view was spectacular and she took a few deep breaths of pine-scented air. It was as if the beauty around her corrected her equilibrium and calmness flooded over her. She turned to Kane and slid one arm around his waist. "Six suspects in less than half an hour. I figure that has to be a record."

"It is. What next? If you want to start hunting these people down, I'd prefer to check them out first so we know what we're walking in to." Kane pulled her against his shoulder and winced.

"Sure." Jenna lifted his shirt and gasped at the blackening bruise across his upper chest. "That looks painful. You need meds."

"I've got something back at the office that will help." Kane shrugged. "It's swollen, is all. I've had worse."

Jenna sighed. Living with a tough man was difficult at times. "Okay, we'll head back to the office and see what's cooking."

ELEVEN

Deputy Zac Rio believed that leaving LA and coming to Black Rock Falls would make life easier, but it seemed the crime rate in town was increasing by the week. He had spent the entire day rushing from one place to another juggling two cases. He'd updated the DA on the meth lab case, as Jake Williams, the person they'd discovered guarding it, was still in custody at county. With the second suspect, Deke Williams, waiting to be interviewed, he needed to know if the DA intended to bring the DEA in on the case.

"Interview the suspect and get back to me. His involvement in kidnapping a law enforcement officer will hold him for now. I figure this suspect will have details of distribution and contacts. I'll run it past the local DEA agents and get back to you. I'm sure they'll want to take this case off your hands, considering the amount of product being produced by these men, and we're talking serious numbers. Send me the statement from the suspect you have in custody and the video. I'll pass it on and I'll get back to you as soon as the DEA has made their decision."

Rio leaned back in his chair. "Okay thanks, I'm going to interview him now." He disconnected.

He made his way down to interview room one and knocked on the door before entering. Inside, the room smelled of fear and stale sweat. He nodded to the attorney, Sam Cross. "Is your client ready to talk?"

"He's willing to answer some questions." Sam Cross was a typical cowboy, and definitely not a typical lawyer.

After turning on the recording device, Rio placed the statement pad beside the notebook on the desk and, stating his name, who was present, the time and date, he turned his attention to Deke Williams. "I regret to inform you that your brother, Dean, is dead. He, along with the group of men who kidnapped Sheriff Alton, died in a shootout about an hour ago."

"The deputies and those FBI agents gunned them down, didn't they?" Deke screwed up his face in rage and hammered his handcuffed fists on the table. "That wasn't how it was supposed to go down. Dean only took the sheriff to trade for Jake, is all. No one was supposed to get hurt."

Unconcerned by the man's outburst, Rio flicked a glance at Sam Cross, to see if he had an objection to his line of questioning. "How it went down is that five men opened fire on one deputy, striking him in the chest. He returned fire. So now you understand if you decide to provide information on the running of the meth lab, distribution, and clients, you won't be ratting on anyone. It's over, Deke." He leaned forward on the table and stared at him. "Right now, you're looking at charges of accessory to the kidnapping of a law officer, obstructing a law officer in his duty, and being the member of a drug syndicate. I strongly suggest you speak to your lawyer and make a decision that could save you many years in prison." He turned his attention to Sam Cross. "The DA will be taking into account the information supplied during this interview. He is considering bringing in the DEA on this case because of the significant amount of drugs this group manufactured. It would be in your client's best interests to cooperate."

"If you give Deputy Rio the basic rundown of what occurred, I'll negotiate a deal with the DA." Cross turned in his seat to look at his client. "I'm sorry for your loss."

Rio stared at Deke. "First, we'll deal with the obstruction of an officer in his duty." He glanced down at the statement Deke made on scene. "You may want to retract your original statement. We have many witnesses to dispute your claim of accidentally driving in front of Deputy Kane and blocking the road. All the witness statements say that he had lights flashing and sirens blaring. You'd have to been blind not to see him. Then you followed up by not getting out of his way. When Deputy Rowley came on scene, he said your engine wasn't running and you were making no attempt to restart it." He gave him a long look. "Did you deliberately block Main to prevent Deputy Kane from pursuing your brother?"

"Yeah, it was part of the plan." Deke shook his head. It seemed that all the anger had drained away and only sorrow remained. "The deputy had been back and forth all day and we figured something was going on, so I parked the truck in an alleyway and waited. The sheriff always goes with the same deputy, so it was only a case of sitting and waiting until they came out. Dean figured the deputy's truck was powerful, but he thought his was faster and would only need a few minutes delay to get away after kidnapping the sheriff. Like I said, no one was supposed to get hurt. Dean planned to keep her for a few hours then call the deputy and negotiate a swap."

Surprised Deke had been so forthcoming, he nodded and moved right along. "How many states have you cooked in? It's obvious you move around frequently to avoid detection."

"All over." Deke shrugged. "We all had a job to do and were able to dismantle the gear and leave within minutes of being detected. We were away delivering the merchandise when you came across our latest hideout. We knew you'd been there because Dean had a security app on his phone. We just waited for you all to leave and then went back and cleaned the place out."

Rio gave Sam Cross a meaningful stare. It was very unusual for him not to object to questioning, but so far he'd said nothing. He made a few notes in his book and looked back at Deke. "So you must have information on bank accounts and clients. Where do we find that information?"

"It's in the cloud." Deke sighed. "Dean's laptop is back at the cabin where we were staying. All the information you require is on there. Look, I'm not hiding anything and I wasn't the mastermind. Dean organized everything and did the cooking. The rest of us were just gofers."

Having enough information to bring in the DEA to take over the case, Rio concluded the interview and stood. "I'll type up this statement and you can read it through and sign it. I'll hand the information over to the DA and then it's up to Mr. Cross to go speak to him." He stood and left the room, pulling the door shut behind him.

As he headed back to his desk, Jenna came in the front door with Kane. Both of them appeared strained. He placed the statement pad on the desk and went to speak to them. "I've interviewed Deke Williams, the guy who used his truck to block the road."

"Did you get anything out of him?" Jenna rubbed her temples.

Rio smiled. "Yeah, we have him hogtied and ready for roasting. He admitted to everything and gave details about the meth lab and why you were kidnapped. I'll send his statement to the DA, but he wants to call in the DEA because these guys were working across states."

"That's good because we'll need you and Rowley to handle any blowback about the shooting." Jenna sighed. "We'll need a meeting as soon as you're able. We have a list of possible suspects for the homicide. I'll be in my office if you need to run anything past me."

Nodding, Rio glanced at Kane and cleared his throat. "Sure, never a dull moment, huh?"

"You can say that again." Kane headed for the stairs to their office, one hand resting on the small of Jenna's back.

TWELVE

Visitation was one of the perks Jimmy Two Cents, aka James Earl Stafford, enjoyed. He had no loyalty to anyone, so when offered the chance of a few luxuries to spill his guts, he jumped at the idea. Although, no one could call him a rat because nobody knew he gave out tidbits of information like candy. He revealed just enough at a time to obtain what he needed. Chained hand and foot, he followed the guard to the visitation room and took a seat in his allotted space. There wasn't any privacy, just a seat and phone surrounded by a Perspex screen. His visitor was sitting there, waiting for him as he'd arranged. He corresponded with many people but had selected three to do his bidding. It hadn't been too difficult to teach the three of them his code. On each visit as they sat face to face, he'd explained it in simple terms. He smiled to himself as a confident person peered at him through the murky screen. He could tell by their demeanor that they'd completed the mission. "Did you visit the forest this weekend as planned? I hear the fishing is really good at this time of year. Did you catch anything?"

"Yeah, three big ones." The person behind the screen

smiled triumphantly. "Do you have any other suggestions? We had so much fun and can't wait to go hunting or fishing again."

Jimmy Two Cents chuckled, seeing the excitement in the eyes staring at him. "This time it's a little different and will demonstrate your loyalty to me. I've never asked anyone to try this before. It takes a special person, one like me, to achieve success. Unless you consider it to be too difficult? I'll understand if you're not ready yet. Hunting bear is a specialty."

"Bear?" The person blinked, realization dawning on them. "That would be complicated."

At first encounter, he'd given them all code names, names they signed their letters with as his pen pals. He could see the concern in his visitor's eyes and shook his head. If this person had a conscience, they wouldn't be able to complete their task. He smiled and leaned a little closer to the barrier. "Any fool can go fishing in a group but it takes skill to be out there on your own. Trust me, you will feel so much better when you've completed this task. You'll be stronger and self-reliant... and you'll enjoy it."

"Okay." The person swiped at their nose and shrugged. "What the heck. I'll do it."

Jimmy waved a finger at his visitor. "Don't forget, bear will be difficult to take down. Use a good rifle, and maybe add a few extra shots just to make it interesting. Or a knife always adds a special thrill. If you succeed, move next onto elk, and don't forget the trophies."

"It will be hard to bag an elk." The visitor narrowed their eyes. "I like elk."

Annoyed, Jimmy glared at the visitor. "If you allow your feelings to interfere, you might as well quit now. You're no good to me."

"I'm not a quitter." The visitor's hand white-knuckled on the phone receiver.

Nodding, Jimmy shrugged. "Fine, prove it to me. Come by

to visit me when you're done. I want to see a change in you. Everything that happens to you, shows in your eyes. You can never hide the truth from me." He hung up the phone, stood, and indicated to the prison guard to take him back to his cell.

"You look happy. Did you just receive some good news?" The prison guard looked at him suspiciously.

"Oh, you know me, every day in here is a blessing." He imagined the slaughter in the forest and smiled. His hand had extended far beyond the prison walls and, yeah, that made him happy.

THIRTEEN

With the team assembled in the conference room, Jenna requested an update from everyone and then turned to look at the list of suspects she'd added to the whiteboard. "This is all the information we have, so I want you to hunt down these people and do a background check. We'll split the list and get to work interviewing them first thing in the morning." She used her pen to point at the white board. "Alicia Palmer, twenty-three years old, out of Fallen Rock Crescent, she works at the local dentist. Bill Ripley is a college student who lives on campus, and Jesse Davis is a rancher from Mustang Creek. They're members of a crossbow club. All are marksmen and they compete in competition together."

"I've known Jesse Davis since grade school." Rowley looked up from his notes. "I don't believe he's capable of killing kids."

"We can't be sure what anyone is capable of doing." Kane leaned forward on the table, his fingers clasped. "These are the only two groups of three people we have discovered who go hunting regularly and compete at a high level. It's a place to start, is all."

Clearing her throat, Jenna looked around the table.

"Moving right along. The other group of three we discovered are Geoff Bannister, a bartender at the Cattleman's Hotel. He lives out at Alpine Ridge. Carl Harper, we don't have any details on him whatsoever, and Lonnie Barlow, a local man who works at the general store and lives out on Maple." She glanced from face to face. "There are six of us and six suspects. I'll take suspect number one and we'll go around the table from Kane and so on, so we each have one to hunt down. Any questions or concerns? Nope? Okay, get at it."

After taking her seat, Jenna pulled her laptop toward her, accessed the DMV, and entered her suspect's name: Alicia Palmer out of Fallen Rock Crescent. She was twenty-three years old and her occupation was listed as a dental hygienist. She currently worked for the local dentist. She had no criminal record and a search of social media confirmed her skill with the crossbow. She had many images displaying her wins at events throughout the state. In more than one photograph, she was pictured beside two men mentioned as her team. After following the links, she discovered the media pages of Jesse Davis and Bill Ripley. She turned to look at Kane. "I've found Bill Ripley's social media page. From what I can see, the three of them were heavily involved in competition."

"Yeah, same." Kane tapped away on his laptop. "Ripley is clean. He's at college and lives on campus. I didn't find too much about him at all. He doesn't have many friends on his media page. I figure he's kind of a loner." He shrugged. "Or he spends all his time studying or shooting his crossbow. Not everybody in college is a party animal." He looked at Carter. "What did you find on Rowley's friend?"

"Jesse Davis runs a cattle ranch out of Mustang Creek." Carter removed the toothpick in the corner of his mouth and smiled. "Squeaky clean, this guy hasn't even had a traffic violation, but then I've seen the most violent murderers with a clean rap sheet, so that doesn't mean much." He sighed. "From his social media pages, he's a player. Over seventy-five percent of his friends are women. He posts a ton of images, many of them are with the group of people he competes with. Some were taken in the forest. It seems his game of choice are elk." He leaned back in his chair, spinning it from side to side. "One thing of interest, he reads true crime and has a passion for serial killers."

Beside him Rowley snorted and Jenna stared at him. "What's so funny?"

"Do you have any idea how many people in this town read books about serial killers?" Rowley turned in his seat to look at her. "Since the true crime series was published, telling all about what happens here, the sales have gone ballistic. The townsfolk read the books to find out what wasn't released to the press in the cases we handled. If you take the time to drop by the bookstore, you'll notice the front window is filled with crime novels. Seems to me that everyone in town who enjoys reading reads crime." He smiled. "Reading about serial killers doesn't make you one."

"I never intimated that it did." Carter held up both hands in submission. "As we're going into the background of all the suspects, it was a point of interest, is all." He rolled his eyes. "Maybe it's time you stepped away from the investigation, seeing he's a friend of yours?"

Feeling as if she was losing control of the team, Jenna stood and glared at them. "In a small town many of the people here are known to us. That is no reason not to investigate them. Being a friend makes no difference whatsoever at this stage of the investigation. If at a later date we discover a close relationship is a conflict of interest, we'll deal with it then. Rowley, you mentioned that this guy went to grade school with you. Is he part of your inner circle of friends now?"

"Nope." Rowley leaned back in his chair with his hands

clasped. "I see him around town occasionally and we've passed the time of day, is all."

Relieved, Jenna nodded. "Okay, but I'd like to bring to mind James Stone, a prominent lawyer in town, a man that I dated who subsequently shot Kane in the head and tried to murder me. He was also credited with the murders of hikers. In the end, I shot him. So just because someone is an acquaintance or friend, and seems fine on the outside, we must never take it for granted that they're not involved."

"That's a given." Jo had been watching the interplay like a tennis match, her head moving back and forth from one person to the other. "It seems to me, apart from the people in this room and our close family members, we can't afford to trust anyone."

"Yeah." Kane blew out a long breath. "Serial killers can be anywhere, in any occupation, any sex or age. I have one rule of thumb and that is look at every suspect as if they are guilty until you can prove otherwise. I know it totally destroys the innocent-until-proven-guilty rule, but so far it's kept me alive."

Needing to keep the investigation moving forward, Jenna cleared her throat and looked at Rowley. "Did you find anything interesting on your suspect?"

"Yeah." Rowley scanned his screen. "I have Geoff Bannister from out of Alpine Ridge. His occupation is a bartender at the Cattleman's Hotel. He has misdemeanors. The bartender is a secondary occupation; his primary occupation is listed as a bull rider. So the majority of his misdemeanors concerns brawling, willful damage of property, and supplying liquor to an underage girl." He rubbed his chin. "He hunts with the same two men, and they attend all the competitions together, and have done for the last five years."

Jenna nodded. "Rio?"

Carter's phone buzzed and he stood and left the room. Jenna stared after him. "Rio, can I have an update?"

"Sure." Rio leaned forward, resting his arms on the table.

"Carl Harper spent some time in jail after a hunting accident in Blackwater. A Blackwater local accused him of stalking him in the forest, finally hitting him in the leg with a crossbow bolt. Apparently, the victim called the sheriff for assistance. Harper was arrested and did three months for aggravated assault." He is currently employed by the local lumberyard in town. He lives in an apartment block on Main. I have the address."

Jenna stared at the door as Carter came into the room and whispered something to Kane. She looked from one to the other as they went outside into the passageway. "Thanks, Rio. Just give me a minute." She followed the men outside and, closing the door behind her, looked from one to the other. "What's up?"

"Nothing." Carter tossed a toothpick into his mouth and grinned. "The DA has cleared Kane. He said he'd reviewed the statements and there's no case to answer. It was a clean shoot. Kane was acting in self-defense."

"I wasn't worried." Kane shrugged. "Going through the process was necessary, although the DA's decision wouldn't stop any of the relatives from seeking revenge."

Relieved, Jenna blew out a long breath. "Let's hope it doesn't come to that. I'll ask Rio to contact the media and put out the statement that Carter suggested. We'll keep the details in house." She glanced at her watch. "It's getting late. I need to hear what Jo has discovered and then we can decide who we are going to interview first." She led the way back into the room.

Standing at the head of the table, she smiled. "The DA cleared Kane, so there won't be any delays in going forward with the homicide. Jo, what do you have for me?"

"Lonnie Barlow works at the general store here in town and lives out on Maple with his parents. He has no priors. His close friends are Harper and Bannister, as we've already established. He seems to be an ordinary guy. I can't find any dirt on him at all." Jo sighed. "Looking over all these suspects, no one jumps out and grabs you by the throat, do they?" She fiddled with her pen. "I mean, the obvious one in this group would be Harper, as he has priors for assault with a crossbow, but he didn't kill the victim did he and the homicides in the forest were executions. It's a big leap of faith to believe someone would go from wounding to murder. We don't know enough about the case to know if provocation was involved."

Jenna sat down and ran both hands through her hair. Her face ached from being punched and she needed some time to think before she proceeded with the investigation. "Okay, if you could update your files, I'll organize the interviews. We'll start fresh, first thing in the morning. Don't forget the autopsies on the homicide victims are at ten." She turned to Rio. "I know I'm not involved with the meth lab case, but could you give me an update? When will you be available to work full-time on the homicide?"

"Now. I took all the information over to the DA earlier. He looked over the case and decided to bring in the DEA. The case is widespread, over many states and out of our jurisdiction. Deke Williams will be picked up and taken to county this afternoon. Once the DEA is through with him, he might never get out of jail. If he does, he'll be back here to face charges of kidnapping you."

"So, it's over?" Kane leaned against the wall. "For now, at least?"

"Yeah." Rio smiled. "Oh, and before you ask, Wolfe said that Dr. Norrell Larson has taken on the mysterious forest graves cases. He said each of the investigations will take months, as she has no time frame to go on. It will be good to watch her work. Forensic anthropology is very interesting."

"I guess it helps that it also happens to be Emily Wolfe's favorite subject." Kane slapped him on the back. "Let's hope we solve this case soon, so you have time to offer your assistance. I'm sure we could spare you between cases."

Jenna smiled. There had been a budding romance between

Wolfe's daughter and Rio for a time, but with Emily's studies to become a medical examiner, everything had been put on hold. Rio was perfect for Emily, and the matchmaker in her would love to see them together. She looked at Kane. "I'm sure we could too. I have a feeling we're going to be involved in the cold cases one way or the other." She looked at her watch and sighed. "Time to head home. I don't figure I'll have trouble sleeping tonight. I'm beat."

FOURTEEN

TUESDAY

A beautiful day greeted Jenna and she stood for a few moments on her front porch to marvel at the way the early morning sun turned the top of the trees to gold. As far as she could see, deep blue sky stretched out in all directions with not a cloud in sight. It would have been a perfect day to take a trail ride or a walk along the riverbank. Her short weekend with Kane had made her realize how much they were missing. They'd spent weeks investigating one crime after another with little or no downtime in between. She smiled as an eagle circled high above and wished in that second she could change places with it. Sighing, she walked down the steps and headed to the stables. She could see Carter moving around inside, with Zorro standing watch at the door. This morning, when Kane neglected to complete his usual grueling workout, she realized just how much the gunshot to his chest had affected him. He'd headed for the hot tub after dinner and completed a few stretching exercises earlier but then decided to go straight to the kitchen to cook breakfast. She'd received a bullet in a Kevlar vest herself. It had been like a kick from a horse.

She went inside the stables and gave Carter a wave. "I figure we should turn out the horses this morning. It's a beautiful day and the grass is growing so long in the corral we won't have to worry about them being hungry if we're late home tonight."

"Yeah, and we won't have to muck out the stalls when we get home either." Carter grinned. "You move them and I'll finish up here." He indicated to Kane's stallion, Warrior. "Are you okay with him?"

Laughing, Jenna nodded. "Yeah, he's a lot like his owner, his bark is worse than his bite." She collected the horses one by one and led them to the corral.

Returning to the stables, she scattered fresh straw into the stalls. "I'm not looking forward to the autopsy this morning."

"I figure it will be pretty straightforward." Carter closed the doors and tipped back his Stetson. "The cause of death is obvious. The autopsy will make it official, is all." He brushed straw from his jeans and walked outside with her. "I contacted Bobby Kalo last night, and we went to work on the victims' phones. They didn't keep much about their social life private. It was all over social media and, from the number of messages, they discussed everything with their friends. It would have been easy to discover where they were going and at what time."

Exasperated, Jenna pulled straw from her hair and turned to slide the barn door shut. "Darn, I was hoping we'd find a lead, but then kids of that age usually have their heads bent over their phones 24/7. I mean, they even take pictures of their meals and share them. I guess telling everyone about a fishing trip is normal these days."

"Do you want us at the autopsies or would you prefer that we head out to interview some of the suspects?" Carter balled his fists on his waist.

Jenna thought for a beat. The faster they interviewed the suspects the better, although discussing the case with Wolfe was an essential part of the investigation. "You should come to the autopsies. Wolfe always has a different slant on things and we don't want to miss anything. Rio and Rowley can get started and we'll head out after the autopsies."

"That works for me." Carter headed toward the cottage. "We'll see you at breakfast."

Jenna headed inside the house and was greeted by the smell of freshly brewed coffee. She went via the kitchen to see what Kane was making for breakfast and caught him sliding a large platter of ham-and-cheese omelets into the oven to keep warm. "Mmm, they smell delicious. I'll grab a shower and then come back and help you."

"It's okay." Kane grinned at her. "I'm just about done here, as soon as I've fried the breakfast potatoes. I'll make toast as well but that can wait."

Jenna kissed his cheek. "I'm so glad you can cook."

Carter and Jo were at the table discussing plans for the day when she walked back into the kitchen. She helped Kane serve the breakfast and then sat down. "I figure Wolfe would have already performed a preliminary examination of the victims, so with luck, we might not be held up too long at the morgue. We need to chase down the suspects before anyone else is hurt."

"I went over their profiles last night." Jo sipped her coffee. "Nothing jumps out at me. I think it's because I'm so used to looking at psychopaths' profiles, although these people all could have the capability of killing under different circumstances. I'm not seeing the cunning I usually see that enables me to create a profile. Looking at the crime scene, and I am sure we've all seen similar on the battlefield, who exactly am I profiling? This group of killers we are assuming are part of a local team or enthusiasts' crossbow club, but if we look outside the box, we might be missing the obvious."

Intrigued, Jenna put down her fork. "Which is?"

"Who are the parents and are they involved in some way?" Jo placed her cup gently on the table, turning it with her fingertips. "What if this murder is a form of payback or a warning?"

"So we should be looking deeper into the parents' backgrounds?" Carter nodded. "I'll get Kalo onto it ASAP."

Jenna stared at Jo. "That would make life a whole lot more complicated."

"Yeah, it would." Kane leaned back in his chair, making it complain, and shook his head. "I can't imagine a cartel or whatever has infiltrated Black Rock Falls. They wouldn't have been established long enough for Mr. and Mrs. Average to become a problem. I mean, killing three kids as a warning is extreme. I know a meth lab snuck under our defenses, but it didn't last long, did it?"

"I see your point." Carter's fork paused on the way to his mouth. "We've heard nothing about gangs or anyone else coming under suspicion for illegal activities in this county. Meth labs pop up all over. They can be very small, have local distribution, and go unnoticed, but usually someone gets greedy and the shit hits the fan." He glanced at Jenna. "I'm with Kane on this one. I figure we stick to the list of suspects. If they don't pan out, we'll try another angle."

After listening to the conversation and theories, Jenna ran both hands down her face. "I agree the list of suspects is sketchy but it's all we have for now. We follow procedure and work through the list and see if we can place any of them in the forest at the time of death. If that doesn't work, we move to plan B."

"Which is?" Carter eyed her speculatively.

Jenna filled her fork. "I'll tell you when I know."

FIFTEEN

After arriving at the office, Jenna received a call from the DA informing her that the DEA had taken over the meth lab case. She would be kept informed, but on the information received, it was obvious that both the Williams brothers would be dealing their way out of life sentences. Glad her team had been involved in removing the manufacturing and distribution of dangerous drugs, she set her mind to the homicide case. With six suspects to interview, she gave Rio and Rowley the task of hunting them down. She needed to know where they would be and when to catch them unawares. She instructed Rio and Rowley to take the first suspect they found and go and interview them. She would head out to the ME's office for the autopsies with Kane, Jo, and Carter. She turned to Rio. "When you're done, keep hunting them down. Message me with anyone else on the list you find and we'll head out and see them after the autopsy."

"I'm on it." Rio stood and headed out the door with Rowley close behind.

Jenna stood and gathered her things. She grimaced.

"Nothing like attending an autopsy to spoil a perfectly good day."

"You can say that again." Kane followed her out of the office with Duke on his heels.

Walking into the morgue had everyone in a somber mood. Coming from a bright sunny day, an inch into a cold white tile environment crushed any happy thoughts. Although Wolfe used every means available to keep the odors to a minimum, underneath the antiseptic smell, the stench of death lingered like an evil entity. Goosebumps prickled across Jenna's skin as the cold air seeped through her clothes. She often wondered how Wolfe and his team appeared to be completely oblivious to the stench and cold. She figured maybe after so long they'd gotten used to it.

Their footsteps on the tile, along with the tap of the dogs' claws, echoed along the corridors as they made their way to Wolfe's office to deposit the dogs and then continue on to the examination rooms. In an alcove opposite, they shucked their jackets, exchanging them for scrubs, face masks, and gloves. Jenna moved her gaze along the three rooms, noting that each of them had a red light burning outside, which suggested that all the rooms were in use. She looked at Kane. "Did Wolfe mention where he'd be completing the homicide autopsies?"

"Nope." Kane frowned. "I'm guessing he would be kind of busy right now. He'd be handling the autopsies for the shooting as well." He turned to Carter. "I don't figure it would be a good idea if I walked in on the autopsies of the men I shot. Take a look for me, please?" He offered Carter his card for the scanner.

"You've got it." Carter plucked the card from his hand and waved it over the scanner of examination room one. As the door slid open, he turned and gave them the thumbs-up. "Right first time." He handed the card back to Kane.

"I'm sorry." Wolfe came out from a back room. "I didn't hear you arrive. Things are a bit hectic around here today. "Emily is assisting Norrell's team in room two, and I have a sudden death that arrived from the hospital early this morning." His attention moved across them. "It's just me today. Webber is organizing the hospital arrival, as there's a rush on it." He was referring to his assistant and badge holding deputy Colt Webber.

Preparing herself, Jenna moved closer to the first of the three gurneys, set out in a line before the stainless steel refrigerated drawers in the wall. It pained her to see three teenagers with their lives ahead of them reduced to three shapeless lumps under white sheets. She folded her arms across her chest in an unconscious barrier against viewing an unscrupulous premeditated murder. This wasn't the act of a mentally disturbed psychopath nor did she believe these murders were organized hits. No, her gut was screaming at her that the people who committed this unspeakable act of violence did it for fun. She swallowed hard as Wolfe pulled back the first sheet. The young girl was so pale and waxlike. Seeing her like this must have destroyed her parents. Tears welled and she tried desperately to force her humanity into a mask of professionalism. Apprehending these thrill killers was paramount. She swallowed hard. To win, this time she'd need to turn her deep-set sorrow into an unstoppable force to catch the people responsible.

"I completed a preliminary examination, first on scene and later on arrival. At that time, I recovered the pennies under each eye. They were placed post mortem and not one of them held any trace evidence. All are of different dates and unremarkable." Wolfe went to an array of screens and displayed the crime scene images taken in the forest. "The time of death we can narrow down to between the time the group left home and when the warden found them. There's little damage from critters, and blood loss on the two single-shot victims was minimal.

This tells us that death occurred within seconds of the sharp force trauma, which we have established was inflicted by a crossbow. The wounds, as Rowley mentioned, are typical in type to those inflicted by a popular deer- or elk-hunting bolt. I used six different types for comparison in a pig carcass. Rowley assisted me yesterday after work by shooting bolts at the correct distance and angle, and an EVO-X CenterPunch premium carbon arrow, used to increase penetration power, gave a positive result, as far as we could estimate, considering the bolts were removed from the victims. The wounds and the surrounding tissue damage due to the velocity and kinetic energy were similar."

Envisioning the horrific few minutes prior to their deaths, Jenna indicated to victim number one, Leo Kelly. "It was different for him, wasn't it? Do you think he saw his attackers?"

"The line of sight for Kelly was minimal." Kane hadn't taken his eyes off the gurney. "We have to assume that he was moving along the trail. They wanted a kill shot, so aimed for the femoral artery."

Jenna nodded. "Would the shooter have repositioned to take the second shot?"

"No." Kane turned to look at her. "I figure that came from shooter number two. Kelly dragged himself to Zoe Ward, so he would have been in their line of sight." He shook his head. "These kids knew nothing about survival or hunting. If someone is shooting at you, the first thing you do is take cover, right? Yet Kelly remained in the open." He shrugged. "In my opinion, the first three shots were simultaneous and the marks from the arrowheads in the dirt would suggest the victims of the neck wounds fell facedown."

"I concur with that conclusion." Wolfe lifted a scalpel and made an incision on Kelly's thigh and folded back the skin and muscle to display the femoral artery. "As you can see, the artery has been bisected. There was no need for the second shot. This alone is a fatal wound." He took a swab and collected the debris inside the wound. "The soil inside the wound is consistent with the bolt being removed. I've collected sample swabs from the clothing of all the victims, and we'll run DNA testing, if the shooters left a trace behind, we'll find it."

"Is the lividity the same in all the victims?" Carter folded his arms across his chest. "Or were they moved?"

"Livor mortis, the purple bruising from when the blood pools after death, is consistent to our theory." He removed the sheets from the other two victims. "As you can see, they all have lividity on the chest and thighs."

"Why do you think they shot across the neck in each case, rather than from behind?" Jo moved closer to the gurney and stared at the bodies.

"It's a failsafe shot and highly skilled, to ensure puncturing the carotid artery." Wolfe shook his head. "I understand that y'all figure that this is a thrill kill, but from my experience in the military, this sure looks like a hit team to me." He waved a hand toward the gurneys. "It's too darn clean. Thrill kills are usually messy, and these guys took the time to clean the crime scene like professionals. Maybe you should be looking a little deeper into what the parents of these kids do. You can't risk neglecting the fact that the homicides could have been a warning."

"We've dug into the backgrounds of these kids and found nothing of interest." Carter blew out a long sigh. "I can see where you're coming from, so I'll get Kalo to dig deeper."

As Wolfe moved from one victim to the other, dissecting and examining the sharp force trauma wounds and explaining each one in detail, Jenna found her mind wandering. Two possible reasons for the murders had her in a quandary. If it was a thrill kill, then the killers could be out murdering unsuspecting hikers again anytime soon, but if it was a warning from a hit squad, then this might be the last they see of them.

After Wolfe concluded the autopsies, she thanked him, walked outside, and went to the alcove to remove the scrubs.

"You were quiet in there." Kane tossed his gloves and mask into the trash and followed her to Wolfe's office to collect the dogs. "What's on your mind?"

Jenna waited for Jo and Carter to join them, and they stood in the corridor in a huddle. "If this is a hit, why the reference to Jimmy Two Cents? Usually anyone involved in a hit likes to keep themselves anonymous, so why leave the pennies? It's an obvious connection to a known criminal. If he is involved, why did it take so long to take revenge on the parents of these kids?"

"Maybe Kalo will be able to discover a connection." Carter tossed a toothpick into his mouth. "Although it might seem like a long time to get revenge, but being in jail, he'd only be able to strike when the opportunity presented itself. I'll look into his case and see if I can hunt down any angles. Maybe one of the parents gave evidence against him and this was his only chance."

Relived the team was steadfastly behind her as usual, Jenna smiled. "Thanks."

"Then again, if it is a copycat thrill kill, then we need to discover more about Jimmy Two Cents." Kane leaned casually against the wall. "I know the general outline of his case but not what motivated him to kill. I'll need to discover what details were released about him to the media and if he has any type of cult following."

"I can find out everything you need to know about him." Jo's face was animated. "I only need an excuse to get an interview with him and we could go straight to the source. It worked well in the past. Also, if I contact the prison, I'll be able to get the details of his activities and if he's been corresponding with anyone in particular. We know we're dealing with a cunning intelligence. If I interview him, I'll have some idea if he has the capability of manipulating people to do his will." She shrugged.

"Although it's very unusual to have three serial killers working together, but we are learning new things about this type of psychosis every day."

"More like a leader and two followers." Kane rubbed his chin. "I figure it gets to a point with these dominant murderers that the people they convince to kill become afraid of them. They keep on going because they're in fear of their life. We've seen this situation before and if you include cults, then it's the perfect scenario. There's always one dominant leader who seemly can convince masses of people to do their bidding, even to the extent of taking their own lives. I've come to the conclusion that nothing is impossible. We have to look at every angle."

Listening with interest, Jenna nodded. "First, we go and talk to the suspects and then we'll have some idea if we're heading in the right direction. If none of them are involved, they might be able to point us toward others they compete against. Right now, we're only surmising that they all live in or around town. Knowing what we do about comfort zones, this group of people could be killing all over. When I get back to the office this afternoon, I'll put out a request to be notified for similar cases and see if we get any callbacks from local counties." She waved them all toward the door. "Let's get at it. We have people to interview."

SIXTEEN

As she walked deep into the forest, his voice ran through her mind, sending shivers of excitement through her. He was a friend but had never looked at her like that before. It was as if she'd been dreaming. His soft sultry voice played like an earwig with each step along the darkening trail.

Little Bear, huh? The name suits you. I could fall into your big brown eyes. Let's meet up in the forest at two. It will be our little secret. Just you and me. We don't need anyone else's company. Meet me on the trail opposite Pine and I'll show you a rock pool I found. It's my secret place and I only tell my special friends about it. You'll come, won't you? I'll be waiting.

He was a flirt and could have any woman he chose, but why the sudden interest in her? She'd finished for the day and he'd dropped by her table at Aunt Betty's Café to chat. She'd listened to his invitation with skepticism and declined to respond. He had to be joshing and she met his amused expression with a sigh. "Don't you have anything to do this afternoon?"

"Nope." He stretched out his long legs and grinned. "I'm all yours. Aw, come on, Bear. You know you want to. I see the way you look at me."

Her face grew hot and she looked away. She cleared her throat. "Okay, I'll meet you, but if this is some sick joke—"

"I'm not joking." He ran the tip of one finger down her cheek. "I'm deadly serious. See you at two."

Idiotic came to mind as she stumbled over a tree root. Had he played her for a fool? Deep down inside, she had to know one way or the other. The forest had an eerie silence, missing the usual sounds of wildlife. The deeper she moved along the trail, the darker it became. High above, dense foliage obscured the brilliant blue sky, and with each step the temperature dropped raising goosebumps on her arms. Ahead she heard a rustling and heart thumping stopped midstride to scan the forest in all directions. Wildlife was in abundance at this time of year, and the fact silence surrounded her was a warning that a predator was close by. The next second, he stepped out of the trees with a wide grin stretched across his face.

"You came." He offered his hand and clasped hers, dragging her forward. "This way."

She followed him, weaving through pastoral tracks until she could hear the rushing of water in the distance. He led her to a sunny clearing. A rock formation alongside the falls had created a deep rock pool. Water trickled into it at one end from the falls thundering down the valley to overflow at the other end, creating a clean swirling rock pool.

"See, didn't I tell you it was magic?" He sat on a boulder and pulled off his boots. "Come on, it's perfect for skinny-dipping." He gave her a long look. "You're not a tease, are you?"

She kicked off her shoes and unbuttoned her blouse. "No, this isn't my first skinny-dip."

"Good." He removed his belt and laid it on the rocks surrounding the pool. The hilt of the substantial hunting knife he always carried poked out of its sheath and glistened in the sunlight. "Last one in the water buys the coffee." He jumped into the rock pool.

She followed and shivered at the icy cold water, but he just laughed and splashed her. Ducking away, she turned back to splash him when sunlight sparkled on the blade of his knife. The smile died on her face as he waded toward her, his face frozen in a blank expression. "What are you doing with that knife? You're frightening me."

"It's your time to die, Bear." He moved closer. "There's no escape. Come here and I'll make it easy on you. Run and I'll slice you like a turkey on Thanksgiving."

Panic gripped her and she glanced over one shoulder, searching for a way out of the pool. If she climbed over the rocks, it was a sheer drop to the falls. She must make him see reason. "Don't be stupid. Everyone saw you with me today in Aunt Betty's, and why me? What have I ever done to you? I thought we were friends?"

"It makes no difference." He moved closer, crowding her back against the rocks. "When it comes to the kill, it's all about me." He raised the knife.

She screamed and ducked away but the blade sliced through her shoulder. All around her the water filled with red ribbons. Uncomprehending, she blinked and gaped at him, slapping at him with both hands, but he just smiled and struck again as if he'd planned each move and was enjoying her suffering. His expression had fixed into a horrific smile as he slashed at her. The swirling water slowed her down as, terrified, she turned her back on him and tried to scramble over the rocks. There was no escaping his vicious attack. Behind her, he grunted with effort, one hand wrapped around her arm to prevent her escape. Each stab he inflicted vibrated through her like punches rather than stabs. Suddenly there was no pain, but the water ran red all around her. In one last effort, she tried to raise her arms to fight back but they refused to move. The next moment, her numb legs came out from under her. Helpless, she lay floating on her back gasping for air and stared at his ruby-splattered face. The metallic taste of blood filled her mouth and all around her seemed to be slipping away. She forced out a breath. "Please... stop."

"Not yet." He leaned over her and grasped her hair. "I need to see you smile, one last time." He held the knife in front of her eyes and then drew it across her throat. "Goodbye, Little Bear."

SEVENTEEN

Back at the office, Carter had made all the necessary calls. Bobby Kalo, the FBI IT whiz kid, was hot on the trail of the parents of the victims. If they'd had a parking ticket anywhere in the US, he'd find it. Carter leaned back in his chair, waiting for Jo to finish her call. She'd been requesting information about Jimmy Two Cents from every source available. Kane had hunted down where and when Jimmy Two Cents had committed his crimes and requested all case files. It was a hive of activity, with Jenna issuing instructions like a general. She was a petite woman, who people who didn't know her underestimated, and yet she had the presence of a giant. He turned as Jenna returned to the long desk in the center of the conference room. "Okay, now it's a waiting game. Did Rowley or Rio leave a list of details for our suspects? Once Jo is ready, we can get at it."

"I have the list. I'll send it to both of you." Jenna tapped away on her phone. "If you take the top two, Alicia Palmer and Bill Ripley, they're both in town, we'll start on Jesse Davis and Geoff Bannister, they are out of town. Rio and Rowley are handling the others." She gave him a long look. "Check in and out with Maggie. If you need to talk to me, use the phone. The radio isn't secure."

To experienced officers, that was a given, but as Jenna covered all the bases, all the time, Carter just smiled. "Copy that."

"I'm expecting a ton of information." Jo disconnected and pushed her phone into her pocket. "Apparently, Jimmy Two Cents has come under the interest of a number of different psychologists since he was first arrested. The local PD was very forthcoming and put me in contact with the first doctor who analyzed him. He in turn was able to give me the names of others."

Raising his eyebrows, Carter frowned. "Is sharing medical information legal? What about doctor-patient privilege?"

"The HIPAA privacy act, which is the Health Insurance Portability and Accountability Act of 1996, is much the same, but it allows medical providers to share information for the good of the patient. It keeps us all on the same page and is essential in following treatment patterns." She gave him a long look. "This is how your physician knew about your PTSD episodes because you discussed them with your shrink. I'm able to obtain this information because, as a psychologist in the field of criminal behavior, I'm planning on interviewing Jimmy Two Cents and need to be updated on his condition."

Astounded he hadn't taken notice of such an important change in the law, he rubbed his chin. "I just figured the FBI knows all."

"No, they don't." Jo collected her things from the desk. "That's not saying they don't have means and ways of obtaining information. Bobby Kalo isn't the only cybercrime whiz kid working with us. They are recruiting more every day." She looked at him. "I'm done here. Let's go. We have a ton of things to do."

They headed downstairs and took Jenna's cruiser from the

parking lot out back. Carter settled Zorro in the back seat, slid behind the wheel, and started the engine. He looked at Jo. "Okay, who's first on our list?"

"We have Alicia Palmer, twenty-three years old, out of Fallen Rock Crescent. She works as a dental hygienist here in town, and Rowley suggests we try there first." She added the address to the GPS and smiled when it popped up on the screen. "It's not far, on Main in the middle of town."

They found the dentist above one of the stores in town and Carter went straight to the counter and rang the bell. The smell inside the dentist's put Carter's teeth on edge and brought back memories he'd rather forget. Although he had to admit he'd received first-class treatment during his time at Quantico, and the childhood mishaps were a thing of the past, but the bad memories always seemed to creep back the moment his next checkup was due. When a man in white stepped out from the back room and smiled congenially, Carter nodded and showed him his creds. "Agents Carter and Wells. We'd like to speak to Alicia Palmer. I believe she works here."

"She does indeed but not this afternoon." The dentist looked concerned. "Has something happened?"

Shaking his head, Carter took a card from his inside pocket and handed it to him. "No, we'd just like to speak to her. She might be able to supply us with some information we need on a case." He wanted to obtain any information he could on Alicia and drummed his fingers on the counter. "How long has she worked for you?"

"Four years." The dentist's brow furrowed. "She's very dependable."

"That's good to know." Jo nodded and smiled as if attempting to allay the man's fears. "We hear she is a marksman with the crossbow."

"Yeah. She often brings in her trophies to show me." He looked from one to the other. "What is this all about?"

Carter smiled. "Oh, nothing to concern you. Do you have any idea where we can find her?"

"She'll be at home, I guess, or shopping." The dentist took one of his cards from a holder on the counter and scribbled a number on the back. "These are her cell and landline numbers. She could be anywhere around town. I have no idea. She didn't mention anything about going anywhere when she left this morning."

"Okay, thanks." Jo picked up the card. "Thank you for your time."

As they walked onto the sidewalk, Carter leaned against the wall of the building as Jo called Alicia. "That's weird. I got an out-of-service message." She redialed and tried again. "Hmm. Same message. I'll try her landline." She made the call and they waited. "She's not picking up. We'll drop by and do a welfare check. She only lives a mile away."

Carter climbed back behind the wheel of the cruiser and added Fallen Rock Crescent to the GPS. As he spun the vehicle around and headed along Main, he turned to Jo. "Check out what vehicle she drives."

"Okay." Jo used the mobile data terminal in the cruiser and soon found the vehicle and registration. "I have it. It's a green Jeep Cherokee."

After driving toward what Jenna always described as the new area of town, they turned onto Fallen Rock Crescent and Carter pulled onto the driveway of a neat wood cabin-style home. There was no vehicle in the driveway, but a dog barked inside as they approached the door. He knocked hard three or four times. "FBI. Are you inside, Alicia?"

Nothing but the snarling of a dog.

"It's a big dog. Bullmastiff, maybe." Jo pressed her cupped hands against the window and peered inside. "Oh, here he comes." She jumped back as the dog hurled itself at the window, barking and slobbering spittle in all directions.

Beside Carter, Zorro's hackles rose and the skin pulled back from his teeth to expose long canines. He lunged forward with a low warning growl and placed himself in front of them. Glad of the barrier between the dogs snapping teeth, Carter glanced at Jo. "We'll walk around and look in the windows, but I figure she's out, seeing the Jeep is gone." He raised both eyebrows. "One thing is for darn sure. I'm not opening that door to go inside to check. If necessary, we'll call in some dog handlers." He turned to Zorro. "With me."

They found no sign of Alicia inside the house as far as they could ascertain. They had views through the windows of a good part of the interior of the house. Nothing seemed out of place, and no signs of a struggle. "We'll make a note to come back later." He called Maggie on the radio to bring her up to date and then added the next suspect's address into the GPS.

"Okay." Jo peered at her phone. "Next, we have Bill Ripley, a college student. He lives on campus and the information we have on him, apart from being in the crossbow team with Alicia and Jesse Davis, is he's described as a loner in his high school yearbook."

Carter headed up Stanton and drove past a green Jeep Cherokee parked off-road and alongside a trail leading into the forest. He waited for a break in the traffic and then backed up and stopped parallel with the other vehicle. "Run the license plate."

He drummed his fingers on the steering wheel as Jo entered the information into the MDT and waited for the confirmation. The Jeep was registered to Alicia. Carter climbed out of the cruiser and went to take a look inside the vehicle. Nothing looked out of place. Nothing around the vehicle had been disturbed, there was no sign of a struggle. "Why did she go into the forest and leave her dog behind?"

"Maybe she was meeting someone?" Jo shrugged. "Or she met up with some of her friends to go hunting. Maybe her dog is not suited to hunting. He didn't come across as a friendly fellow to me."

Nodding, Carter made his way back to the cruiser. "Yeah, and I'd switch off my phone too. If your phone rings when you have an elk or deer in your sights, it's game over." He sighed. "We'll call her later."

"Isn't it a bit late in the day to go hunting?" Jo looked at him as they drove through the college gates. "I figured people left at dawn."

Smiling, Carter glanced at her. "Yeah, most times." He pulled up in a parking space outside the office building. "It might be spring break but there's always office staff here. I'll go and ask where we can find Bill Ripley."

"I'll go." Jo smiled at him. "You call it in. Jenna would want to know that we haven't spoken to Alicia and where we found her vehicle."

Reaching inside his pocket for his phone, Carter smiled. "You got it."

He made the call and brought Jenna up to date. "We're not overly worried at this stage. She could be meeting friends in the forest."

"Just a minute, I'll check on something." Jenna went away for a few minutes. *"Yeah, there is a designated area for elk not far from there. She is known to hunt and not only with her crossbow friends. She has images all over social media. Concentrate on Bill Ripley. We'll meet back at the office when you're done."*

Blowing out a sigh, Carter stared out of the window as Jo came hurrying back. "Okay. Catch you later." He disconnected and looked at Jo as she slipped into the passenger seat. "Any luck?"

"Yeah." She pointed to buildings set in a line on the far side of the campus. "The building is the one on the far right. We go through the courtyard and take the stairs. He's in room 103. We're lucky. The receptionist said he hasn't been home long."

Carter backed out of the parking slot and turned the cruiser around. "Did you get anything else from them? Any background?"

"Yeah, he's here on a full scholarship." Jo frowned. "He was raised in Black Rock Falls but spent three years in foster care after his parents died in a fire. He's very quiet, has a few people he calls friends, and they mentioned the crossbow club. Apparently, discussing the club is the only time he becomes animated and, apart from designing video games, is his life's passion. He studies computer science. That's all I have."

Amazed, Carter smiled at her around his toothpick. "I wasn't expecting them to volunteer so much information. That's gold."

"Well, I did have an edge." Jo's cheeks pinked. "One of the receptionists was reading my latest book and I autographed it for her."

Laughing, Carter drove toward the student residences. It was eerily quiet, with the majority of students away on vacation. The long empty windows of dark lecture halls resembled a skull with teeth missing. He pulled up outside and they climbed out. He looked at Jo. "You take the lead. He's a young guy, and I don't want to intimidate him. If he's one of the killers, seeing us might frighten him into doing something stupid. Thrill killers are known to be unstable. If he makes a move on us, I don't want to take him down before we've extracted information from him."

"Okay, then we'll approach the questioning from a different angle." Jo collected a statement book from the glovebox and climbed out of the cruiser. "Leave it to me. I know just how to proceed."

The noise of battle from a video game echoed down the corridor as they moved closer to Ripley's room number. Carter cleared his throat. "I guess, as there's nobody else here, he can make as much noise as he likes." He hammered on the door.

The sound stopped immediately, followed by footsteps on tile. The door opened a crack and all Carter could see was one blue eye looking at them. "Bill Ripley? Do you mind if we have a word with you?"

"That depends on who you are." Ripley eyed them with suspicion. "How exactly did you get my room number?"

"We used our creds." Jo held up her cred pack. "Please open the door, Mr. Ripley."

"Why do you want to speak to me?" Ripley open the door a little wider and looked from one to the other.

"Can we come in?" Jo's face showed no emotion whatsoever. "We've been trying to locate a friend of yours, Alicia Palmer. We dropped by her place of work and her home and she's not there. Her phone has been switched off and we're concerned about her welfare."

"No, you can't come in and I don't know where she is." Ripley shrugged. "It's not as if she's a girlfriend or anything. She's way older than me and we shoot together sometimes, is all. She does have other friends apart from me. She likes to hunt and I prefer targets. We don't hang out socially."

"Do you know any of her other friends?" Jo held a pen above her notebook and stared at him. "Can you give me any names?"

"Not really. I don't socialize with her crowd." Ripley snorted. "Like I said, she's older than me. Maybe ask some of her old college friends."

Unable to stop himself, Carter leaned in a little closer. "We were told she went into the forest yesterday morning to do some target practice. Maybe she was hurt. Do you know where she went? When did you last see her?"

"It would be difficult to get injured during target practice." Ripley chuckled. "The last time I saw her was when we practiced on the range about a week ago. Before you ask, no, she didn't tell me what was on her social calendar for the week."

"Were you in the forest at all this week?" Jo made a few notes and then looked at him.

"Nope." Ripley sighed. "I've been here all week, apart from when I run out of junk food." He stared at them. "Is that all? I'm playing online."

"That's all for now." Jo handed him a card. "If you hear from her, give me a call."

"Why do you want to speak to her?" Ripley pushed a hand through his untidy hair. "Is she in trouble with the law?"

Carter shook his head. "Nope."

"You went to the same high school as Leo Kelly, Zoe Ward, and Ash Rogers. Are they friends of yours?" Jo raised her pen expectantly.

"Nope, and you're wasting your time if you figure they're Alicia's friends. She doesn't like teenagers. She barely copes with having me around at competitions." Ripley shook his head. "You olds don't understand the way of things, do you? Gamers don't need friends. We live online. Offline, my spare time is devoted to crossbow target shooting. It's my exercise, if you like, but apart from that, I spend all my time developing games. That's where the money is and I aim to get my fair share."

Carter turned away. "Okay. Thank you for your time."

As they walked back to the cruiser, Carter turned to look at Jo's concerned expression. "I figure we handled that pretty well. Did you get anything from him?" He tossed a toothpick into his mouth.

"Well, if you were expecting a psychopathic reaction from him, you'd be disappointed." Jo tucked the statement book under one arm. "This crime doesn't display any psychopathic tendencies or makes me believe that they're the work of a serial killer. I'm still convinced this was some type of organized thrill kill." She shrugged. "After speaking to Rowley about the location of the murders, he informed me only one or two people go there. The falls has a sheer drop on that side. There is a fishing hole at the bottom of the falls they call Dead Man's Drop, because people have fallen from many places along that edge. He said, because of the very low volume of hikers in that area, it wouldn't be feasible for three shooters to space themselves out and wait for the opportunity to kill a passerby. This tells me it was an organized kill, which opens up realms of possibilities."

Carter opened the back door to the cruiser to allow Zorro to jump inside. He regarded Jo over the roof of the vehicle. "How so?"

"We've already discussed the murders as a warning to the parents. This is still a possibility, but don't discount the fact that a group of people might plan to kill a bunch of kids for fun. It's harrowing but it does happen." Jo folded her arms across her chest, fingers gripping the statement book. "The thing is, if they knew the exact time the kids planned to be on the trail, they must know them to have access to their social media."

Thrill kills meant that the killers were unpredictable, volatile people who could snap at a second's notice. Something in Carter's gut told him that this was the case here. "Well, Ripley knows the victims but I'm not sure if he's involved. He came over as defensive."

"So, the opposite of what you'd expect from a serial killer." Jo smiled. "That isn't reason to discount him, as we're not looking for a serial killer personality in this case. Ripley has freedom of movement, no parents to check on him. He can come and go as he pleases, so in fact, he could be anywhere, and unless someone has seen him, who's to know?"

Carter nodded and swung inside the cruiser. He waited for Jo to fasten her seatbelt. "He has the skill set, and knowing his background in IT, likely has the knowledge to wipe out or disguise any incriminating communications between the group responsible."

"Okay." Jo wrote in her notebook. "I'll do a more detailed profile on him when we get back to the office." She pulled out her phone and called Alicia again. "I'm getting the same message. Do you think we should head through the forest and see if we can find her?"

Carter started the engine. "Nah." He swung the cruiser around and they headed back to town. "We'd never find her, and as it's a designated elk-hunting area, we should stay clear. "He picked up the radio and called Maggie. "We're leaving the college now, but we'll be stopping in town." He waited for her response and looked at Jo. "Jenna and Kane haven't returned to the office yet. Want to drop by Aunt Betty's Café?"

"I thought you'd never ask." Jo smiled. "I'm famished."

EIGHTEEN

Rowley disentangled himself from his twins, Cooper and Vannah, and placed them back inside their stroller. He might be on duty, but meeting his wife, Sandy, outside the general store was a common occurrence. After enrolling the twins in a play group, held in one of the reception rooms in the town hall, he was seeing more of them than ever before. He grinned at Sandy and waved the finger-painting Cooper had given him. "I had no idea they did this sort of thing at this age."

"This is why I'm taking them to the play group." Sandy hoisted Vannah on one hip. "It's all very well raising them on a ranch, but they need interaction with children of their own age. This way, they get to do kid stuff."

Lifting Cooper high into the air, Rowley smiled as his son giggled. "I'll help you get them into the truck and then I gotta go. We're interviewing suspects." He settled the wiggling little boy into his car seat and clicked the harness.

"Okay." Sandy kissed his cheek. "See you tonight. Don't forget to eat lunch."

Catching Rio's eyeroll, Rowley straightened. His ears growing hot. He ignored Rio and waited for Sandy to secure

Vannah. When she slid behind the wheel, he leaned in the truck's window. "See you tonight. Love you." He waited for Sandy to drive away and turned to Rio. "I know you have a thing about Emily Wolfe, and probably even considered marrying her sometime, but marriage is more than the sexual attraction that you have now. Having someone who really cares for your wellbeing is really special."

"That's why I like Emily." Rio shrugged. "She doesn't try to mother me. I'd find it embarrassing if my wife told me to make sure I ate in front of my work colleagues."

Shaking his head, Rowley stared at him. "Then you shouldn't marry her because the relationship you're having right now sounds more like a business partnership. Trust me, you'll need a stronger bond than that to make it through the first year."

"What do you mean by that?" Rio glared at him, hands on hips.

Chuckling, Rowley sighed. "Marriage isn't business as usual. It's a life changer. Every minute you have to consider the other person and what your actions might do to upset the balance. When kids come along, you suddenly have to share them, their time and affection. It's all about give and take. It also means you need to care so much you'd willingly die for them. If you can't give that kind of commitment to somebody, then you should look for the person that you can." He headed into the general store and walked up to the counter. A man in his mid-twenties came to serve him and Rowley smiled. "I'm looking for Lonnie Barlow, is he working today?"

"I'm Lonnie Barlow. What can I do for you, Deputy?" He pressed two hands down on the counter and gave him a puzzled expression.

Slowly pulling out his notebook, Rowley heard Rio coming up behind him and caught the troubled expression in Barlow's eyes at the sight of him. He clicked the top of his pen. "We're chasing down three people with crossbows sighted in the forest near the Devil's Punch Bowl on Sunday morning. You hunt with a crossbow and are part of a crossbow competition team, so you're on our list."

"I see." Barlow frowned. "I'm not the only person on a crossbow team, or the only shooter. I meet many at the range. I've seen you there as well. Are you part of the investigation too?"

Rowley shook his head. "No, I'm not and I've seen you around, but we're hunting down teams of marksmen."

"Ah, I see. There are only two championship teams in town and we all know each other. It's friendly rivalry. Our team is sponsored by one company and there's another, is all. The rivalry is within the teams as we compete against each other... we all do." Barlow shrugged. "What exactly have these three people done? I wouldn't be comfortable giving you their names if it causes a problem."

"Oh, we have the names of the people in the teams you've mentioned. This is probably some other team and we just need to talk to them, is all." Rio stared into the glass counter as if perusing the stock.

"Yeah, well it just happens I was in the forest on Sunday morning hunting wild turkey, but not near the Devil's Punch Bowl. That area is designated for hikers." Barlow shrugged. "I did hear tell there was a hunting accident, which I find hard to believe because most people who live in these parts follow the rules. I'd suggest you look for unlicensed outsiders, because they cause trouble for every hunter in the county."

After speaking to the forest warden at the scene of the crime, Rowley was already aware of that fact. "Where exactly did you hunt on Sunday?"

"Near Bear Peak. I was with a few buddies from the crossbow club. We checked in with the forest warden station around six-thirty, again around eleven to have my tags checked, and I was home before twelve." Barlow shrugged. "I didn't see anyone else with a crossbow. The few people I did see had rifles and everyone was doing the right thing."

Nodding, Rowley made a note of the times. He could easily check who was with him with the forest warden station at Bear Peak, and Barlow would know this, so he believed him. He glanced up from his notebook. "Did you bag any turkeys?"

"Yeah, the legal limit." Barlow narrowed his gaze. "You're welcome to come and look in my freezer, if you have a problem with that?"

"Nah, we're good." Rio raised one dark eyebrow at Rowley. "I figure we're done here. Thanks for your time."

Rowley stared after Rio as he strode out the store. He turned back to Barlow and took a card out of his pocket and handed it to him. "If you hear anything or see any rogue crossbow shooters, can you give me a call? That was an accident in the forest, and we need to find the people responsible. I'll keep your name out of it if you call me with information."

"Okay, sure." Barlow pushed a card into his top pocket.

Outside, Rio was leaning up against his truck with his arms folded across his chest. Rowley went up to him. "What's caught in your craw?"

"Nothing." Rio blew out a long breath. "He's not one of the killers. We have time to go and see Carl Harper before we eat. How far away is the lumberyard?"

Climbing into the passenger seat, Rowley waited for Rio to slip behind the wheel. He preferred to be driving his own truck, but it was his turn to ride shotgun. "It's next to the recycling yard." He busied himself with his notes on the next suspect. "Head down Main and I'll direct you."

"I know the way." Rio backed out onto Main. "I have the map of the town in my head."

Laughing, Rowley looked up at him. "Wow! You have a built in GPS. Cool. Then you have details of everything in that head of yours. I can't imagine how good it would be to have a retentive memory like yours." He closed his notebook. "Save me the time and give me the rundown on Carl Harper."

"He did time in jail after a hunting accident in Blackwater. A Blackwater local accused him of stalking him in the forest." Rio headed down Main. "At the time, the victim was in fear of his life and called for assistance. Before help arrived, Harper shot him in the leg with a crossbow bolt. The Blackwater sheriff arrested him and he did three months for aggravated assault." He flicked a gaze at Rowley. "That's the MO of one of the forest shooters, so we need to be careful with this suspect."

Rubbing his chin, Rowley nodded. "He won't have his crossbow at work, so we'll be safe enough and I doubt he'll be armed." He grabbed a statement book as they parked outside the lumberyard. "You take the lead as you know all about this guy."

Walking into the lumberyard brought back a flood of memories for Rowley. The smell of freshly sawn wood, the ever-present dust in the air reached them as they walked through huge metal doors. Inside, the sound of machinery was deafening. On one side under a FOR SALE sign sat a row of sacks overflowing with wood shavings. As a kid, he would come here to collect the wood shavings to use as kindling. At that time they were offered free and he used to take a sack to the pile and help himself, like most people in town with wood stoves. Things were sure different now. Under the huge saws cutting the lumber, a conveyer belt took away the sawdust and dumped it into a container. From there it was sent to the particle board factory on the other side of town. Any branches and leaves were put through the woodchipper and used on people's gardens. Every part of the tree was used.

Men wearing helmets, goggles, masks, and gloves moved around under a sign that stated that visitors to the work area were strictly prohibited. Rowley recalled standing beside some of the great saws, watching as the giant logs slipped through. How times had changed. He followed Rio into the office and went to the counter. A woman sitting behind a computer screen looked up at him expectantly. "Is Carl Harper working today?"

"He is." The woman stood and frowned at them. "He's not gotten himself into trouble, has he? I told my husband not to employ convicts, but he figures every man deserves a second chance."

"They do." Rio rested one hand on the butt of his pistol. "He's not in trouble. We're just trying to locate one of his friends, is all. Is there someplace we can speak to him in private?"

"Out front." She lifted a section of the counter and walked through. "I'll go and get him. You can wait outside. I don't want him walking sawdust all through my office."

They waited outside until she returned with a thick-set man in his mid-thirties. As he walked toward them, he removed his goggles and mask. He was covered from head to foot in wood dust. Rowley glanced at Rio. "We'd better keep this short. Dragon Lady will likely take the time out of his pay."

Carl Harper had obviously being given instructions to take it outside and he led the way through the gate and turned around on the sidewalk to stare at them.

"Did you have to come to my place of work?" Harper balled his hands on his hips and paced around in circles. "Do you know how difficult it was to get a job?"

"I figure you got away easy, after stalking a man and then shooting him in the leg." Rio straightened. "Or do you have a different sequence of events?"

"Man, I was given a court-appointed attorney who didn't really care what I had to say." Harper stopped pacing and glared at him. "The guy I shot just happened to be in the wrong place at the wrong time, is all. He was wearing brown and green, which made him practically invisible. I was stalking a wolf in the forest but not him. He walked across my shot. I was aiming for the wolf, and the jerk ran up a slope right behind it. He alerted the wolf, which vanished, and the bolt caught him in the calf muscle. If I'd wanted to kill him, I'd have aimed for his heart or throat." He shook his head. "Trust me, I don't miss at that range."

"Did you know him?" Rio glanced at Rowley and back to Harper.

"No, I'd never met him before in my life." Harper looked from one to the other. "This isn't about him though, is it? What have I been accused of doing this time?"

"We're not accusing you of anything, Mr. Harper." Rio stared nonchalantly into the distance before returning his attention back to him. "We've been speaking to your hunting buddies about a trip into Stanton Forest Sunday last."

"Well, you can talk to them all you like, but I wasn't in the forest last Sunday." Harper folded his arms across his chest. Go speak to my neighbors. They came over and complained because I was making a noise. There was a leak in my roof and I was up there for all to see fixing it."

"What time was this?" Rio made a few notes in his book. "For the record."

"I don't recall the exact time. Between nine and noon, I guess." Harper glared at them with a disgusted expression on his face. "I haven't seen my hunting buddies for a few weeks. The last time I saw either of them was down at the range. With the melt and all, it was so muddy down there, we gave it a miss."

Rowley needed a piece of important information. "What type of bolts did you use the last time you hunted?"

"Twenty-inch carbon with LED nocks." Harper snorted. "Anything fancier is too expensive for my budget. I use different types depending on the game or when I'm target shooting."

Rowley kept his face emotionless. "Have you ever used an EVO-X CenterPunch premium carbon arrow?"

"Can't say that I have but I've heard about it." Harper narrowed his gaze on Rowley. "Have you?"

Watching Harper's body language, Rowley nodded. "Just so happens I have, so you wouldn't mind if we went by your residence and checked out your gear?"

"Go right ahead but you'd be wasting your time." Harper slapped his gloves against his dust covered jeans. "Is that all?"

"Not quite. Have you been to the Devil's Punch Bowl anytime in the last week or so?" Rio straightened. "The forest warden mentioned seeing three people carrying crossbows in that area."

"Nope. Why would I want to go there? They don't have a season for hunting hikers yet, do they?" Harper gave them a long stare and then snapped his fingers. "I heard tell of a hunting accident up that way. You figure I'm involved in that? I'm not. Now, if you've finished with me, I need to get back to work. They don't like it when we take breaks."

"Okay." Rio handed him a card. "If you hear any gossip, give me a call."

"Yeah, sure I will." Harper turned on his heel and tossed the card into the woodpile inside the gate.

Rowley stared after him. "That went well."

"He's angry." Rio headed back toward the truck. "Maybe he did the time but didn't do the crime."

NINETEEN

Jenna waited for Geoff Bannister, the bartender at the Cattleman's Hotel, to walk to the end of the bar to serve them. He gave them a curious look as he came toward them. It wasn't a place that Jenna usually entered wearing her sheriff's department jacket. As he came closer, she placed her notebook on the bar and took out her pen. "Mr. Bannister?"

"Yeah, what's the problem, Sheriff?" Bannister wiped down the bar moving his hand in circular motions ignoring a direct stare.

She glanced at Kane and raised an eyebrow. The body language of this man was very telling. He was hiding something for sure. "I'll come straight to the point, Mr. Bannister. Were you in or around Stanton Forest on Sunday, in the vicinity of the Devil's Punch Bowl?"

"You know I was." Bannister lifted his gaze from the bar. "The forest warden checked my fishing permit. I was there for only about an hour when all hell broke loose. I knew something was going down. Two forest wardens came on horseback and then blocked the trail back to the fire road. It was lucky I didn't come in that way or I wouldn't have been able to get back to my vehicle."

"Who else did you see in the forest?" Kane leaned one elbow on the bar. "From all accounts it was a busy place on Sunday morning."

"No one at the fishing hole apart from the forest warden." Bannister rubbed the back of his neck. "I did see a woman carrying a crossbow. I figure it was a woman, with long hair tied back in a ponytail, like, low on the back of her neck. She was wearing camouflage gear and carrying the crossbow on her back. I figured at the time she was heading to a designated hunting area because the Devil's Punch Bowl is for hikers."

Jenna made notes. "I see. So no one else at all?"

"No, not in that area. I didn't see anyone else until I reached Stanton." He shrugged. "It was a waste of a morning. I didn't catch any fish or get any peace of mind." He shot a glance at Kane. "That's what we go fishing for, right?"

"I guess." Kane straightened. "You compete with the cross-bow, don't you?"

"Yeah, on occasion. I hunt with a crossbow too." Bannister shrugged nonchalantly. "Why?"

"We noticed that there are two prominent teams in this county, your team and another team that has a woman member by the name of Alicia Palmer. I assume you've met her before?" Kane stood feet apart and back straight. "Could the woman in the forest have been her?"

"Possibly, but I was over one hundred yards away and, yeah, I've spoken to Alicia during competitions and at the dentist. She's a great shot." Bannister lifted one shoulder in a half shrug. "I don't know if it was her."

After making a few notes, Jenna looked up. "Have you ever hunted with her or met her socially?"

"Nope." Bannister smiled. "She isn't my type and I find women are usually a problem when hunting."

Frowning, Jenna stared at him. "What do you mean by 'a problem' exactly?" Her phone was vibrating in her pocket but she ignored it.

"Oh, you know." Bannister looked straight at Kane. "Most of them can't stop talking or they're asking to stop for a bathroom break every five minutes. Then others always find a need to wear perfume. You should try hunting down an elk or deer with a woman stinking of perfume."

"I figure you've made your point." Kane pushed his Stetson firmly on his head and looked at Jenna. "Are you just about done here, Sheriff?"

Unfazed, Jenna nodded. "Just a second. You mentioned you hunt with your crossbow. Do you hunt with any of the other team members?"

"Yeah, all the time." Bannister rolled his eyes skyward. "Anything else?"

With a shake of her head, Jenna handed Bannister one of her cards. "If you see this person around town and recognize them, please give me a call. Thank you for your time." She followed Kane out of the bar and stopped in the foyer to look at her phone.

She checked the missed calls and, seeing that it was Maggie trying to contact her, she returned the call. "What is it, Maggie?"

"*A fisherman out at Dead Man's Drop snagged the body of a naked female. The man's name is Jud Cole. I'll text you his details. The FBI agents are here and Rowley and Rio are on a break. Who do you want me to send?*"

Jenna stared at Kane and he shrugged. They had one more suspect to interview but dead bodies took precedent over everything else. "I'll go. We're at the Cattleman's Hotel. Contact Wolfe and give him the details. We'll meet him at the office." She disconnected and turned to Kane. He'd been moving slower and it was obvious his chest hurt. He hated her fussing over him, so she rubbed her cheek. "My head is a little sore. I need something to eat and some Tylenol. What about you?"

"Yeah, I'm hungry and Tylenol is looking good, but we haven't got time to stop." Kane frowned and touched her face with gentle care. "Is it hurting bad?"

Jenna leaned into his hand and sighed. They really didn't have time to spare. "Nope. We'll grab some sandwiches from the bar and eat on the way."

"That works for me." Kane turned around and headed back into the bar, returning a few minutes later loaded up with sandwiches. He walked beside her to the truck. "Did Maggie mention any obvious cause of death?"

Thinking over the conversation, Jenna frowned. "No, but the body is naked." She opened the truck's door for Kane and he dumped the sandwiches on the seat before turning to get Duke into the back. She piled the food into the console and waited for him to climb behind the wheel. "Dead Man's Drop isn't a place anyone goes skinny-dipping. You've been there before. It's way too deep and the water is dark. Cold as ice too."

"I recall the place." Kane's stomach rumbled as he unwrapped a sandwich and bit into it. In three bites it had vanished. "Drowning is a possibility if anyone is stupid enough to jump in." He started the engine. "I guess we'll find out soon enough." He looked at her. "Best we take Rio and Rowley with us. We can't send Rowley out to interview Jesse Davis. He's an acquaintance. Why don't you send Jo and Carter to speak to Davis?"

Jenna selected a sandwich and nodded. "We can ask them. Right now, they're here as consultants. I can't order them to do anything."

"Well as Carter mentioned being bored stupid in Snakeskin Gully, he'd be happy to be involved." He flicked her a glance. "I believe we've gone past the 'calling in the FBI to assist us' with them. They're friends and as friends they'll help out when they

can. They don't want recognition for an arrest and as field officers they go where they're needed."

Nodding, Jenna swallowed her food and sipped water from
her bottle. "I guess. I'll need to change into hiking boots back at
the office. Rio and Rowley are on a break. They should be back
by the time Wolfe arrives. It's quite a trek to Dead Man's Drop.
Will we make it there and back before sunset? I don't want to be
out in the forest at night and that body isn't going anywhere."

"It will only take ten minutes or so if we ride the dirt bikes.
We can set up a travois to carry the body. In fact, I'm sure Wolfe
has one. Call him and catch him before he leaves the office."

Jenna made the call and explained. She disconnected and
looked at Kane. "Yeah, he has a travois and he figures we can
use his trailer to carry four bikes to the forest. It will save time.
Two will fit on the back of Rio's truck."

"That sounds like a plan." Kane pulled into his slot outside
the office and, grabbing sandwiches, climbed out. "Get Duke.
We'll leave him with Maggie. He won't be able to keep up with
the dirt bikes. I'll get the bikes gassed up." He shouldered his
way through the glass door.

Imagining the pain Kane would suffer riding a dirt bike,
Jenna shook her head, grabbed Duke, and followed. After
explaining the situation to Maggie and bringing Carter and Jo
up to date, she listened with interest about the sighting of Alicia
Palmer's Jeep Cherokee. "Well, if it's still there when you
return from Mustang Creek, call me. If she was hunting, she'd
have been seen by someone. You could call the forest warden's
station. I'll give you the number. They'll call whoever is in that
region and ask if they've seen her."

"Okay." Carter stood. "Oh, and Kalo called. He found
nothing on the parents of the college kids. They're clean. So we
have no motive for the murders." He gathered his things from
the desk. "Are you ready, Jo?" When she nodded, he turned
back to Jenna. "We'll head out now. When we get back, we'll

discuss the suspects we interviewed. Jo has some interesting theories."

Jenna smiled at Jo. "I'll look forward to it." She headed to the locker room to change.

Fifteen minutes later, Wolfe arrived in his van with a trailer hitched behind carrying two dirt bikes. After Kane had added two and loaded another two onto Rio's truck, they were ready to leave. They drove in a convoy to the edge of the forest, unloaded the dirt bikes and, pulling on helmets, headed out in the direction of Dead Man's Drop. The wind was cold on Jenna's face and she was glad of the Kevlar vest Kane insisted she wore. Lightweight, a liquid Kevlar vest would protect her from an arrow or bullet and had the added benefit of warmth. Under her jacket it served as a shield from the icy wind as they followed the trail through the darkening forest.

It was strange but whenever they visited a crime scene, she always had the feeling someone was watching her. She constantly scanned the deep shadows cast by the afternoon sun for movements. Trying to push away uncertainty, she inhaled the delicious scent of the forest. Although slightly tainted by exhaust fumes from the dirt bikes, she could still smell the snow on the mountains. She had the comfort of Kane in front and Rowley close behind to watch out for danger, but other things concerned her. Dirt bike riding was a new skill for her and she wasn't as confident as she'd like to be. She'd been out riding many times now, but when her deputies jumped over obstacles, she took a slower approach. For them it was usually a crazy mud-splattered rush through the forest, but she preferred to take her time, gaining skills along the way. This time they moved at a more sedate pace due to the gear they carried to process the crime scene, but they still made good time bumping along the narrow trails. The way back would be slower dragging a travois, but the contraption Wolfe had pulled from his van at least had wheels. It folded into a saddlebag, which made carrying it a breeze.

They turned into the clearing surrounding the fishing hole known as Dead Man's Drop, named because long ago many people exploring the mountain caves high above had fallen to their deaths into the water. Ahead, a man sat on one of the boulders with his back to the water, a blue cooler at his feet. Leaving her team to process the scene, she pulled up and approached him. "Jud Cole?"

"Yes, ma'am." The man wore blue jeans, a sweater, and a cowboy hat, and long gray hair fell to his collar. He stood and a weathered face looked at her. "She's out in the middle. My hook is still in her, caught on her arm. When she came to the surface, it scared the bejesus out of me."

Removing her helmet, and leaving it on the dirt bike, Jenna picked up the cooler. She led him away from the fishing hole to a fallen log and sat him down. "What time was this?" She set the cooler down beside him.

"I'm not sure." He scratched his head under his hat and stared at her. "I called 911 immediately, so there should be a record of the time, right?"

Pulling out her notebook, Jenna nodded. "Yeah, we'll have the time you called it in. How long before that do you figure you were here?"

"Maybe twenty minutes or so, but I do recall hearing a splash as I came along the trail." His brow furrowed. "It made me extra cautious in case it was a bear. They're known to fish here as well. You see, fish get washed down here from the falls. If you've ever taken the time to see how the lakes are set out, they come down in graduated layers, each with its own small waterfall. Those waterfalls split up and spread out all over, some into small creeks like this fishing hole, others join the river that flows right through to Blackwater. Several of these small catchment areas make fine fishing holes." He stared into the forest as if thinking. "Maybe she fell from the caves. Tourists take no heed to warning signs and they're all over right now."

Processing the information, Jenna made a note in her book about the splash. If this was suicide, the splash could indicate the time of death. If not, someone threw her into the waterfall and the time they did this would be crucial evidence. "Well, she didn't fall from the caves. After an accident a year or so ago, the entrance to the cave that leads to a rock pool that drags people over the edge and into the falls was sealed with iron bars. She either jumped or was pushed from the edge of the falls."

"Well, if she fell, Sheriff, wouldn't she be screaming?" The old man raised both eyebrows. "All I heard was the splash, and when I got here, I took a long look around to make sure I didn't have company. There was no sign of a bear, no scat or claw marks on trees." He waved a hand to encompass the entire area. "I didn't see anyone, man or beast." He pointed upward. "The only possible way she fell into the water was from up there. If someone dumped her in the water from here, they wouldn't have known I was coming, would they? For sure, I'd have seen them leaving the area and like I say, I was looking."

Jenna turned to see Wolfe and his assistant Colt Webber lifting a body out of the water and onto a large rock on the side of the pool. Wolfe unhooked the fishing line, wound the reel, and handed the rod to Kane, who headed toward her. She kept Jud Cole's attention away from the body retrieval. "My deputy has your fishing rod." She pulled a card out of her pocket and handed it to him. "You've been very helpful. If anything else comes to mind, please give me a call. We have your details if we need to speak to you again. I would greatly appreciate it if you could keep this to yourself until we have time to notify the next of kin. It would be such a shock to the family to hear about a loved one's death on the news."

"I understand." Cole nodded sagely. "I've been walking

these forests since I was a boy. There aren't many places a person could fall or be pushed over the falls above Dead Man's Drop. Two places come to mind. One is the plateau at the top of the falls, the one that is accessed by the rope bridge. I see tourists up there all the time taking photographs, and the other is a small rock pool. I found it at the end of an animal track one day when I was hunting. The trail into the forest that leads there, I figure, was cut out by animals over the years. The rock pool makes a fine watering hole. The entrance to the trail is on Stanton opposite Pine."

"Thanks." Kane smiled and handed him the fishing rod. "That's very useful information."

"I'll be on my way." Cole bent to pick up his cooler and then vanished into the trees.

"He was a font of information." Kane led the way back to the group surrounding the body. "We have another homicide and this one is vicious."

Preparing herself to look at another murder victim, Jenna's heart raced. She recognized the brutally murdered girl from the photograph of one of her suspects. She gripped Kane's arm. "That's Alicia Palmer, one of the suspects. When I spoke to Carter earlier, he said that they hadn't been able to locate her. The dentist she works for said that it was her afternoon off and she usually went shopping." She pulled out her phone and called Carter. "We've found Alicia Parker. She's been murdered."

"*Dang. That's a turnaround we hadn't expected. When we noticed her Jeep Cherokee parked on the edge of the forest on Stanton opposite Pine, we stopped to check it out. Nothing seemed to be disturbed. We searched all around for signs of a struggle and found nothing. If she left that vehicle, she did it by her own free will. No footprints, scuff marks, zip.*" Carter heaved a deep breath. "*We're coming up on Mustang Creek now to interview Jesse Davis. I'll see you back at the office. It will be too late to search the forest for clues by the time we're done. Maybe get Duke to follow her trail in the morning?"*

Jenna stared at the body of the once vibrant young woman as Wolfe straightened and held up something to show her. "Yeah, sure. We'll be here for a time yet. Just a minute." She gaped in astonishment. "This case just got crazier. Wolfe just removed two pennies from her eyes."

TWENTY

James Earl Stafford, aka Jimmy Two Cents, pushed a cart up and down the rows of books in the prison library. By all accounts, the prison staff believed him to be an exemplary prisoner. Since his conviction, he'd convinced a variety of shrinks and officials that he'd found God. To say his urges to murder had vanished was laughable. In fact, if he ever stepped out of prison again, he doubted there would be anyone left. He smiled to himself as he read detailed messages secreted inside the books he'd collected from other inmates. Each small scrap of paper had become an ongoing saga of the exploits of each of them. The notes being moved around the inmates via various volumes. The scheme had been easy enough to organize. Jimmy kept a detailed record of what books went to which prisoner, so everyone received each installment of a vicious crime in order. He often wondered if the prison guards knew what was going on and turned a blind eye, mainly because this form of communication kept them busy and subdued to some extent. Although, that didn't stop the out-of-control crazies from killing each other.

Lifers in his wing of the prison had certain privileges for

good behavior. These included paper and pen to write to their pen pals, which they obtained via a webpage. Restricted internet use gave them access to the site. Much like a dating app, a prisoner could post his profile and within a few days a ton of letters would appear. Some of these pen pals would become romantically involved with them and even go so far as to request visits. Jimmy had been lucky. It seemed the more vicious and brutal the killer, the more women he attracted, although he had his fair share of men too.

He arranged the books in order, ready to be delivered to the cells the following morning, and glanced at the clock on the wall. The wait for the phone call he knew would be coming sometime today was killing him. He needed to know what had happened and if Bear had met the end he'd designed for her. Had the boy come through? He had relived the hunt so many times in his head he could almost smell the blood on his hands. When the guard's footfalls came along the row of books, Jimmy's heart picked up a beat in anticipation. He pushed the cart to the end of the row and smiled at the guard. "Is it dinnertime already?"

"Nope. You have a phone call." The guard waited for him to hold out his hands. "Someone called Eagle. He's on your list. Third time he's called in a month. You planning on a homosexual relationship with this guy? Want me to arrange a conjugal?" The guard chuckled and attached the chains.

Ignoring the guard's usual coarse humor, Jimmy shook his head. "Nah, he's just the son of a guy I used to go hunting with in the day. We talk about hunting, is all."

Moving outside the library meant shackles, and he shuffled along beside the guard to the bank of phones in the hallway. He was only granted a few minutes and the caller understood the time limit. He lifted a receiver and gave his name. A familiar voice came down the line.

"You asked me to call the next time I hunted bear."

Jimmy smiled. "Yeah. I do so love hunting bear. How did it go? Did you bag one?"

"Yeah, it went smooth. I found it just where you suggested but taking it down was harder than I anticipated. It refused to go down and I cut it up real bad. Ended up slitting its throat. I had blood all over."

Exhilarated, Jimmy's hand shook on the receiver. He could see the kill in his mind as clear as if he'd been there. The smell, the feel of warm blood on his hands, the fear in the eyes of his victim, followed by the acceptance that he'd won. He sighed. "I used to get it up to my elbows. Dominating them is the thrill, don't you think? The final sigh as they die used to play like an earwig in my head. I hated washing the blood away. If I'd had a chance, I would have rolled in it."

"I can't get it out of my head. I keep hearing it moan." The caller cleared his throat. *"Does that ever go away?"*

Snorting, Jimmy laughed. "Why would you want it to? If you plan to keep hunting, you can't have a conscience. The idea is to have fun, push on to greater experiences. Wallow in the thrill of killing." He suddenly realized what the man was asking him. Unlike him, this person needed praise. It was a weakness but after a time it would pass. "I'm impressed with how far you've come. Hunting alone can be difficult but if you really want to make me proud, take down a young buck, field-dress it, and leave it where it lies, then come and give me a blow by blow."

"How do I select the right one?"

Jimmy rubbed his chin. "Take out the weakest in the herd, the loner. Sometimes these can be the most challenging."

"Okay. I'll talk to you soon."

Jimmy smiled. "You did good, Eagle. Real, good." He hung up the phone.

TWENTY-ONE

In his time in the service and investigating some of the horrific crimes in Black Rock Falls, Kane had witnessed atrocities that would give normal people nightmares. As a sniper, he'd managed to slip into the zone, a mental trick to leave the horror behind and out of his dreams. He never forgot those he'd killed in the line of duty nor would he keep a tally or brag about it. In his time in the service, the people he killed were referred to as "targets" in the field but this wasn't to dehumanize them. It was to keep their names off the airways. He'd always been fully aware that each person he'd killed left a grieving family behind, but in warfare, people who threatened the freedom of his country unfortunately became casualties of war.

As his gaze moved over the brutalized body of Alicia Palmer, compassion for the young woman filled him. It was obvious from the stab wounds she'd fought for her life. When Wolfe and Colt Webber rolled her over to view her back, beside him Jenna caught her breath. It was obvious Alicia had tried to escape a frenzied attack. From the deep cuts across her torso and arms, her killer had shown no mercy. The lacerations also told him that her attacker had never been trained in hand-to-hand combat. From behind, anyone skilled with a knife could have murdered her with one strategically placed stab wound. The same with the front of the torso, the stab wounds were random and frenzied, none of them hitting vital organs. One single thrust with a knife, pushed up under the sternum, would kill instantly. He walked over to Wolfe, his attention moving to the cut across the woman's throat. "That was done from the front. Right-handed killer." He looked at Wolfe for confirmation.

"Yeah, I agree." Wolfe picked up the victim's hands. "Defense wounds, but this body is fresh. She hasn't been in the water long, less than an hour. Her killer must be covered in blood. She would have been bleeding profusely and you know as well as I do cutting the carotid artery produces a spray of blood forward and with considerable force. If the killer was bending forward, I would expect him to be covered."

Kane nodded. "Maybe someone saw him leaving the forest?"

"The problem with that is it's bear-hunting season, and many people who field-dress their kills are covered in blood." Rowley removed his hat and wiped his brow. "It's not something anyone would take notice of around these parts." He looked from Kane to Wolfe. "I know you guys aren't partial to hunting but it's the way of life here."

Nodding, Kane cleared his throat. He'd done enough killing to last him a lifetime and he could still see the faces of the men who'd kidnapped Jenna. At the time it was kill or be killed, an instinct drilled into him. He shrugged. "It's not for me. I prefer fishing. I like the thinking time."

"What are you seeing here, Shane?" Jenna moved to Wolfe's side.

"I figure she knew her attacker. There's no evidence her clothes were torn from her body. I would usually see burn marks on the skin. So maybe this was a romantic liaison gone bad. I figure he attacked from the front. I'll examine the sharp force trauma incisions more closely later, but my first impression is he attacked from above. She tried to defend herself, and then turned and ran. He caught up and attacked from behind. She has grazes to her knees and shins, which would indicate she tried to climb over rocks or maybe the edge of the waterfall."

Imagining the scenario in his head, Kane nodded. "He must have turned her to face him." He glanced at Jenna. "This makes him particularly dangerous. He wanted to see her face as she died." He looked up at the jagged rocks climbing high into the air and then turned to Wolfe. "I figure he cut her throat and then tossed her over the edge, so your theory of trying to climb rocks to get away would fit." He ran a hand through his hair. "The guy who found her, Jud Cole, mentioned a trail through the forest to a rock pool. He said it was opposite Pine on Stanton, right where Carter found her Jeep."

"If she was murdered in a rock pool, it would likely be fed by the falls." Wolfe rubbed his chin thoughtfully. "I figure the chances of finding any trace blood evidence would be remote in that situation, but in a crime scene anything is possible." He glanced at his watch. "It's getting late, but we should hunt down the murder scene as it's still fresh. Once we get the body on the travois, we'll be good to go. Do you want to leave now and see if you can find the rock pool?" He looked at Rowley. "You've lived here all your life. Do you know this place?"

"Nope." Rowley shook his head and pointed upward. "As you can see, the edge of the falls is very steep and dangerous. It's not a place most people would venture voluntarily. The forest wardens have it on the list of no-go areas for hikers and warn hunters to keep away from it. I can't ever remember it being a designated hunting area."

Kane looked at Jenna. When she nodded her approval of the plan, he looked at Rio and Rowley. "Head off now. We'll help Wolfe with the travois and be right behind you. If you find the place, send us the coordinates."

The forest roared with sound as the dirt bikes started up and headed along the trail back to the road. Kane noticed Jenna staring at the pool. She was working things through in her head. He went to Wolfe's dirt bike and pulled out the travois, assembled it, and attached it to the back. Wolfe needed to be astride the dirt bike to keep it balanced when they added the body. After spending some time getting everything ready, he walked back to Jenna. "Ready to go?"

"Yeah." She shivered. "Do you recall the last time we were here and Atohi Blackhawk told us about this place? He said his people never fished here because they believed the souls of the dead occupied the lake. It's the darkest lake I've ever seen. It looks sinister. Whenever I'm here I feel as if someone is watching me." She sighed. "I hope she was dead before she hit the water. It would be a terrible place to die."

Slipping an arm around her shoulder, Kane pulled her hard against him. "I can assure you she was dead before she went over the edge. There's no doubt. Come on, we'll go on ahead. There's little doubt the killer is covered in blood, and I doubt he'd be staying around but I'd like to be there when Rio and Rowley find the murder scene."

"Okay. Let's get out of here." Jenna headed for her dirt bike. "Stay close, I can't keep up with you."

Kane smiled. "You lead the way. Follow Wolfe. He'll find his way back to the road." He waited for her to start her dirt bike and smiled. He'd considered building her a Harley, but he loved the way she squeezed him so tight when they rode together. He pushed on his helmet and sighed. "Dave Kane, you're becoming sentimental. Go figure."

TWENTY-TWO

Carter and Jo arrived at Mustang Creek to find a large spread. Rowley hadn't mentioned that Jessie Davis owned such a prestigious cattle ranch. The ranch house spread out with wide verandas all around. Outbuildings by the dozen—pens, barns and cattle dips—were dwarfed by the open ranges surrounding the property. Herds of prime beef cattle roamed lush pasture. The business would be worth millions. Carter rolled the cruiser to a halt in the neat driveway out front of the house. They climbed out and went to the front porch and knocked on the door. Through the screen, he made out a long hallway leading to a kitchen. The smell of meat cooking wafted toward them, making him wish it was dinnertime. A dog barked and a small mixed-breed came scampering down the hallway, its nails clattering over the polished floor, followed by a woman wearing an apron. As they were going onto a ranch outside of town, Carter and Jo had worn their FBI jackets. Often, being recognized as law enforcement officers prevented problems when entering people's land.

As the woman came to the screen door, picked up the growling dog, and peered at them, Carter touched the rim of his hat in a friendly manner and smiled. "Good afternoon, ma'am, we're looking for Jesse Davis."

"He's over at the bunkhouse." She pushed open the screen door and pointed to a building in the distance. "One of the ranch hands had an accident earlier today and he's checking up on him."

"I'm Agent Jo Wells and this is Agent Carter." Jo smiled at her. "Are you his mother?"

"No, I'm his housekeeper. As far as I'm aware, Jesse is all alone in the world." She frowned. "I'm Ada Crabtree. I've been here since he was a boy. His pa died and left him the ranch, must be six years ago. Time moves so fast these days."

"So he was out this morning?" Jo moved closer to the screen door. "Do you know what time he returned?"

"No. He is in and out all the time." The woman shrugged. "This is a big spread and he can be anywhere at any time. That's why he carries a satellite phone."

Wanting to keep moving, Carter nodded. "Thank you, ma'am. We'll go and see him now." He headed down the steps, wondering why she hadn't asked him the reason they wanted to speak to Jesse. He turned to Jo. "We'll drive. That bunkhouse is farther away than it looks." He swung into the driver's seat.

"She didn't ask why we wanted to speak to him." Jo echoed his thoughts as she turned in her seat to pat Zorro's head. "Don't you figure that's strange? People are naturally inquisitive. It would be the first thing I'd ask two FBI agents if they were standing on my doorstep."

Nodding, Carter shot her a glance. "I was thinking the same thing. Maybe it's not unusual for law enforcement to turn up on his doorstep. In the cattle business, I'm sure the turnaround of employees is great. Out here, I'm sure many of them are hiding off the grid and move from ranch to ranch as soon as someone notices them. Not just criminals, men trying to avoid alimony or child support, maybe they have people chasing them for money.

I could think of a thousand reasons why someone wants to live off the grid."

Carter found the bunkhouse without any problem and parked outside. He led the way to the open door, knocked, and ducked inside. As his eyes accustomed to the gloom, he made out a central living area with kitchen attached and hallway beyond with doors along each side. It was a rough log-built structure with unsealed wooden floors worn gray from years of cowboy boots stomping over them, and a stark contrast from the luxurious ranch house. A heavy stench of sweat permeated the air as if those inside believed that *deodorant* was another word for *sissy*. Two men sat around a wooden table drinking beer. "Sorry to bother you but we're looking for Jesse Davis."

"That would be me." A tall brown-haired man wearing a cowboy hat, snakeskin boots, and a bull-riding buckle on his belt waved them over. "Come over and join us. You'd be the FBI agents working with Jake Rowley?"

Carter nodded. "The same." He stood his ground. "We'd like to speak to you in private if that's okay?"

"Not a problem." He emptied his bottle of beer, dropped the empty in the trash, and headed toward them. "What can I do for you?"

Carter had been considering how to conduct the interview with this man and decided to take a different angle after discovering that Alicia Palmer had been murdered. Once they were outside the bunkhouse. He took Davis to one side. "Rowley mentioned that one of your crossbow team members is Alicia Palmer."

"She is, why?" Davis tipped back his Stetson and stared at him.

Carter cleared his throat. "She was found dead this afternoon. We don't have any information about her next of kin and need someone to identify her body. We were wondering if you could give us any information?"

"Not about her family, no." Davis shrugged. "We met at the crossbow range a few years back. We needed another member to join our team and she stepped in. I can't recall her speaking about her family. She mentioned working for the dentist in town, but she didn't discuss her personal life with either of us."

The man standing in front of Carter was relaxed. Davis' hands hung loose at his sides and his direct stare gave him the impression he was confident with nothing to hide. "Who do you mean by 'us'? Who was the other member of your team?"

"That would be Bill Ripley." Davis smiled. "It seems I attract loners. Bill is as introverted as they come until you get him behind a crossbow. He beat me in the last competition we entered. Although we ran one, two, and three in our section."

"Do you hunt together as well as compete?" Jo looked up from her notebook. "Black Rock Falls is the perfect place to live if you like hunting. Don't you agree?"

"We all hunted together once but it didn't go well. Our relationship with Alicia is strictly to do with competing." Davis shuffled his feet and leaned against the bunkhouse wall. "I don't usually get the time to hunt since my pa died. I need to be here to run the ranch, but if I do, it's usually with one of the guys from the crossbow club."

Carter had been on many cattle ranches and recognized the small cabins set aside for the permanent workers and their families. He knew darn well a working ranch of this magnitude would have at least a manager and other people in supervisory positions. It would be near impossible to run a place of this size alone. "I can imagine it would be a ton of work. How many men do you have working for you?"

"It varies." Davis shrugged nonchalantly. "If you know anything about the cattle business, we have busy times and quiet times. Moving the cattle, cutting out the steers to be sold, moving them from one pasture to another happens at different times of the year. Most of the time, it's just maintaining the ranch, which is a big enough job on its own."

"Getting back to Alicia Palmer." Jo inclined her head as she looked at him. "Did other members of the local crossbow teams have any social contact with her, apart from hunting and competition?"

"Not that I'm aware." Davis smiled. "She's one tough cookie. More like one of the boys if you get my meaning?"

"How would you define a tough cookie?" Jo had an interested expression on her face. "Not feminine?"

"Aw, there you go getting all defensive." Davis chuckled. "Us guys can't say a word without you gals taking it the wrong way. The day we hunted together, Alicia brought down an elk and field-dressed it herself. I've never seen her happier than that day, when she was up to her elbows in blood and guts. Maybe that's why she liked working with the dentist. It was the masochistic side to her." He gave Jo a direct stare. "The type of woman who interests me is the high-maintenance type. I hope saying that isn't sexist, but I mean if they're squeamish, frightened of spiders, and hate breaking their nails, they're my kind of gal."

The hair on the back of Carter's neck tingled. There was something not right about this guy. He wasn't acting as if the news of his friend's death was a surprise. "I couldn't help noticing that you didn't ask how Alicia died. That's usually the first thing people ask when hearing news of a friend's death."

"That's because I assumed something happened to her in the forest. Alicia is reckless and that's why we don't hunt with her. I know she hunts alone. It's not unusual for accidents to happen when people go out alone, even someone like her." Davis shrugged. "We'd had words, you know, about her not following the rules and risking lives. She mentioned wanting to leave the team, which was fine by me. There was no love lost between us and I was hoping Jake... ah Jake Rowley would take her place."

"When was the last time you saw her?" Jo lifted her chin and stared at him.

"I saw her this morning when I was driving through town." Davis met his gaze. His expression was nonplussed. "She was coming out of Aunt Betty's Café."

Interested, Carter narrowed his gaze. This information was crucial. "What time was this and do you recall what she was wearing?"

"Oh, around noon, I guess." Davis shrugged. "She wasn't dressed for hunting, now I come to think on it. She was wearing white, like she does at the dentist. Maybe she'd stopped by the diner for lunch. I don't know."

Knowing Aunt Betty's had CCTV cameras, Carter smiled. "Was she alone?"

"Yeah, I was held up in traffic or I wouldn't have noticed her." Davis frowned. "She climbed into that old Jeep of hers, but I'd gone by before she pulled out. I don't know which way she was heading."

"How did she appear?" Jo lifted her pen from her notebook and looked at him. "Happy? Sad? In a hurry?"

"Dang! I don't know. She looked normal, I guess. Whatever that is for her." Davis shook his head and then rolled his eyes skyward. "I didn't take that much notice." He gave Carter a direct stare. "Just how did she die?"

Feeling the interview slipping away and Davis getting annoyed by their questions, Carter straightened. "The cause of death is undetermined at this time. I haven't been on scene. I'm just conducting inquiries about her next of kin."

"Just one more thing. Do you know the rock pool alongside the falls. On Stanton opposite Pine?" Jo exchanged a glance with Carter and raised one eyebrow. "Is that a place she'd go to hunt?"

"No way." Davis stared at them. "It's dangerous, the edge of the falls is deceptive and overgrown. The ground is unstable." He looked from one to the other. "Oh my God, don't tell me she fell over the falls. Did you find her in Dead Man's Drop?"

"I'm not at liberty to say. The rock pool, does it have a name?" Jo's expression had turned to stone.

"I don't figure it has." Davis stared into space for a time as if he was thinking. "Nope, can't think of a name. It's above Dead Man's Drop, like twenty feet above it and cut into the side of the mountain beside the falls. It's steep and animals fall over the edge all the time and into the fishing hole below. That pool runs directly into the river, forming its own mini falls. The Native Americans say it holds the souls of the dead, so most people leave it be."

Sure he'd covered every angle with Davis, Carter nodded and tried a bluff. "So, you wouldn't have been seen in the area this afternoon?"

"Me? Nope. I grabbed a pizza and then came home. I fixed some fences on the northern pasture, then got a call about one of my men hurting his knee." Davis pulled out a strand of wheat grass and chewed on the end. "Is there anything else I can do for you? I have calls to make."

"Can anyone verify the time you got back from town?" Jo raised one eyebrow.

"I don't need to check in with anyone, ma'am." Davis snorted. "I come and go as I please. That's the pleasure of being the owner." He gave her a long look. "You'll just have to take my word for it, unless you can persuade one of the steers to talk."

Carter glanced at Jo, who shook her head slightly, signifying she had no other questions. "Would you be willing to drop by the morgue to identify the body?"

"Me?" Davis shook his head. "No way. Ask the dentist. He'll know her by her teeth."

"Okay." Jo handed him her card. "If you think of anything else, call me. Thank you for your time."

Carter walked slowly back to the cruiser. He waited for Zorro to jump into the back seat and slipped behind the wheel. "What do you make of him?"

"Smooth, confident, and sure of himself." Jo stared at Davis as he headed toward the house. "Like you, I noticed he didn't ask about her cause of death, which if a friend had died is usual. However, I'm not really surprised that he assumed she fell into the falls as it is a common occurrence. In his favor, he didn't have to admit being the last person to see Alicia alive, did he?" She pushed a hand through her hair. "What makes him a possible suspect is that no one can give us the time he returned to the ranch and he admitted to being in town around the time of death. He had time to kill her and then return to the ranch."

Carter pulled out his phone. "Everyone is heading for the rock pool. They figure we'll have time before dusk. I'll call Jenna and let her know we'll meet them there." He added the coordinates to the GPS and stared at the screen. "It's easy walking distance from Stanton." He looked at Jo. "Just as well you're wearing hiking boots."

"I never leave home without them." Jo smiled at him. "Not in Black Rock Falls."

TWENTY-THREE

Jenna and Kane returned to the office briefly to collect Duke and then hurried back to Stanton to meet up with Wolfe and the others. Carter and Jo had brought her up to date and were in transit. Rowley had gone ahead with Rio to send them the coordinates to the rock pool. Wolfe would be waiting on Stanton and then go with them to the rock pool and send Webber back to the morgue with the body. Everything should run smoothly unless they ran into a bear.

After allowing Duke to sniff the body of Alicia Palmer, they set off at a brisk walk along animal trails that wound through the trees. It was about ten minutes before the roar of the falls and cold clouds of water vapor surrounded them. She looked over one shoulder at Kane. "It can't be much farther."

"Nope." Kane held up his phone to check the coordinates. "Duke is still on the scent. I've scanned all over. It's impossible to make out prints along these trails. There's too many pine needles. It's difficult to tell if she was alone."

The forest didn't end, rather boulders had invaded the forest to create a small clearing. In the center, dangerously close to the raging falls was a small swirling pool, fed by a constant stream of water from the falls. It overflowed into the raging torrent cascading down the mountainside. As Jenna stepped into the sunshine, Duke barked and sat down beside a pile of clothes carefully laid out on a boulder some ways from the pool. "We have something."

"Coming on scene, Sheriff." Rowley stepped out of the trees with Rio close behind. "We've searched the perimeter and found nothing unusual. It doesn't look like anyone else was here."

"We'll need to take a closer look." Wolfe came into the clearing and stood hands on hips scanning the area. "Someone killed her. He's left a trace behind somewhere. We just have to find it, is all."

Taking charge, Jenna ran through procedure in her mind. She had a memorized list and it helped especially when confronted by horrific murders. "Okay, spread out and search everything withing a five-yard area of the pool. Look for hair strands on tree branches, fibers, anything at all. Leave the rock pool and clothes to us." As the deputies spread out, Jenna pulled on examination gloves and went to examine the pile of clothes. She kneeled down beside them and examined each item before sliding it into the evidence bag that Kane was holding open for her. She looked up at him. "She removed these herself. No buttons ripped off or tears, everything is neat and tidy. I smell perfume as well. This isn't a uniform. She was meeting someone special, so must have gone home to change before coming here."

"For skinny-dipping, maybe?" Kane indicated to a towel draped over a branch. He squatted beside a rock and pulled out a purse. "Keys, cash, lipstick, and hairbrush." He bagged the purse and frowned. "She lives alone with a dog. So she must have gone home to change and then headed here."

"You'll need animal control to go get her dog." Carter walked into the clearing with Jo. "It's a bullmastiff and it's angry. No one is getting inside that house anytime soon. Want me to call someone?" He glanced around the clearing. "If you have her house key, we can get someone to collect the dog and take a look around the house. We have a forensic kit in the cruiser. We'll suit up before going inside."

Standing, Jenna nodded. "Yeah, that would be great but leave the car keys, Wolfe will want to do a forensic sweep."

"There you go." Kane extracted the house key from the bunch and handed it to Carter. "When you're done, we'll meet back at the office."

"Yeah, but before we head home, I'd appreciate a steak at Antlers." Carter stretched his back. "It's been a long day and we can discuss everything over dinner."

"I can't." Rowley shook his head. "Sandy will have dinner waiting."

"Me neither. My housekeeper is making pulled pork." Rio grinned. "And I need to be home for the twins or they'll figure they can stay out to all hours."

"I'll be working late at the morgue." Wolfe frowned. "Emily will come by with food. She always does if I'm working late."

"I'd love a steak." Jo leaned against a tree. "I'm exhausted."

Seeing Kane's eager expression, Jenna nodded. "That works for me. She looked at Kane. "Make a reservation for eight. We'll eat and then head home to tend the horses. We can bring the files up to date tonight."

"I'll make it for seven-thirty, and then we'll miss the dinner rush." Kane pulled out his phone. "I know it's early, but we have a ton of things to get through tonight and we're all bushed."

Jenna looked at her watch and nodded. "Okay, can you make it back to the office by six?"

"Yes, ma'am." Carter grinned and led Jo back through the forest.

Jenna looked at the others. "Okay, let's get at it." She followed Wolfe to the edge of the rock pool and moved around slowly, searching the ground for evidence, but the rocky surrounds gave nothing away.

"No trace of blood in the water." Wolfe held up a test kit. "I'm not surprised. The way the water is swirling around before rushing out the other side is similar to the action inside a washer. It's as if it were designed to change the water frequently. We need to search around the rocks for any blood spatter. If we find anything at all, it will prove this is the murder scene."

When Duke went to the edge of the waterfall, Jenna got Kane's attention. "Has he found something?"

"What have you found, boy?" Kane moved to the edge of the waterfall, dislodging small rocks. Spray from the rushing water glistened on his arms as he moved dangerously close to the edge and peered over. "There's blood spatter here." He stood feet wide apart to balance and gripped a nearby sapling. "Hand me a swab, Jenna, and I'll try to get a sample."

Jenna could hardly hear him over the roar of the falls. The noise here was incredible. She removed a swab from the glass tube and handed it to him. She raised her voice. "It's not worth dying for, Dave."

"It's all good." Kane leaned forward and stretched one arm out, straightened, and then handed the swab back to Jenna. "I'll need to take photographs. I can't get my phone out and access the app while I'm holding on. I'll need to use your phone." He moved his attention to Wolfe, who was watching with interest. "It looks like bloody handprints. I think she tried to climb out of the pool to get away from her attacker."

After accessing the camera on her phone, Jenna handed it to Kane and waited with bated breath as he hung dangerously out over the falls. With the phone safely in her hand, she reached out to steady Kane as he slid back down the rocks. As Kane and Wolfe looked over her shoulders, she scrolled through the photographs. Bloody handprints suggested Alicia fought for her life, even preferring certain death in the falls to the attack. The image of her body and the damage inflicted flashed into Jenna's mind. She glanced around the peaceful sunlit clearing. The grass here was soft, and small patches of wildflowers had sprung up around the perimeter. She could imagine it would be a very private place to visit with a special friend. Had Alicia believed she was meeting a close friend, only to find a monster waiting for her?

"This is a perfect place to commit murder." Kane removed his Stetson and shook off the water droplets. "Think about it. The killer lures Alicia here with a promise of romance. She agrees to go skinny-dipping, gets undressed, and as soon as she's in the water he attacks her. As she tried to escape in that direction." He indicated with his chin toward the area where they'd discovered the fingerprints. "I figure he attacked from the shallow end, closing in on her so she couldn't escape. He likely stabbed her in the chest first. She turned to get away and that's when he inflicted the wounds to her back."

"I would agree to that scenario." Wolfe nodded and rubbed his chin. "I've examined the incision across her throat. It didn't happen quickly." He glanced at Kane as if expecting him to explain.

As Rio and Rowley were crowding around Kane and listening intently, Jenna gave him a nod. "You mentioned earlier you'd seen something like this before. Can you give us a rundown?"

"It would have been easier to grab the hair, tip the head back, and slice across the throat. This in itself takes a lot of force and isn't easy by any means. The throat is very muscular, and cutting through almost to the spine, it's more difficult than you imagine. In this case, Alicia's attacker obviously wanted to look her in the eye when he killed her. I can see from the initial puncture wound in the area of the carotid artery he knew how to inflict the most damage. From what I could see, he used that initial stab wound as a starting point."

"Yeah, cutting from the front requires more of a sawing motion and it would be extremely bloody. Not fast and easy like you see in the movies." Wolfe grimaced. "The problem we have here is, if he dumped the body over the falls, he likely spent the time to wash off the blood. The flow of water being so rapid, it would have been easy enough, although there might have been traces under his nails. There are places where blood is very hard to remove."

They spent another hour meticulously searching the entire area and found nothing, no hairs or fibers. It was as if nature had reclaimed the area and turned it back to a pristine condition. Jenna straightened after bending over for some time and groaned. It had been a very long day and every part of her was aching. Her team all looked the way she felt. She went up to them and turned to Wolfe. "Are we done here?"

"Yeah, I can't think of another thing y'all can do." Wolfe pushed back his Stetson and wiped his brow. "If I can get a ride back to the morgue, I'd appreciate it. With any luck, Webber will have prepared Alicia Palmer and gotten her on ice. When I get back to the office, I'll hunt down the dentist. I figure he'll be the best person to identify the body."

"I'll give you a ride." Rowley smiled. "Do you want me to stop by Aunt Betty's for some takeout? If you call now, it will be ready by the time we get to town."

"Yeah, I'd appreciate it. I haven't eaten since breakfast." Wolfe collected his things. "I'm ready when you are."

"Ma'am?" Rowley raised one eyebrow at Jenna. "Are we good to go?"

Jenna waved them away. "Yeah." She glanced at her watch. "Head back to the office. We'll need to discuss the interviews and bring the suspects list up to date."

"We should drop by Aunt Betty's too and speak to Susie.

It's likely she or Wendy was working this morning when Alicia stopped by. I'd be interested to see if she met anyone." Kane removed his examination gloves before tossing them into the garbage bag that Wolfe was holding. "Maybe while we're looking at the CCTV footage, she can fill a few to-go cups with coffee for us. I'm sure everyone would appreciate a drink when they get back to the office."

Jenna nodded. "Yeah, right now I need a gallon."

TWENTY-FOUR

As usual, Susie Hartwig was more than happy to assist. Jenna crammed into the small office in Aunt Betty's Café to view the morning's CCTV footage. "Were you working this morning?"

"No, Wendy wasn't either. Luckily, I have a few very reliable people I can leave in charge." Susie scrolled through the morning's footage, slowing it when the time stamp came up to around eleven-thirty. "She must have come in around this time if she left around noon."

She moved the video forward slowly as each person came up to the counter. Not everyone who ate in the diner came up to the counter. Most went to sit down and waited for a server to bring coffee and take their order. Other customers liked to peruse the specials board or peer inside the glass case at the delicacies on offer. Alicia Palmer was one of these and stood for some moments deciding what to buy. She then walked away but the table she chose was out of view of the camera.

"When we installed the new CCTV cameras, we decided to concentrate on the front counter, rather than the entire room. I think people like their privacy when they're eating. It seemed so intrusive filming their every move. Although it doesn't really help you if you're looking for a killer in town, does it?"

"We have a time at least, and it looks like she came in alone." Kane rubbed his chin thoughtfully. "I doubt if she came in with a date, he'd go and sit down without her. Does she usually come in for a meal after a shift?"

"Yeah, she comes by all the time." Susie stared into the distance thinking. "I don't recall her ever coming in with anyone. I don't think that girl had many friends. Every time I spoke to her all she could talk about was hunting with her crossbow. She'd get this real strange look in her eyes, like she really enjoyed blood sport." She closed the screen and stood. "I never encouraged the conversation because people at the tables next to us don't really need to know how she gutted her last kill."

Considering what Carter had told Jenna about the Jessie Davis interview, it seemed that his impression of her was the same. "No, I imagine they wouldn't, especially as half of them are tourists. Thanks, Susie, this has been very helpful. We needed to verify the time that she was in town."

"Your coffee should be ready by now. I'll get it packed up. We baked a ton of cherry turnovers today and cinnamon sticky buns. I have three dozen each left. Can I add them to your order... on the house? Father Derry usually comes by and collects all our leftover pastries for the shelter, but they had their cake and cookie bake drive today, so he'll have more than enough."

When Kane's stomach rumbled, Jenna nodded. "The team has been out all day, so they'd really appreciate it." She looked at Kane. "Don't forget we're dining at Antlers at seven-thirty."

"That's not something I'd forget in a hurry, Jenna." Kane grinned and looked at Susie. "You are an angel, thanks, but I'll happily pay for them."

"Oh, don't be silly." Susie grinned at him. "You're the only man I've met who turns down a free meal." She headed back to the counter.

"Well, I tried." Kane shrugged.

A short time later they arrived back at the office with coffee and pastries. Jenna peered into the second bag Susie had given her and found two juicy bones. She handed one to Carter. "Is Zorro allowed to have a bone?"

"Yeah, but he won't take it from you." Carter took the bone, unwrapped it, and sniffed it before handing it to Zorro. "There you go. Look what Jenna got for you."

Jenna was sure she could see the dog's lips curl into a smile. She could actually see his front teeth. He took the bone delicately from Carter's hand and went to sit in the corner of the conference room. She didn't need to call Duke. He was sitting at her feet, staring at her with adulation. His big brown eyes watching her every move and his tail thumping on the floor. "Here you go, Duke. You did real good today." She headed to the sink to wash her hands and then sat at the table and opened her files. "Okay, give me a rundown on the suspects interviews. Rowley and Rio, what have you got for me?"

After discussing the interviews, they concluded that all five of the remaining six suspects should remain as possible suspects. Jenna looked over the file notes and then at Carter and Jo. "You sure this college kid, ah... Bill Ripley is capable of murder? He sounds like a recluse."

"Sometimes it's the quiet ones who are the most dangerous." Jo leaned back in her chair, fiddling with her pen. "He could be the psychopath who's leading the team. I want you to think outside the box with these murders. We are only assuming that the hiker murders and Alicia Palmer's murder were committed by the same person or group of people. Although we have no proof whatsoever that Alicia's murder was committed by more than one person. If Wolfe proves to me that she was attacked from different angles, using different width blades, then I will be open to suggestions, but right now, from the evidence there was only one perpetrator in that murder."

Jenna nodded. "Agreed." She blew out a breath. Tiredness was dragging at her. The last couple of days had been very stressful. "Problem is, any one of these five men could have a team and just decided to kill Alicia for the thrill of it. We selected the suspects because they were marksmen in their sport. That doesn't mean there aren't any other marksmen in the county. I would assume that Rowley is a marksman, especially as his friend Jesse Davis suggested he joined their team, but that doesn't make Rowley a killer, does it?"

"So you're taking the ringleader approach?" Rio nodded slowly. He looked at Jo. "In your experience, could a ringleader of a group like this be influenced by someone like Jimmy Two Cents, because to me that sounds more like a follower or hero worship."

"Research tells us that certain things trigger certain behavior, not just in psychopaths." Jo smiled. "We've all heard the term 'followed like sheep.' I've actually seen where the leader of a flock of sheep jumps over a shadow and all the ones following it jump over nothing as well. So the first sheep triggered all the others to do the same action. It's possible, even using peer pressure or authority, to influence people's responses."

Scratching her head, Jenna stared at her. "Can you explain?"

"Okay, say you seat a variety of people in an auditorium. On the stage is a person they consider a person of authority, a doctor, cop, or a firefighter. If the person in authority tells them to stand up, the majority—the sheep—will follow his orders and stand. These people are easily manipulated because they comply without thought." Jo smiled. "The others who remain seated will never be controlled. They are the leaders in society. It's a fact of human behavior. We have leaders and followers. In a crisis, someone always steps up to take charge. This is why cults are successful. The unscrupulous wolves lead the sheep to their demise."

"Wow!" Rowley blinked. "That really happens. I've seen that."

"Nevertheless, I'm still convinced that Jimmy Two Cents has something to do with these murders." Jo moved her attention back to Jenna. "I took the opportunity to call the prison and speak to the warden. He confirmed that as an inmate trustee he was allowed certain privileges. We discussed pen pals, visits, and limited use of the internet, and he certainly does have all these privileges. This gives him access to many people, maybe hundreds of people. Psychopathic serial killers like him get thousands of fans, most of them wanting intimate details of the murders. This rarely happens because most of the psychopathic serial killers insist they're innocent. If they did happen to write it in a letter to one of their pen pals, it will be classed as a confession and legal action would proceed."

"Then why don't we arrange a visit to see him?" Kane leaned on the table, a to-go cup of coffee dwarfed in his large hands. "You mentioned they like to brag. He might want to brag about his pen pals or the people who visit him. We could also get a look at the visitors book and be able to discover who's been stopping by recently."

Mind reeling with possibilities, Jenna nodded. "Okay, Jo, see what you can arrange." She turned back and looked at Carter. "Did you find anything of interest at Alicia Palmer's house?"

"No, I took her laptop and asked Bobby Kalo to help me access it later tonight." Carter sighed. "Her dog's name is Butch and very much loved, by the photographs of him by her bed. No family pictures but she sure loved hunting. The dog reacted positively when animal control came to get him. He was protecting his house, is all. There's not a bad bone in his body.

They figured they'll be able to rehome him, if you can't find a family member to take him."

"We haven't found anyone locally." Kane sipped his coffee and sighed. "I've sent her information to Kalo. He might find a distant relative, but at this stage we don't even have anyone to claim her body."

Jenna thought for a beat and leaned back in her chair. "It's strange, in the last case we were talking about victims. At the time, they didn't own a dog. It seemed that no one who was getting murdered owned a dog. If she had been at home or had taken Butch with her, she would have been okay. If the dog was as aggressive as you say guarding the house, he wouldn't have let anyone near her. As she wasn't going hunting, why did she leave the dog behind?"

"Maybe the man she was meeting had an aversion toward dogs? Or was allergic maybe?" Kane smiled at her. "That's a good point and one we should follow up."

"Oh, I don't know about that." Carter cleared his throat. "I've had the experience of an angry pooch trying to attack me the moment I tried to make a move on a woman during a date. I mean, just putting my arm around her shoulders made the dog sink his teeth into my leg. If Alicia was planning to have a romantic liaison at the rock pool, skinny-dipping and all, she might not have wanted to take the dog with her for that very reason. Butch being overprotective, he'd certainly destroy the mood, and from all accounts, Alicia didn't attract many men. Well, I figure she wouldn't want to spoil her chances."

"The woman is dead, Carter." Jo rounded on him. "That's not a very nice thing to say. Have some compassion. Her death would have been horrific."

"I wasn't being unsympathetic, Jo." Carter stared at the ceiling as if waiting for divine intervention. "I was just making a point. She knew she was going into the forest, right? She'd left her crossbow and hunting gear behind. This was plain to see as she had a room with everything set out on the wall. If something was missing, we'd have known about it." He dropped his gaze back to Jo. "She was familiar with the dangers of the forest, so any sane person would take her dog with her if she was going for a walk. It's obvious she'd made plans to meet someone at the rock pool. It's a remote place that nobody visits because it's dangerous, so this wasn't an opportunistic thrill kill. It was planned. She knew her killer well enough to undress and climb into the rock pool with him."

Taking in everything he said, Jenna nodded. "Which takes us back to the people at the crossbow club. It seems to me these were her only friends. So it has to be one of them who killed her, as we believed in the first place." She glanced at her watch. "Okay, people, let's call it a day." She turned to Kane. "I'm going to freshen up and change my clothes before we go to dinner." She smiled at his expression and quick glance at his watch. "We have time. I know the reservation is at seven-thirty."

"Me too." Jo stood, collected the empty to-go cups and threw them in the trash. "I'm sure glad we leave changes of clothes in the locker room. We never know what's going to happen in this town." She headed out the door.

TWENTY-FIVE

Miles Nolan stared at the ceiling. So what, he hadn't done his chores? It was spring break and he'd gotten spectacular grades. All the other kids' parents rewarded their kids for doing well at school. They gave them time to enjoy their vacation before the next grueling semester began, but not his pa. What was the big deal about forgetting to take out the trash twice this week? It wasn't life threatening? Surely his brother, at twelve, was more than capable, but no, his brother's nice little chore was to unload the dishwasher. Now he was grounded for the rest of the week, his phone, laptop, and car keys confiscated. His pa's voice boomed in his brain. *"Driving is a privilege at your age, not a right. You earn luxuries in this house by doing your chores. You need to learn that it's hard work that gets rewards, not being lazy."*

He tossed and turned in bed and punched the pillow. The most humiliating was being sent to bed at eight-thirty, especially when he needed to explain things to his girlfriend. Without his phone or laptop, he had no way of contacting her, and Betty-Jo, being Betty-Jo, would assume he was ghosting her. He wanted to tear out his hair because no matter how many times he tried to explain this to his pa, he refused to listen, and the more he insisted, the more punishments his pa added to the list.

He just knew the moment his back was turned one of the guys would move in on his girlfriend, especially as they'd had a fight, which he'd smoothed over by inviting her to a party. It was the perfect makeup situation and he'd make everything right, but now he couldn't go. The problem was Betty-Jo was gorgeous and the captain of the cheerleading team. If he didn't show, she might give up on him and take up with one of the other jocks. The idea made his stomach cramp. He'd lose her for a couple of lousy bags of garbage. He pressed the pillow to his face and swore. All his friends were going and they'd planned to meet up under the bleachers at the football stadium at ten. It was a onetime deal. The keys "borrowed" from the janitor's room must be returned by the following morning. One of the guys had scored two twelve-packs of beer; some of the girls had managed to obtain bottles of wine. He'd been looking forward to going and told his folks he'd be staying over at a friend's house. They'd covered for each other and the plan was golden —until now.

He switched on his bedside lamp and stared at the clock on the wall. It was generic, a white face inside a black circle, with large black numerals, black hands, and a red second hand ticking by the seconds of his life. He couldn't remember how long he stared at that clock. As a young kid, he would sit up all night waiting for it to tick so slowly down to Christmas morning, too scared to peek down the stairs in case he scared Santa Claus away. Other times it moved so fast. When he fell out of bed, running late in the morning, he'd swear the hands sped up, and he'd need to run to catch the school bus.

The hand ticked past ten and his mind went to Betty-Jo. He slid out of bed and opened the bedroom door and listened. The TV in the family room blared out the news but if he went downstairs, his mom would see him walk by the kitchen. Her soft humming drifted toward him as she made a snack, so the back door was out of contention. The stairs in the old house creaked and would alert his parents if he tried to slip out of the front door. There was only one other option. He dressed fast and, pulling on his sneakers, opened the window and, heart pounding, eased out, grabbing for the drainpipe. He'd climbed down this way a thousand times before as a kid, but he was a whole lot heavier at seventeen. The drainpipe creaked and groaned and he fell the last five feet or so, landing heavily on his backside.

Pain shot through his hip and he lay on the damp grass panting. Had his parents heard the thump as he hit the ground? He rolled under the window and waited before limping away. Walking softly, he kept to the bushes around the perimeter of his yard. It was a long walk to the stadium unless he took the alleyways that joined most of the properties facing Stanton Forest and linked roads for pedestrians. He face-palmed his head the moment he got to Stanton and peered along the dark road. Only a few streetlights spread their yellow light, the side-walk in between was cloaked in shadows. How did he forget to take a flashlight? He knew darn well the alleyways were pitch black at this time of night.

Grim determination spurred him on. He must get to the party and sort things with Betty-Jo. Shaking off the warnings nagging him about walking the streets at night, he zipped up his jacket and picked up his pace. Light from a vehicle illuminated the blacktop and he turned to stare into the halogen beams. A truck drove past and stopped a few houses away. A man climbed out and opened the back door, leaning in as if searching for something. Miles nodded as he walked past and kept going, taking the first alleyway. He'd used the alleyway network like most of the locals many a time, but during the day. A shiver of apprehension went through him as he entered the seemingly endless dark tunnel. Stanton was opposite the forest, and anything could be lurking in the alleyways. They were different to the ones in town; they had sidewalks and buildings along each side. The alleyways along Stanton ran alongside someone's yard and acted as a property line. Thick bushes lined each side of the alleyway. Some of them neatly tended by the owners of the houses, others left to run riot, with branches reaching out to touch the opposite side, creating a tunnel of vegetation and blocking out the moonlight.

Gathering his nerve, Miles took a deep breath and kept moving into the darkness. Behind him, the wind from the mountains rushed down Stanton in blustery waves and with each step leaves rustled and branches groaned. Nerves on edge, he shuffled forward deeper into the dark unknown. Behind him an engine started, and the sound of the truck moving slowly along Stanton left him frighteningly alone. No one was about to help him. Hurrying on into the darkness, he kept to the middle of the alleyway, with both arms outstretched and fingers trailing along the bushes. Relief flooded him when the streetlights of the road ahead came into view and he increased his pace. As he crossed the road, he noticed an identical truck parked some ways from the entrance to the next alleyway, but many people drove trucks in Black Rock Falls.

The streetlights gave off an eerie glow, as he jogged across the misty blacktop and headed into the dark pathway. Confident a bear or wildcat wouldn't venture this far from the forest, he moved silently into the entrance, his sneakers not making a sound on the gravel.

Keeping alert, he listened for any warning sounds coming from ahead but only the sound of wind rustling the leaves came in the silence. He'd reached about halfway, when the distinct sound of footsteps, like boots on gravel, echoed down the alleyway toward him. He stopped and turned, looking both ways, but saw nothing. Uneasiness crept over him as he strained his eyes trying to peer into the darkness, but nothing moved ahead of him

Crunch, crunch, crunch.

His heart pounded as the footsteps came closer, but no one loomed out of the darkness. The hairs on the back of Miles' neck stood to attention and fear gripped his stomach. He shook his head trying to dispel the stories of ghouls prowling these alleyways at night. The footsteps stopped suddenly, and Miles stared into the pitch black. "Hello, is somebody there?"

Nothing.

Terrified, he forced one leg in front of the other and shuffled forward, one hand against the bushes, the other held out in front of him like a blind man. Stuck midway through the alleyway, it was too far to go back. He must keep moving forward. Trying to calm shattered nerves, he gave his head a shake, wondering if he'd imagined the footsteps. His pulse pounded in his ears as he moved onward. Wind whistled around him and shadows moved. Each small sound was magnified. He forced his feet to take each step, sure someone was close by. An odor came to him on the breeze, thick, musky. Was he smelling his own fear? No bear or cat smelled like that. He turned, peering into blackness over one shoulder, and a crunch on gravel cut through the silence. Pain shot through his head and he turned, shaping up ready to fight. Something cold hit his stomach and he cried out as white-hot pain sliced into his belly. He dropped his arms, hugging the leaking mass seeping through his fingers, and fell to his knees. The smell of blood surrounded him as he shuddered in agony. Under his palms the slippery mess of intestines, moved like snakes fighting to get free. Gasping, he stared into the darkness, seeing nothing, but someone was there. He could sense the menace hanging over him.

Footsteps moved away, and he tried to take a breath to call for help, but blood filled his mouth. He rolled onto his back and using shaking legs pushed himself along the gravel on his back.

He must get to the end of the alleyway to get help. It was his only chance. Slowly, inch by excruciating inch, he moved along.

Crunch, crunch, crunch.

Terrified, Miles listened with horror as the footsteps came closer. Slow, deliberate strides, but this time the light from a phone illuminated the alleyway. He stared down in horror at the bloody mess filling his hands and sobbed in fear. The light came closer, a tall shadow behind it. Miles lifted his head. "Help me, please, help me."

No words were spoken, no comfort given. The person just stood there, ignoring his pleas. His killer had returned to watch him die. Sobbing, he stared into the sky seeking divine intervention. The bushes overhead moved against the moonlit sky, like the long fingers of an exotic dancer dancing to the song of the wind. No help came. Cold seeped into him and his heart jittered, beating erratically as if trying to leap from his chest. Warm blood leaked over his fingers, in a horrifying rush. A smiling face came out of the darkness, so close, he could make out the neat straight teeth. The flash of a bloody knife waved across his vision. Terrified, he cried out. A thump of pain hit the center of his chest without warning. As the world slid away, Miles stared into the face of his killer.

TWENTY-SIX

WEDNESDAY

The blue sky stretched on forever and not a cloud interrupted the view from Jenna's front porch to the Black Rock Falls mountain range. It was another beautiful day. A light breeze rustled the grass and Jenna leaned against the porch railing, watching the horses frolic in the corral. When Kane came up behind her, encircling her in his arms, she sighed with contentment. "The last thing I want to do right now is head into the office to try and solve a crime that seems to be spiraling out of control. After our discussion last night, with Jo and Carter even taking all the interviews into account and everyone's opinion, we still really don't have anything positive going forward. The only reason our suspects list has reduced is because one of them became the victim. Personally, I'm not convinced that Alicia Palmer wasn't involved in the first murder. From what everyone was saying, she was more than capable."

"Yeah, well Kalo is digging into her background a little more." Kane rested his chin on her shoulder. "From what Davis said about her, my gut is telling me to take a closer look. She may well have been killed to keep her from running her mouth."

He blew out a breath, moving her hair. "Which is a complete turnaround for what I would normally consider, as her injuries are more like a crime of passion."

Jenna leaned into him. "So what would make you change your mind?"

"I figure her killer is inexperienced." Kane stared off into the distance. "He might be skilled with a crossbow, but he doesn't know how to kill with a knife. Alicia had so many injuries it was as if he panicked. Most hunters, or anyone trained to kill, would be able to kill a person with one stab wound. She had her back to him, which gave him many choices. For instance, he could have stabbed her in the base of the skull by sliding the knife between the vertebrae to severe the spinal cord. Or stabbed her under the ribcage in one thrust and hit the liver, or an easy one would be under the arm." He turned her to face him. "He stabbed her once or twice and she didn't go down and he panicked. The only part of this kill that concerns me is the need to look into her eyes when he did the final blow. The cut throat was more like butchery. And from Wolfe's account, the pennies were pushed under her eyelids with some force."

Running the murder through her mind as Kane described sent a shiver down Jenna's spine. "Do you think this is the same killer or these killers know each other? Maybe they have a thing for Jimmy Two Cents."

"I'd like to know how they got the details of his murders." Kane turned and followed her back inside the house. "I've read over the court transcripts and the details regarding the coins never made the press. This was to prevent copycats and to allow the investigation of similar crimes. How did they know about the coins?"

Jenna checked her watch. "I don't know but we have to go. Carter and Jo left half an hour ago." She buckled her weapon around her waist and then pulled on her jacket. "Jo mentioned that Jimmy Two Cents is allowed pen pals and visitors. I know that his mail is censored but who knows what they talk about during a visit."

"As an inmate trustee, he has contact with other prisoners as well." Kane pushed on his black Stetson and followed her out of the door. "It's possible he told them about the coins, and the information was passed on through less supervised prisoners. There are two different types of visits: one is behind a screen and the other is in an open room with other prisoners and their families or whoever is visiting them at the time. Anything could be said during these visits and information passed on wouldn't normally get out."

Jenna climbed into the Beast and thought for a while as they headed for the office. "Jo would be able to get us into see Jimmy Two Cents. Maybe we need to go to the source. She has a way of extracting information from psychopathic serial killers." She looked at Kane. "I know this is Serial Killer Central, but I don't think we're dealing with psychopathic serial killers. This feels different to me. A psychopath seems to follow a pattern of sorts, but these killings are random and different. Too different. Three neat murders, the body's untouched apart from the coins, then a woman brutally stabbed to death. This can't be the same person."

"If our suspects had any connection to Jimmy Two Cents, they'd have shown up in Kalo's report. He ran their names against the visitors books and the current list of pen pals, which is substantial, although there is a chance we missed someone. I'm sure not all of them use their real names." Kane pulled into his slot outside the sheriff's office. "It was the first search Kalo did for us."

Unconvinced, Jenna gathered her things. "You always say to follow your gut instinct and mine is telling me we've missed something important. I'm going to go over everything again today and see if I can find out what it is." She climbed out of the truck and waited for Kane to get Duke. "I'll at least have a couple of hours before we go to the autopsy."

She walked inside the office and at once noticed Atohi Blackhawk leaning on the counter chatting with Maggie. She smiled. Blackhawk was a good friend and she laughed as Duke did his happy dance at seeing him. Duke had been raised on the res and considered Blackhawk family. "It's good to see you. Are you waiting for us?"

"Yeah." Blackhawk shook Kane's hand and gave Jenna a hug. "The puppies are almost three months old and will be ready to go soon, if you want to come and see them." He pulled out his phone and proudly displayed a set of photographs.

Enthralled, Jenna looked at each one, enlarging the image with her fingers. "Oh, they are so pretty." She sighed. "We can't leave town until we've solved this case."

"Oh, no rush." Blackhawk nodded and took back his phone. "We like having them around." He looked at Kane. "I just dropped by. I'm heading out today with Dr. Larsen. She is taking a team to look over one of the gravesites I found. She said it may take months to excavate and make a determination. I figure I've given her a few years' work." He dropped his voice to just above a whisper. "Has Wolfe found the woman of his dreams?"

"I think it's a work in progress." Kane grinned. "We all hope it works out for him. Norrell is a very special lady and perfect for him."

"They sure look happy when they're together." Blackhawk slapped one hand on the counter. "I've gotta go. Call me when you're ready to see the pups and bring Duke. He'll need to accept the puppy before you take it home or he'll believe it's a replacement. You do know how intelligent he is, I'm sure."

"I do indeed." Kane grinned and waved as he walked out the door.

Jenna turned and headed for the stairs. "Come on, every-one's going to believe we've taken a personal day."

"Ah, don't worry." Kane followed close behind. "Maybe they've solved the case in our absence."

"Sheriff!"

Jenna turned to see a man running toward her, his coat flying out behind him and face flushed. Before she could open her mouth to ask what was wrong. Kane had stepped in front of her.

"Whoa, hold up." Kane held up a hand like a traffic cop. "You can't come running at the sheriff like that. What seems to be the problem?"

"It's terrible, I've seen something in the alleyway." The man was grasping his chest and panting. "You must come."

Stepping out from behind Kane, Jenna beckoned the man forward and then sat him down in Rowley's cubicle. Concerned the man might be having a heart attack, she took his pulse, but he shook her hand away. "Take a few deep breaths and then explain what you saw in the alleyway."

"I figure it's a person with their guts hanging out. The light isn't good in there and I didn't get close enough to take a better look. I just turned around and ran to my friend's house and they gave me a ride into town."

"Okay, let's start with your name and details." Kane unfolded his notebook and took a pen from his pocket.

"John Forester." Forester gave his details.

Cracking open a bottle of water and handing it to the man, Jenna sat at Rowley's desk. "Where exactly is this alleyway? And what were you doing there?"

"I live on Maple and was taking the alleyway to get through to Stanton. I wanted to catch the bus into town." Forester was shaking like Jell-O. "That's when I seen it lying there with blood all around, black like tar. Flies buzzing around and stinking. I figure it's been there for a time. I turned around and ran back to a friend's place and ask him to drive me here."

"Why didn't you call?" Kane leaned against the filing cabinets and stared at him.

"The network's been down in our area all night." Forester shrugged. "Apparently, there's a work crew on it now. I don't have a landline, neither does my friend. There's really not any use for them anymore, is there?"

Jenna stood. "Would you be able to come with us and show us exactly where you found the body?" She couldn't help noticing his expression of revulsion. "We'll be happy to give you a ride home or back into town if you wish?"

"Yeah, okay. I'm not feeling so good and figure I should go back home." Forester went to stand and Kane laid a hand on his shoulder.

"Just sit awhile." Kane took Jenna's place. "The sheriff will have to notify the other deputies what's happened. It will only take five minutes or so."

Taking the steps two at a time, Jenna rushed to the conference room, bursting inside. She instantly got everyone's attention. "We might have another victim. Rio and Rowley, I'll need you to take Mr. Forester to show us where he found the body. Cell phones are down in the area, so you'll have to use the coms to keep in contact. Go and take a look. I'll contact Wolfe as we are due there for an autopsy at ten, and explain things. If it is a body, set up a crime scene perimeter, and we'll get everyone out there as soon as possible."

"What about Mr. Forester?" Rio pushed to his feet and gathered his things. "What do you want us to do with him. We can't exactly leave him on scene, can we?"

Jenna pulled back her hair and secured it with an elastic band from around her wrist. "Once he shows you where he found the body, ask him to remain in the cruiser. As first on scene, we will need his DNA, and more details than what I got from him downstairs. He is very unsettled. When he's been left to sit for a while, he might recall a few more details. Don't worry, as soon as I get there I'll speak to him personally, then maybe you can drop him home. Apparently, he only lives a short distance away."

"Not a problem." Rio looked at Rowley. "We'll take your truck. I'll ride shotgun."

"Works for me." Rowley grinned and, attaching his com pack to his belt, followed him out the door.

"We'll come." Jo shot to her feet. "If this is another victim, with pennies under his eyelids, I'll need to compare the murder with Jimmy Two Cents' MO. I'm sure there's a link to him, and if so, we'll need to go to the source and speak to Jimmy Two Cents."

"That's what Jenna said on the way here this morning." Kane was filling to-go cups with coffee and handing them around. "Right now, we don't have enough evidence to pin these murders on any of the suspects. Circumstantial evidence linking them to the time or place of one of the deaths won't be enough." He shrugged. "If one of them has a link to Jimmy Two Cents, we can expand it and start building a case."

Jenna used the landline to call Wolfe to explain. "I'll get on scene in five but we're not even sure it's a person yet. The witness was a little vague. We're using coms as the cell phones are down in that area, so I might not be able to call you."

"I'll come. What I find at the scene may be crucial." Wolfe sighed. "The autopsy can wait. I've done a preliminary examination and have enough information for you to use. Type of knife for instance, depth of wounds. I'll need to open her up for a cause of death, but from my initial examination, the severed carotid artery is likely the cause of the blood loss resulting in cardiac arrest."

Jenna thought for a beat. "Meet us on Stanton. Rio and Rowley have gone ahead with the witness and will be able to give us the coordinates over the com. There are alleyways all over this part of town."

"I'm on my way." Wolfe disconnected.

TWENTY-SEVEN

John Forester was babbling by the time they arrived at the entrance to the alleyway. Rio tried to keep the mood upbeat, talking to the guy about football and ice hockey, but it seemed that nothing would work. The man's sheet-white face and staring eyes were exaggerated by his trembling hands. When they pulled to the curb, no amount of encouragement would lure him from the back seat of the cruiser, although Rio had little doubt they were in the right place. A cool breeze rushed up the alleyway, bringing with it the stink of death. One thing was for sure, something lay dead in its murky depths. "Okay, Mr. Forester, if going any farther is distressing for you, stay here until we come back. How far are you from your home?"

"Not far." Forester pointed vaguely behind him. "Over there, not more than five minutes away. I can walk from here."

"No, stay in the back of the truck." Rowley gave him a condescending smile. "The medical examiner will be here soon and I'm sure he'll want to speak to you. I understand this has been extremely unsettling for you, but it would be better if you get the interviews out of the way, then you can go home and rest."

After grabbing the crime scene kit from the back of the truck, Rio pulled on examination gloves and a mask before switching on his flashlight and heading down the alleyway. The beam from his flashlight illuminated a humped shape against the hedge lining the dirt track. All around it, what he assumed was blood had run in rivulets along the alleyway. As they got closer, it was apparent the victim was a young man, perhaps a teenager. Appalled, Rio's gut tightened as he moved the beam over the slumped figure. The carnage before him was brutal, and sadistic. He kept a good distance away as it was obvious the victim was dead. The blue tint to the face and the liver mortis evident in one forearm suggested the body had been there for some time, possibly overnight. He turned to Rowley. "He's been gutted and left to die."

"Do you figure it's the same killer?" Rowley pulled crime scene tape out of the forensic kit and tossed it in his palm.

Avoiding the congealed patch of blood around the victim, Rio bent and shone his flashlight on the face. Under the eyelids, the shape of two pennies was unmistakable. "Yeah, unless it's become fashionable to push pennies under the eyes of murder victims this week." He straightened and cast his light around, searching the immediate area for evidence. Finding nothing of interest, he tapped his com and gave Jenna the exact position of the alleyway. He turned back to Rowley. "Hand me another roll of tape. I'll head back to check on Mr. Forester. You go and seal the opposite end of the alleyway; we don't want people walking through the crime scene."

"I was already on my way." Rowley tossed him a roll of tape and headed off in the other direction, his flashlight bopping in the distance.

Walking slowly back to the road, Rio noticed a few drops of blood on the dead leaves lining the edge of the alleyway. He'd stuffed his pockets with marker flags before leaving the office and marked each spot of blood. The trail, which had started with noticeable droplets, dissipated to nothing as he got closer to the road. Right at the entrance to the alleyway sunlight illuminated a small hole, as if the ground there had been stabbed with a knife. He marked the spot and scanned the immediate area. He crouched down to examine the grassy verge and discovered what he had been looking for. It was a small patch smeared with blood. The killer had used the dirt and surrounding grass to clean the blood from his knife. He added a circle of markers and straightened as Kane's black truck, with the ME's white van close behind, pulled up nose-to-tail with Rowley's cruiser.

"What have you got for me?" Jenna came straight to his side, wrinkled her nose, and pulled on a mask. "Is it a body?"

Nodding, Rio waited for Kane and Wolfe to walk into earshot. "Yeah, it's a young guy who's been gutted. He has pennies under his eyelids, the same as the others. Rowley is at the other end of the alleyway, sealing it with crime scene tape."

"Did you find a murder weapon?" Jenna was staring down the dark alleyway, as the beam from Rowley's flashlight came into view.

Rio shook his head and pointed to the evidence markers. "No weapon, but from the trail of droplets, this killer is as cold as ice. His knife was dripping with blood, and from the distance between the drops, he murdered the young guy and then walked calmly away."

"Okay." Jenna looked at Mr. Forester sitting in the back of Rowley's truck. "Get a written statement from Mr. Forester and then give him a ride home. When you're done, I'll need you back on scene."

Rio touched the brim of his Stetson. "Yes, ma'am."

TWENTY-EIGHT

The smell of death was the same for most people. The sweet rancid stench was one of the most recognizable on earth, but as Shane Wolfe ducked under the crime scene tape, he detected a variety of different odors. The smell of decaying flesh usually overlaid the more subtle aromas. He detected the smell of congealing blood, spilled intestines, fecal matter, and the sweat of fear. It was no surprise when he reached the body and viewed the extent of the injuries. He turned to his assistant Colt Webber and daughter Emily. "Set up the portable lights but keep to the perimeter of the alleyway."

"I can't see any signs of a struggle, Dad." Emily moved her flashlight around the scene. "Do you think the killer was waiting for him?"

Glad that Emily was taking in the whole picture, he nodded. "It sure looks that way, but we'll leave it up to Jenna's team to decide how it went down."

"Attending homicides, especially when they're young people, makes me kinda sad." Emily looked at him. "Do you feel like that?"

Wolfe met her gaze and she stared back, chin high and

confident. He couldn't be more proud of her. "Always. That's why I became a medical examiner. If you lose your compassion, it's time to walk away."

From the light of the halogen beams, the full extent of the attack became evident. Cold encircled the pit of Wolfe's stomach. The victim was a teenager, and his face held the fullness of a young boy on the brink of manhood. A shock of light brown hair fell over one eye and reddish stubble brushed the chin of a handsome face. His lips had drawn back during rigor, showing even white teeth. He shook his head. Even after attending so many crime scenes, he'd never become hardened to the sight of a homicide. He swallowed hard, more determined than ever to speak for the young man.

All around him, Jenna, Kane, and Rowley scanned the area for evidence. The scene was videoed and photographs taken for the record before Wolfe moved closer to the body to do his preliminary examination. After finding a wallet in the man's back pocket, he handed it to Kane. "Miles Nolan, just turned seventeen."

Wolfe took out his voice recorder for taking notes. Jenna and Kane moved closer to him, listening with interest. Jo and Carter stuck to the edge of the blood spatter. "Pennies under the eyes the same as the other victims and there's a bruise on the left side of his temple and an imprint of a ring, maybe? I'll look at it more closely back at the lab." He flipped open the victim's torn jacket and heard Jenna's sharp intake of breath behind him as the full extent of the man's injuries were revealed. "The victim received an incision approximately ten to twelve inches in length, midsection, to expose the bowel." He paused his recorder and turned to look at Kane. "This looks more like field-dressing than a kill. I don't figure the intention here was to kill him but to watch him bleed out. From the blood loss, the victim was alive for some time before death." He pointed to the dirt on the man's fingertips and then indicated to the bloody drag marks on the ground. "He tried to crawl away after he was injured."

"Yeah, that sure looks like an experienced hunter's work to me." Rowley straightened and walked away, taking deep breaths.

"If you need a break, take it before you spew." Kane gave Rowley a sympathetic look.

"I'm okay." Rowley turned to look at Kane. "It's the smell, is all. You would think that after changing diapers I'll be used to anything by now."

Wolfe needed Kane's input. "Hunter or assassin?"

"Hunter. It has an almost delicate touch." Kane crouched down beside him. "It looks unrushed to me. Anyone intending to kill outright would stab the knife under the sternum in an upward thrust. This looks more like he was intending to skin him." He indicated to the head injury. "I figure he came up to him in the dark, stunned him first with a punch, and then used the knife. He'd have time to draw a knife before the victim knew what was happening."

"Hunting knife?" Jenna leaned closer, examining the wound. "I agree with you, Dave. It looks almost surgical."

Wolfe's attention moved over the edges of the incision. "Hunting knife, most like. They would be sharp enough to do this type of injury. When I look at it under the microscope, I'll be able to determine if it was a serrated edge or straight blade." He lifted the shirt higher, displaying one deep sharp force injury to the heart. "From this, it looks as if he watched him suffer and then decided to finish him off. The trail of blood that Rio discovered would indicate he walked away slowly and took the time to clean his knife."

"He wanted to watch him die, the same as with Alicia Palmer." Jo folded her arms across her chest, leaning into the hedge. "Apart from the coins, he is starting to show an individual pattern. I would say, from what we see here and from the Alicia Palmer murder, this is the same killer. If you look at the murders of the teenagers in the forest, one of them was struck in the leg first. If I created a profile on the killer in this case, I would say he was the one who killed Leo Kelly. The others were clean death shots. The murderer of the other three enjoys seeing people suffer. He has psychopathic tendencies. He must be the leader, and the others are followers." She sighed. "When I get back to the office, I'll sift through the crime scenes again and see if one of our suspects stands out."

"I've walked up and down the alleyway from one end to the other." Carter walked casually up to the body and stared at the forlorn figure on the floor. "My boots made a distinctive noise in the gravel, and yet when Webber came in before, he didn't seem to make a sound. This kid is wearing sneakers. He could move through this alleyway almost silently, but I noticed, following back from where he's lying, slight indents in the gravel, as if he ran a few steps and then turned around here." He pointed to the ground where there was a slight disturbance in the gravel. "I figured he did this to see who was following him. No one was hiding in the bushes. The killer just walked straight up to him and punched him in the head."

"I couldn't help noticing he's not carrying a phone and a kid of this age would be." Jenna crouched down and pointed a flashlight under the bushes and then turned to look at the other side of the alleyway. He is not carrying a flashlight either and you can see how dark this place is now. It would have been pitch black last night." She turned to look at Wolfe. "If this played out like you figured, the killer was carrying a light, probably the one on his phone. It makes sense if the victim was walking alone up a dark alleyway and heard footsteps behind him. A kid of his age might have been frightened and picked up his speed. He's seventeen, maybe he was second-guessing himself about being afraid and turned to see who was following him. The light would have blinded him. He would never have seen the blow coming."

Impressed, Wolfe nodded. "I agree the killer had a flashlight, he wouldn't have been able to see much in the dark, and as he obviously likes to watch his victims die, it makes perfect sense." He looked at Jenna. "I've seen enough. I'll get him back to the morgue. From the photo ID he lived on Stanton." He handed Jenna the evidence bag containing the wallet. "Call me when you've spoken to the next of kin to confirm a viewing at one. I won't be conducting his autopsy until tomorrow. I'll reschedule Alicia Palmer's for three this afternoon. Will that give you enough time?"

"Yeah, sure." Jenna took the wallet out of the bag, extracted the driver's license, and turned to Kane. "374 Stanton." She shook her head. "I bet they don't even know he's missing." She turned to her team.

"We'll head back to the office." Carter removed his gloves and turned to Jenna. "Jo will need to contact the state pen and wrangle an interview with Jimmy Two Cents."

Wolfe looked from one to the other. "Make sure you make it after the autopsy tomorrow. I can move it to nine to give you more time?"

"I can work with that." Jo nodded.

"Okay, let's get at it." Jenna headed out of the alleyway. She stopped to speak to Rowley. "You'd better get a ride back to the office with Jo and Carter. Rio has given the witness a ride home."

Moving his attention to Emily, Wolfe indicated with his chin to the departing team. "I'm sure glad you decided to become an ME. The investigation side Jenna has to deal with looks like organized chaos."

TWENTY-NINE

Jenna's stomach went into freefall as Kane pulled to the curb outside a neat redbrick home. She turned over the wallet belonging to Miles Nolan in her hand and stared out of the window, trying to find the words she'd need to deal with distraught parents. Five homicides over a few days had pushed her resources to the limit. Her mind was overflowing with information, but right now she couldn't put anything together to make a case. Had she lost her edge? Pushing her mind back to the horrible task at hand, she turned to Kane. "It never gets any easier, does it? I know this is my job, but it sure helps when Wolfe talks to the next of kin. He has a way with people, a deep compassion, and it shows that he cares. I seem to freeze up and I know dealing with notifications of death should be professional. Sometimes I just want to hug the people. Is that such a bad thing?"

"Yes and no." Kane took her hand and squeezed gently. "It depends on how the recipients of the news regard law enforcement. You know the 'kill the messenger' syndrome. Sometimes the relatives need someone to blame, whereas Wolfe is a doctor. They understand he is trying to discover the truth of what happened." He gave her a long look. "Do you want me to take this one?" He sighed. "I figure it's going to be a shock. As it's spring break, they probably believe their son is still in bed or they'd have called the office to report him missing by now."

In two minds, Jenna stared at the wallet in her hand. She removed the driver's license and then pushed the wallet inside her pocket. The wallet was evidence and may contain a clue to why Miles Nolan was walking through dark alleyways at night. She sucked in a deep breath and nodded to Kane. "Okay, I'm ready."

Suddenly glad of her SHERIFF'S DEPARTMENT jacket, she led the way up the garden path and knocked on the front door. When a woman came to the door and stared at her open-mouthed, she held up the license. "Does Miles Nolan live here?"

"Yes, he does, Sheriff." The woman glanced over her shoulder and then back at Jenna. "I'm his mother. Is there a problem?"

Wishing she could be anywhere else but here, Jenna met the woman's troubled expression. "Is your husband at home?"

"No, he's at the office." Mrs. Nolan pointed over her shoulder. "Miles is in his room. His pa grounded him and he didn't come down for breakfast, so he's probably still sulking."

Heart sinking, Jenna nodded slowly. "We need to speak to you. Can we come inside?"

"Has something happened to Jerry?" Mrs. Nolan's hand went to her mouth. "Did he wreck his truck on the way to work?"

Swallowing hard, Jenna shook her head. "No, we're not here about Jerry. Is he your husband?"

"Do you have his office number?" Kane took out his notebook. "I need to speak to him."

"Yes, of course." Mrs. Nolan gave Kane the details and then

stared at Jenna when Kane walked away to make the call. "What's this all about?"

Getting the next of kin inside and sitting down was a priority. Jenna moved closer. "It's about Miles. May we come inside?"

"I guess so." Mrs. Nolan walked into the hallway and, placing one hand on the banister, looked up the stairs. "Miles, get down here. The sheriff wants to speak with you. Pa is on his way, so move your sorry ass." She led the way into a kitchen, leaned against the counter, and folded her arms across her chest. "Okay, what's he done now?"

The remains of a breakfast littered the kitchen table, and the scent of coffee still hung in the air. Jenna turned as Kane walked into the kitchen behind her. They exchanged a meaningful glance and Kane gave her a slight nod. He'd informed the father. Sucking in a deep breath Jenna pulled out a chair. "Maybe you should sit down?"

"Look, just say what's on your mind." Mrs. Nolan shook her head. "How bad can it be?"

Bracing herself, Jenna lifted her chin and handed the driver's license to Mrs. Nolan. "Is this your son, Miles?"

"Yes." She turned the license over in her hand. "Where did you find it?"

There was no easy way to tell a mother her child had died. Straightening, Jenna stared at her. "On the body of a young man we believe is Miles."

"That's impossible." Mrs. Nolan ran from the room and headed up the stairs. Footsteps ran down a passageway and the sound of a door hitting the wall. "Noooo."

"Go upstairs." Kane squeezed her shoulder. "I'll wait for Mr. Nolan. I didn't tell him. I just said he was needed at home. I'll speak to him when he arrives."

Concerned for Mrs. Nolan, Jenna took a glass from the shelf, filled it with water, and headed for the stairs. She found

Mrs. Nolan sitting on an unmade bed, staring into space, a high school letterman jacket clutched in her arms. "Have a drink of water."

"What happened to my boy?" Mrs. Nolan ignored the water, folded the jacket with care, and placed it on the bed before raising her ashen face to Jenna. "Don't sugarcoat it. Tell me the truth. Where did you find him?"

Clearing her throat, Jenna sat beside her and pushed the glass into her hands. The woman needed information but not the gory details of her son's last moments. "In an alleyway, not far from here. Someone stabbed him."

"Where is he? I want to see him." Mrs. Nolan trembled but hadn't shed a tear.

Mrs. Nolan's cold, matter-of-fact tone concerned Jenna. Was the woman going into shock? Then when she caught a flash of malice in the woman's eyes, she quickly reassessed the situation. Not in shock, she was angry. "Miles is with the medical examiner and you'll be able to see him shortly. I'll be happy to give you a ride to his office, but I think we should wait until your husband arrives."

A truck pulled onto the driveway and Jenna got to her feet, but not in time to stop Mrs. Nolan from leaping to her feet and dashing out of the door. Following close behind, Jenna watched in dismay as the woman pushed past Kane and flew at a man walking up the driveway.

"It's your fault." Mrs. Nolan ripped her nails down her husband's cheek. "You know how important that party was to him last night. If you hadn't taken his keys and grounded him, this would never have happened. You killed our boy for not putting out the trash. I'll never forgive you, not ever."

Mr. Nolan stared at Jenna, eyes wild. He grasped his wife's arms and held her away from him. "What does she mean? Has something happened to Miles?"

"We'll talk to you inside." Kane took a firm grip of Mrs.

Nolan's arm and led her back to the kitchen. He lowered her into a chair and waved her husband into one opposite. "We found the body of your son in an alleyway close by. He'd been stabbed. I'm so sorry for your loss. Is there anyone I can call? A minister, family members?"

"My youngest is at a friend's house." Mrs. Nolan sipped the water. "He's just twelve years old. I can't tell him over the phone."

"Give me the number. I'll call the family to explain and ask them to give him a ride home." Kane took out his notebook and pen. "The news is best coming from you."

"Stabbed?" Mr. Nolan looked at Kane and scrubbed both hands down his face. "When did this happen?"

Jenna handed him a glass of water and sat beside Mrs. Nolan. "We don't have the time of death. We came straight from the scene. The medical examiner will make a determination after the autopsy."

"Did your son have any enemies or anyone who had a reason to harm him?" Kane leaned against the counter.

"No, everyone loved him." Mr. Nolan shook his head slowly. "He even mowed old Mrs. Jones' grass and never asked for a cent. He was always happy and generous."

"So, what happened between the two of you recently?" Kane cleared his throat. "Why did you need to ground him?"

"He wasn't doing his chores, is all." Mr. Nolan shrugged. "You need to keep a firm grip on teenagers. First, it's not taking out the garbage, and then it's a downward slide. I was constantly reminding him that he needed good grades for college. It's not all about football." He gave Kane a long look. "I know some parents allow their kids to go out and stay out without any regard to what they're doing. We have rules in our house to keep our boys on the straight and narrow. He wanted to go to a party with his girlfriend to make up after they'd had a fight, and I grounded him. It wasn't like him to disobey me and climb out of the window. I know where he was going. He was heading to a party at the high school. I imagine he would have taken the alleyways as a shortcut. He was complaining to me that the party started at ten and he'd have Betty-Jo home by eleven-thirty. His girlfriend is the captain of the cheerleading team. He was concerned that she would hook up with one of his friends." He let out a long sigh. "I tried to explain that if she couldn't be trusted with his friends, she could never be trusted. He was the quarterback and had girls falling all over him, yet he wanted the captain of the cheerleaders. Betty-Jo was a status symbol, I guess."

Jenna listened with sympathy, glad the couple had calmed down at last. "Did he take his phone? We didn't find anything other than his wallet."

"No." Mr. Nolan stared at his hands. "I confiscated his phone and his laptop. He had no way of communicating with her at all. It was only for a few days and it's the only type of punishment that works. I don't believe in beating my children."

Saddened, Jenna took her phone out of her pocket. "You shouldn't blame yourself. You were only doing what you considered to be best for him." She looked at Mrs. Nolan. "I can arrange for you to see Miles at one this afternoon to identify his body. Would you like me to call Father Derry or your minister to accompany you?"

"Yes, and please call Father Derry." Mrs. Nolan got unsteadily to her feet and cleared the table. "I need to keep busy." She looked at her husband. "Don't just sit their staring into space. Call Miles' friends and see if anyone saw him last night. I'll make a fresh pot of coffee."

Jenna stood. "We'll go outside to make the calls." She followed Kane out of the open front door and turned to him. "She is like a drill sergeant. Have you noticed she hasn't shed a tear?"

"You wouldn't fall to bits and lie around wailing either."

Kane thumbed a number into his phone. "She'll wait until she's alone. Some people never shed a tear. I'm not sure that it's healthy but everyone deals with tragedy in their own way."

As Kane walked down the pathway with his phone pressed to his ear, Jenna made the calls. Wolfe would have Miles ready for viewing at one and Father Derry was on his way. She would wait until his arrival before returning to the office. After slipping her phone inside her pocket, she waited for Kane to disconnect. "Mr. Nolan is calling Miles' friends. I'll ask him to email me a list. We know that Alicia Palmer was known to all our suspects. The first three victims attended the same high school as Miles. I would be interested to see if he knew Bill Ripley as well."

"If Ripley knew all of the victims and everyone on the crossbow teams, it's a link we can't ignore." Kane stared blankly at the open front door. "That's just too much of a coincidence. If we discover he's one of Jimmy Two Cents' pen pals, we have a slam dunk."

Nodding, Jenna stared at him. "It seems to me that Bill Ripley has just moved to the top of our suspects list."

THIRTY

Excitement shivered through Jimmy Two Cents as he pressed the phone to his ear. His mouth watered at the exquisite detail delivered by his protégé. He could almost taste the victim's fear and smell the steam rising from his entrails. Hand trembling on the receiver, he glanced left and right. He'd earned extra time for his phone calls and to his delight the guard had walked way down the end of the corridor. Of course, anyone listening in would hear exactly what he wanted them to believe. The conversation always centered around hunting and in these parts what they were discussing was a normal topic of conversation. Along the way, he offered his usual amount of encouragement, too much and he would lose the dependence his protégé needed, too little and the man at the end of the line would refuse to do his bidding. He needed the contact. His memories often faded, and without his trophies, he had nothing to trigger the delightful details of his kills. Craving more information, he picked his words with care. "It was brave of you to stun the young buck. Getting that close, he might have injured you."

"It went down, so I gutted it." The voice on the end of the line quivered slightly. "It just looked at me, like it couldn't believe what had happened. It was on its back and its legs were running in the air. I watched for a time and then stabbed it in the heart. It would have been easier using my crossbow."

Savoring every word, Jimmy Two Cents checked the time. He didn't have much longer to set the next task. Each step forward, he increased the level of difficulty. He'd thought long and hard on how he should proceed. He did not intend to lose his protégé but being able to manipulate him and see everything through his eyes was too tempting. The next kill would be dangerous but the rewards greater. Trying to hide his excitement, he cleared his throat. "I hear the pigs have been increasing in town of late. Now they're dangerous, so your crossbow would be the best choice. You could strike at a distance or lure them into a trap. I'm sure you'll think of something interesting. Call me when you're done and tell me all about it. I've really enjoyed our conversation today. It takes me back to old times. When I talk to you it's just like being there. I sure miss hunting in the forest."

He waited for his protégé to disconnect and then leaned against the cold brick wall gathering himself. His hands still shook and he pushed them into his pockets. The images he'd been given would feed his memories for years to come. When the prison guard came over to escort him back to his cell, he smiled at him as if he were an old friend. "It's sure good to talk about hunting. I can almost feel the mountain air brushing against my cheeks."

"If you'd stuck to hunting, you wouldn't be here." The guard didn't put the shackles on him but walked beside him with them dangling in one hand, jingling as they walked. "The warden wants to speak to you." He held up the restraints. "He figures you're trustworthy enough not to jump across the table and attack him." He gave him a sideways look. "Seems some hotshot behavioral analyst is writing a book and wants to interview you. I told him you wouldn't spill your guts to anyone, but apparently this young woman has a way of extracting information." He burst out laughing.

Grinning, Jimmy Two Cents straightened. "Most guys in here would spill their guts just for the scent of her. She sounds like an intriguing challenge." *And maybe someone my protégé can kill.*

THIRTY-ONE

Emotionally drained, Jenna carried the takeout they'd collected from Aunt Betty's Café and dumped it on the table in the conference room. From the information added to the whiteboard, her team had been busy. She went to the counter and poured two cups of coffee and added the fixings. After placing the cups on the table, she looked around at the group of people, all of them engrossed in what they were doing. She sipped her scalding coffee and sat back in her chair with a sigh.

"That bad, huh?" Carter removed the toothpick from the corner of his mouth and peered into the sacks containing the takeout. He pulled out a ham on rye and removed the plastic wrap. "Jo has some news for you."

"Yeah." Jo dragged her eyes away from the screen and looked at Jenna. "We can visit Jimmy Two Cents tomorrow morning at eight-thirty. The warden doesn't honestly believe that we'll get any information out of him but said he's easily bribed. He has a long visitors waiting list and wants more time on the phone speaking to his pen pals. All of his calls have been monitored and none of them have given up any type of information whatsoever. He never speaks about the murders and makes no reference whatsoever to any of the victims."

"You know as well as I do, Jo, most psychopathic serial killers love to relive their kills." Kane waved his egg salad sandwich toward the whiteboard. "I figure he's speaking in code. The next time he receives a phone call, maybe you need to get a copy. You need to remember he has access to other prisoners, who for a favor would ask their visitors to pass on messages. In prison information is currency, traded for favors, protection, and benefits."

"I'll keep that in mind when we speak to him." Jo helped herself to a donut. "Carter will be taking us in the chopper, so we can be back here for Miles Nolan's autopsy at two."

Exhausted, Jenna nodded. "That's great, thank you. I had a thought when we were over at the Nolans'. Do all the victims know each other? Think about it. It's likely they all met the local dentist's assistant, but the three in the forest and Nolan all attended the same high school." Jenna sipped her coffee. "Our suspects know each other, but they have two solid links to the victims. Alicia Palmer could have overheard conversations between the dentist and the victims about going fishing."

"But not Miles Nolan. She'd been murdered before him." Kane shrugged. "Why would the killer murder her if she was a good source of information?"

"I can think of a ton of reasons." Carter shrugged. "Maybe she wasn't trustworthy."

Blowing out a breath, Jenna looked from one to the other. "The second one everyone would know for sure is Bill Ripley. He is some kind of genius and was in the same year as the victims in high school until he jumped a year and went straight to college." She looked at the faces around the table. "He plays violent video games, hunts with a crossbow, and knows everyone. I figure he's our man."

"From what you said in your notes"—Jo scrolled through the

files on her screen—"he's a loner and introverted. Someone led a group of three people into the forest to hunt humans. He doesn't fit the profile."

Shaking her head, Jenna shrugged. "We'll see." She glanced at her watch. "Heads up on the time. The autopsy is at two."

Thirty minutes later, they filed into examination room two for Alicia Palmer's autopsy. To Jenna's surprise, Norrell was waiting inside for them. "Hi there." Jenna nodded to her. "Are you conducting the autopsy today?"

"No, I just dropped by to speak to you. Shane will be right in." Norrell's blue eyes twinkled above her mask. "I just wanted to tell you not to expect too much information about the graves in the forest just yet. Excavating graves of this type can be a very complicated process. It's not something I intend to rush. If for instance they're ancient Native American burial sites, we have to take into account the customs of the local tribes. We can't just go hell for leather and disturb them. If I uncover artifacts of any kind, the dig must be postponed until they can be identified. The list of gravesites Atohi Blackhawk has given me could take as long as six years to complete. I figured you would appreciate why I won't be sending you weekly reports. If, however, I do find anything of interest, you'll be the first to know. These people all have the right to have their stories told, just the same as any murder victim of today."

Sobering, Jenna nodded. "I wouldn't expect any of less of you, Norrell." She smiled behind her mask. "How are you settling in?"

"Like one of Shane's family." Norrell's eyes danced with amusement. "I've never been so contented." She looked at Kane. "Thanks for introducing us. How did you know we'd get along so well."

"Just a hunch." Kane shrugged. "You both like playing with dead things."

The door whooshed open and Wolfe walked in. "Who likes

playing with dead things? Has Emily been visiting the body farm again?"

Jenna laughed, which seemed so inappropriate at the start of an autopsy. "No, Kane was saying what you and Norrell have in common."

"It seems to run in the family." Emily followed close behind him. "And no, Dad, the body farm was last week. Do you think we're creepy, Jenna?"

"Time is getting away from us." Wolfe's tone stopped the conversation in its tracks when his cold gaze moved over everyone. He hated discussing his private life and his budding relationship with Norrell was a no-go zone. "Alicia Palmer is waiting for us to find answers. Let's get at it." He went to the gurney and pulled down the sheet.

Jenna stepped forward. "The on-scene examination was very detailed. What more can you tell us?"

"As you're all so busy, I went ahead and completed an initial examination. If you want to stay for the full autopsy, that's fine by me, but I'll only be validating what I already know and Colt will be here as your representative."

Nodding, Jenna met his gaze. "Okay, that works for me. With all the murders, we are snowed under."

"There are some key points." Wolfe turned away from the gurney. "I've examined the incisions of both victims microscopically and measured the depth of each one." He lit up the screens behind him to display a hunting knife. "This is the type of hunting knife used in the murder. I cross-referenced these incisions with the ones inflicted on Miles Nolan and they match. I have no doubt the killer used the same knife in both murders."

"The depth would indicate the strength of the killer, and type of attack." Carter moved closer to examine the wounds. "These look even and deep."

"They are." Wolfe indicated to the screen again. "I usually

use a pig carcass for experiments with knives and to determine the force used to inflict incisions. We have three different types of people here, and all of us stabbed the carcass with force, as we would during an attack. The depth of the blade would indicate someone with the same body mass as Colt and without the experience of hand-to-hand combat is the perpetrator. The knife didn't enter the flesh up to the hilt, but deeper than the blows inflicted by Emily. For her, I recognized a drag on the edge of the incision, which would indicate her difficulty in removing the knife before striking again. This wasn't evident in the incisions on either victim."

Jenna shrugged. "So really, you're eliminating the fact it might be a woman or a younger man without the upper-body strength of Webber?" She turned to Kane. "That would blow my theory to shreds. I figured that the killer is Bill Ripley. Emily could take him down with one hand tied behind her back."

"I wouldn't discount him just yet." Kane moved to her side. "Rage or anger play a very important part in strength during combat. From what I'm seeing here, my first instinct would say it's a frenzied attack, but as Wolf will tell you, usually the incisions are deep at first and then as the killer tires, they become shallow. Here the depths of the incisions are the same. I've seen torture victims with similar cuts. As I'm sure Wolfe will agree, it is almost as if he avoided hitting any vital organs."

"Yeah, I agree." Carter adjusted his face mask. "It was the same in the alleyway with Miles Nolan. He was slit open just enough to make him suffer, when a close-up attack like that should have been fatal."

Considering what had been said, Jenna turned to Wolfe. "How long would it have taken her to die?"

"She had many superficial wounds, so he could have kept her alive until she bled out, but he didn't choose to, did he?" Wolfe indicated to the neck wound on Alicia Palmer's throat. "The incision on her neck is consistent with sharp force trauma directly to the carotid artery. I figure he had hold of her hair, pulled her head back, stabbed, and then cut. The stab wound would have killed her in a rush of blood."

"You've obviously examined Miles Nolan." Kane looked at Wolfe. "Do you have any conclusions? It would save us time attending another autopsy."

"I have theories but no conclusions as yet." Wolfe straightened and gave Kane a direct stare. "From the injuries, he died from sharp force trauma to the heart. I've completed an MRI on both victims. Miles Nolan's heart was dissected. He died instantly from the final blow. From the blood loss, he lay in the alleyway for maybe as long as five minutes before the death blow. It would have been an agonizing death." He gave Kane a short nod. "You need to catch this guy."

"We will." Kane frowned. "The coins?"

"No trace evidence. He's very careful." Wolfe shook his head slowly. "Washed in bleach before use, inserted post mortem. I guess that's a blessing."

"That's the same MO as Jimmy Two Cents." Jo shook her head. "Nobody knows that information. How is this happening? Did he have an accomplice we don't know about?"

"I spent most of last night reading the casefiles." Carter folded his arms across his chest and blew out a long breath. "He worked alone. Trust me, from his profile, he wasn't sharing his kills with anyone."

It was an impossible mystery, like the chicken or the egg. How could anyone know? Jenna facepalmed her head and winced. "I've just had a thought. We know about the case, right? Who else, the lawyers involved? The cops all along the way. It only takes one of them to let it slip to a friend and then it spreads like a virus. She pulled out her phone. "I'll ask Google."

Jenna waited for the results to come up for James Earl Stafford and got the sanitized version, but when she used the name Jimmy Two Cents, there it was, how James Earl Stafford had gotten his name. She passed the phone to Kane and shook her head. "Some secret. It's all over the internet." She looked at Carter. "Now what?"

"Oh, my goodness." Jo barked a laugh. "How would Jimmy Two Cents deflect suspicion away from his involvement in these murders? He'd get someone to leak information. What if he's been grooming some of his followers to kill for him and then report back?"

Jenna nodded. "That makes sense. It's just as well we're going to see him in the morning. Maybe you can pry some information from him?"

"I'll be sure to wear perfume. It always makes them pliable, plus I have a few prearranged inducements for him." Jo smiled. "He knows something and I mean to find out what it is."

THIRTY-TWO

THURSDAY

After breakfast, Jenna climbed into the Beast, and with Jo and Carter following close behind in the cruiser, they headed for the medical examiner's office. Carter had parked the FBI chopper on the helipad on top of the building. Excitement thrummed through her, mixed with a little nervous tension at the thought of meeting Jimmy Two Cents. During a long discussion the previous evening with Jo, they had all decided after considering the prisoner's profile that Jenna would be the best person to go into the interview room with Jo. James Earl Stafford, aka Jimmy Two Cents, clammed up when speaking to male cops and Jo believed it would be unproductive for them to be in the room at the same time. Kane had been very quiet on the journey into town and Jenna turned to him. "Are you concerned about me going into the interview?"

"Nah." Kane shot her a white smile. "I'll be right outside the door and although Jo believes that an unshackled prisoner is safe, the prison warden thinks otherwise, and one of his conditions was that Jimmy Two Cents remained shackled." He shrugged. "Trust me he's not going anywhere."

Slightly confused, Jenna frowned. "So what's been on your mind? Something is troubling you I can tell."

"Rowley and Rio." Kane glanced her way and then returned his attention to the road. "They've been working seven days straight and long hours. Considering we have Jo and Carter to take some of the caseload, we need to give them at least one day off duty this weekend. We don't know when we'll need them for backup and mistakes happen when people are exhausted."

Nodding, Jenna could see his point. "Yeah, they haven't been trained in endurance like the rest of us. Rowley has the twins at home, which means he doesn't get to rest when he actually gets there. Talking about twins, I'd say Rio's life isn't much easier, with teenagers to watch over. I guess raising his siblings, he doesn't get much life at all." She tapped her bottom lip thinking. "I wonder if Emily has ever considered what would happen if she married Rio?"

"How so?" Kane frowned. "Ah you mean, would she become a mother figure to kids not much younger than herself? I doubt it. Cade has settled down over the last twelve months and Piper is very sensible. I don't figure they need a mother figure and they'll probably be leaving home before Emily is ready for marriage. She won't compromise her career just yet." He barked a laugh. "You worry over the silliest things. Whatever happens, it's none of our business."

Sighing, Jenna stared out the window at the mist swirling like dancers with long white dresses across the glossy blacktop. "I guess it's the mother instinct in me to worry about Emily. We are close, as you know." She watched a falcon fly high in the air from a cluster of trees and then disappear in a dive, marveling at the way it hunted so efficiently.

"Had any thoughts about giving the guys some time off?" Kane turned onto Main and the smell of freshly baked apple pie wafted through his open window.

Almost tasting the crumbly delight, Jenna inhaled and looked at Kane. "Yeah, we'll manage and if we can't, we'll call them back in. Right now, we're just chasing our tails. We've interviewed the suspects and all we need to do is chase down if there's a link between them and the victims. We can do that ourselves and we always have Bobby Kalo to lend a hand. I'm just hoping that we can get some information out of Jimmy Two Cents."

Jenna thought for a beat and then pulled out her phone. She called Rowley. "Hi, Jake, we've reached a stalemate in this investigation, so we're heading for the state pen to interview Jimmy Two Cents. I'll need you and Rio to handle the office today."

"Not a problem." Rowley was as laidback as usual. "I'm here with Maggie. Rio is just parking his truck."

Flicking a glance at Kane, Jenna smiled. Her deputies always arrived at the office early, both of them could handle any callouts or problems during her absence. "Thanks, I figure we might as well take advantage of the lull in the case, so I'm rostering you off on Friday and Rio on Saturday."

"Are you sure you won't need us?" Rowley sounded concerned.

Jenna chuckled. "Trust me, I'll call you in if we need you. Take tomorrow and get some rest."

"I might go fishing. The twins will be in playgroup and Sandy is going out to lunch with her mom." Rowley chuckled. "It will be nice to have some quiet time."

As Jenna disconnected, Kane swung the Beast into the parking lot behind the ME's office. Within ten minutes, she boarded the chopper, and they were winging their way toward the state pen. On the way, she studied the notes Jo had given her about the interview. What to expect and how to react along with some questions. Her mind was buzzing with information by the time they landed on the helipad on top of the prison. They'd left the dogs enjoying playtime on the ranch. It had taken Zorro a time to relax without Carter, but he'd found a good friend in Duke, and seeing him run wide ecstatic circles around Duke and acting like a dog for a change, warmed Jenna's heart.

"Stay close." Kane looked from her to Jo. "I'll be one side and Carter the other. You know they'll spit and catcall. Don't react."

Jenna nodded and pulled earplugs from her pocket and pushed them into her ears. It was a trick Jo had taught her to block out most of the inmate noises. The walkway inside to D block went through the exercise yards and although they couldn't be touched, somehow the inmates knew they were all law enforcement and made it perfectly clear what they intended to do with them. It was an unnerving experience to be surrounded by so much hate. The guard who met them and escorted them to the warden's office had found the ordeal through the walkway amusing and smiled at the inmates as he paraded them in front of them. It was a relief to reach the warden's office.

"It's nice to see you again, Agent Wells." The warden stood behind his desk, cheeks flushed and with an inquiring expression. "Ah, I see you have the entire team with you today. Sheriff Alton, Agent Carter, and Deputy Kane, welcome to my humble abode." He grinned. "The rules have changed slightly since the last time you were here. James Earl Stafford has been an exemplary prisoner and has gained the status of inmate trustee, but during the talks with the prison psychologist we've uncovered his deep desire to murder women, so he will be shackled during the interview, as I explained previously."

"I'll be interviewing him with Sheriff Alton, and Agent Carter and Deputy Kane will be watching through the two-way mirror as before." Jo lifted her chin. "I'd prefer if the guard remains outside the door. It's impossible to get a psychopath to talk with a prison guard overhearing every word they say. They have to believe what they say to me is confidential, even though they know it is going to be included in a book. I guess they figure that none of the prisoners here will get to read it."

"That won't be a problem." The warden waved them to the door. "The guard will take you down. Stafford is being taken to the interview room as we speak."

"Are you ready?" Jo looked at Jenna.

Drawing in a deep breath, Jenna nodded. "Yeah."

THIRTY-THREE

In the small space outside the interview room, they all peered through the two-way mirror at Jimmy Two Cents. The fact that he looked so absolutely normal surprised Jenna. Even though she understood that most psychopaths blended into society without a ripple, she somehow thought that a man who had killed so many would show some signs of madness. Although in his prison orange, the man appeared relaxed without a care in the world. He could be your local shopkeeper, the doctor, or even a teacher. Someone you wouldn't hesitate to trust because he looked so darn normal. She leaned into Kane and when his strong arm came round her and squeezed, the world seemed to drop into focus. He would never allow anything to happen to her and she drew strength from that. Taking a deep breath of the musty air, she turned to Jo. "Let's get at it."

Inside the interview room, the smell of stale sweat seemed to creep across the air toward them like an entity. Beads of sweat formed on James Earl Stafford's forehead and his eyes betrayed his excitement. When he inhaled deeply and his lips curled up at the edges, Jenna's stomach rolled in revulsion. Jo was wearing a dab of perfume, and from the way Stafford's nose flared, he was savoring it. Avoiding eye contact, she placed her iPad on the table and sat down. She'd been very careful with her dress this morning. She'd chosen jeans and a long sweater that came down to her thighs. Jo on the other hand was wearing a black suit with a knee-length straight skirt and heels. It was obvious she was using Stafford's lack of female company to encourage him to cooperate. She understood that Jo had requested that, the warden intimated, if the interview went well, she would be returning on a regular basis. This was true to some extent, as Jo liked to leave the door open for further visits if the information received from the psychopath was valuable.

The silence in the room was almost deafening, with only the heavy breathing of Jimmy Two Cents. Perhaps the fear of sitting before a mass murderer was getting to Jenna. She had the very strange notion that he couldn't possibly kill them because she didn't have any pennies with her.

"Mr. Stafford." Jo introduced them and started the voice recorder she'd placed on the table. "You do understand that any interesting information you give me on your crimes may be included in my latest book?"

"Yeah." Stafford grinned at her. "Do I get a copy?"

"That will depend on just how juicy the information is you give me." Jo leaned back in her chair and crossed her legs, gaining his immediate attention. "The fact you placed coins under the eyelids of your victims has never been in the public domain until recently. Have you ever discussed this fact with anyone?"

"Maybe." Stafford shrugged. "Time and conversations all roll into oblivion inside these four walls."

"Can you tell me what significance the coins are to you?" Jo looked down as if examining her notes, but Jenna had seen this ploy before. Her seeming disinterest in him was having an effect.

"Don't you know about the ferryman?" Stafford leaned back

in his chair and grinned. "When you die, you need money to pay him to get to the other side."

"I find it hard to believe you had any feelings for these people, let alone worried about if they passed through the pearly gates or not." Jo uncrossed her legs and, after lifting her briefcase onto the table, took out a folder and spread crime scene photographs over the desk. "These injuries don't look like they were inflicted by someone who cared."

"Oh, I wasn't doing it for them." Stafford's shackles jingled as he moved his hands. "I was doing it for me. No one is going to put coins on my eyes when I die, so I was building up a credit." His fingers stretched out to touch one of the photographs. "I enjoyed this one. Are you going to include the pictures in your book?"

"Maybe." Jo crossed her legs again. "The warden mentioned that you have many pen pals. Do you discuss the murders with them?"

"I'm not allowed to discuss the murders with anyone outside the prison." Stafford towered his fingers and stared at her with an unsettling directness. "I can't take a dump in here without them knowing. Being able to speak freely with you, without anyone listening in, is like a vacation in Miami for me." He scanned the photographs again and then lifted his gaze to Jenna. "This one isn't mine." The chains clanked as he tapped the table in front of an image. "Nice work. The pennies are there, but pennies don't make them my kills." He snorted. "That's why you're here isn't it? I have a copycat and they know things they shouldn't about my MO."

The image was of Alicia Palmer, and Jenna watched his face closely when Jo pushed it toward him. To her surprise, he ran his fingers over the young woman's face. His expression had changed, hardened, and his eyes had become hawklike. Before her eyes, he'd changed from the guy next door to a predator. It was a startling transformation and one Jo had mentioned in her books.

"Do you recognize her?" Jo had picked up on the change in him too. She took more photographs out of her briefcase and then spread them over the top of the others. "Her name was Alicia Palmer and she was a dental hygienist from Black Rock Falls. It was a frenzied attack as if someone lost control. Have you ever lost control?"

"No." Stafford stared at her with dead eyes. "I probably would with you, but then there's always a first time." He wet his lips as if enjoying the thought of killing her and then stared at the image again "Yeah, I know her, but you already know that or you wouldn't ask me. She was one of my pen pals and visited me a few times." He rolled his shoulders. "They told me you were a doctor, some fine analyst writing a book, and you're really a stinking pig."

"I *am* a behavioral analyst writing a book." Jo reached into her briefcase and pulled out her latest release. "See for yourself, my picture is on the back." She slid it toward him. "Many men just like you are immortalized in my books."

"Okay." Stafford flicked through the pages and then slid it back to her. "Ask the questions. I'm getting bored."

"You have many pen pals. Are they both male and female? Do men visit you as well?" Jo leaned back in her chair, with her attention fixed on him. "What do you talk about if not your crimes. What's the interest?"

"The women are like buckle bunnies." Stafford snorted and his chains clanged. "They write about sex and relationships. They want to be my girlfriend. Even though I killed my wife, they still want to share my bed." He laughed. "Go figure."

"And the men?" Jo looked at her notes and then at Jenna.

"Hunting." Stafford shrugged. "They want details of my kills, but that's not allowed, so we talk about the times they went hunting."

His statement slammed into Jenna's head. Suddenly everything made perfect sense. She scanned the files on her iPad, rereading the information in Stafford's file. Convinced she'd finally made a breakthrough in the case, she turned to Jo. "I need to step outside for a minute." She looked at Stafford and gave him an apologetic smile. "Are you good with that?"

"Don't leave me sitting here too long or I'll call the guards and go back to my cell." Stafford glared at them. "I'm doing you a favor answering your stupid questions. Don't forget that."

"And I'll show my appreciation by making sure you're given extra privileges." Jo stood and pushed the photographs toward him. "I'll leave the pictures for you to look at. Maybe you can let me know if any of the others don't belong to you?" She stood and gave Jenna a long stare but followed her from the room.

"Is there a problem?" Kane stared at her with one eyebrow raised.

Bubbling with excitement but keeping her voice to just above a whisper in case Jimmy Two Cents overheard her, she moved closer to her team. "Did you hear what he just said? He discusses hunting trips with his pen pals and visitors." She looked from one to the other, waiting for a reaction and received blank stares. "He receives phone calls at least one a week, and from the notes Jo received from the warden, all his conversations are about hunting, and yet I don't recall any mention of hunting game in the information we received about his life prior to imprisonment. So I checked it again. He liked to go fishing. He went to the firing range and was a member of the crossbow club. When they searched his house after the murders, the only trophies they found were from his victims." She stared at them, waiting for the penny to drop. "He is using his conversations about hunting to instruct his followers to murder for him."

"That makes perfect sense, but he's never mentioned anything in any conversations about the coins." Kane rubbed the back of his neck. "They were on a list of flagged words, and I doubt very much they would have slipped through the net."

"Part of being an inmate trustee is he has access to the library." Carter moved a toothpick across his lips and smiled. "In fact, he enjoys working in the library and collects books for the other inmates and distributes them. He is not allowed to converse with them, but they fill in a form that they hand to him for any book they require. It would be too easy to use the distribution of books as a mail service."

Stafford's communication system was falling into place. Excited, Jenna nodded. "Yeah, many prisoners have conjugal visits, and social visits in an open room where what they say isn't recorded. It would be easy enough to get a note to the right person, and they in turn would pass the information to their visitor. The visitor would then contact the person involved and give them the message."

"Stafford already has a ton of privileges, which I gather includes deliveries of food and candy from the outside. He would have the resources to use as bribes." Jo shook her head slowly. "There are no rules to say a prisoner can't give another prisoner candy, for instance. It would be checked when it arrived, so it's not like contraband."

"He'd probably distribute it along with the books." Carter leaned against the desk. "He has the perfect setup."

"There is another angle we should be looking at." Kane frowned. "How does he choose his victims? What if he is taking out witnesses or people who may have snitched on one of the other inmates. His mail system could control a ton of things inside and outside the prison."

"We need to get back to it." Jo moved toward the door. "I'll try some different questions and see if I can pull anything out of him. He will be expecting me to ask him certain questions, so I'll move with care."

Schooling her excited expression, Jenna followed Jo inside

and took her seat. She looked across the table at Stafford. He appeared to be sleeping but his eyes opened slowly and anger flashed. Jenna's fight-or-flight response happened so fast her adrenaline peaked. She wanted to be anywhere but inside a confined space with a serial killer. Jo had retained her composure and sat down without taking her gaze off Stafford.

"We won't be keeping you too much longer, Mr. Stafford." Jo leaned forward to peer at the photographs. "Did you find any that don't belong to you?"

"I can't rightly say." Stafford clasped his hands on the table and shrugged. "Looking at images of crime scenes is like looking at a garbage dump. Once you mix it up in a pile, it's hard to tell who it belongs to."

Jenna looked up from her iPad. "I hear you have a regular delivery of candy bars delivered to the prison, among other things. Do you keep them for yourself or do you share them?"

"You don't know too much about the goings on in a prison, do you, honey?" Stafford grinned at her. "Candy, cigarettes, cookies, and cakes are currency. Moving them around for favors never hurts anyone."

"Have you ever discussed with your psychologist why you murdered people?" Jo crossed her legs slowly and looked at him.

"I've never needed a reason, but if you mean 'how did it make me feel?'—Stafford snorted with amusement—"it's a stupid question, but they all ask it. It felt good. No, it felt spectacular. I never wanted to stop." He stared at her and then slowly moved his attention back to Jenna. "In fact, I'll never stop. It's only a matter of time. You figure being in prison will stop me? It would be like shooting fish in a barrel."

"How did you decide who to kill?" Jo lifted her chin. "Did they remind you of someone in your past?"

"You mean, did I need a reason to kill them, like my daddy abused me or some girl embarrassed me at school?" He chuckled. "There are plenty of those twisted freaks in here."

Needing to know, Jenna leaned on the desk. "So why?" She gave him a direct stare. "Why did you kill your wife?"

"She disrespected me." Stafford shrugged. "I'll ask you a question now." He slid the chain through the loop on the desk so he could scratch his cheek. "Have you ever had some young punk driving a tricked-out truck overtake you and almost run you into the gutter? Or maybe make you spill your beer? Or the woman at the bank who looks at you like you're trash when you go to the counter?"

Jenna shook her head. "No, not often. So do you mean people who disrespect you become victims?"

"There you go." Stafford nodded slowly. "See, it was their fault. If they hadn't dissed me, they'd be alive today."

"That doesn't sound like a valid reason to murder someone." Jo stared down her nose at him. "Those people had families and didn't deserve to die."

"In your opinion." Stafford's eyes blazed with controlled rage. "Not mine."

"If you were released tomorrow, what's the first thing you'd do?" Jo's expression hadn't changed since she sat down. "No, let me rephrase that. What are the first three things you'd do?"

"Three is generous." Jimmy Two Cents snorted with amusement. "First, I'd buy me a hunting knife, and the second, I'd kill you." He swung his gaze to Jenna and his lips curled into a satanic grin. "Sorry, honey, you'd come in third, but it would be worth the wait."

THIRTY-FOUR

They arrived back in town a little after one and Kane drove straight to Aunt Betty's Café. They had things to discuss, and Jenna and Jo needed time to unwind. They hadn't been able to talk in the chopper. The noise was restrictive to any real discussion, although questions burned in his mind. After they'd placed their orders and taken their usual table at the back of the diner, Kane looked at the others. All appeared to be deep in thought. Jenna had cracked the case and placed Jimmy Two Cents slap bang in the middle of the murders. He'd been an accessory and Kane had obtained a list of people who'd visited and called the prison to speak to Stafford. The pen pals were endless and it would take the prison some time to make a list. He ran his finger down the visitors' list, hoping to match any of them to the suspects. Unfortunately, he found none of them on the list apart from Alicia Palmer. "He was telling the truth. Alicia Palmer is on the list of visitors. She is listed as a girlfriend."

"Well, we can't interview her, can we? Anyone else of interest?" Jenna leaned toward him to peer at his screen.

"Hmm." Kane frowned. "I've read everything about Jimmy

Two Cents. I know he murdered his wife, but I didn't know he had a son. From these records he's visited him."

"Yeah, he is on my list from Kalo. James Earl Stafford Jr." Carter lifted his gaze from his phone. "No one of interest. He was just a kid when his father went to jail. Strange he visited his father. Most kids would have hated him for murdering their mom and disassociated themselves from him."

"You don't know the circumstances." Jenna shrugged. "Maybe he wanted to know what really happened. There could be a ton of reasons why he wanted to speak with him. I would if my father had done something like that. I'd want to know if he really did kill her and why."

"What happened to him when Stafford went to jail?" Jo sipped her coffee. "Is he a person of interest?"

"I don't think so." Carter scrolled down his page. "No priors. Not much info on him at all. His last known address is Big Sky. That's all I have. That's a ways to travel to visit him." He held up a finger. "Ah, this might be why. It says in Kalo's report that Stafford's mom died recently. Maybe he went to tell him?"

"Maybe." Jo ran her finger through a scattering of sugar on the table. "I've run a few profiles using other cases but this killer is so diverse it's difficult to produce a solid profile. I'd say, if he is leading others, he's charismatic, a strong alpha male, easily liked and trusted. I'd say maybe around thirty. He'd mix easily with a group or is happy alone."

"That kinda fits all our suspects apart from Bill Ripley. He's the complete opposite." Carter added cream to his cup and shrugged. "I'm finding it hard to believe he competes in competitions. He's introverted. Being a friend or in a group doesn't make him a serial killer, or even a thrill killer."

Not wanting to waste time, Kane checked the lists again, going down the most recent, and lifted his head. "Well, maybe he's playing a character. A psychopath can change on a dime if needs be. I have found a phone call to Stafford from someone called Bill made last week. He is another of Stafford's pen pals. What if this is Bill Ripley? Think over what we know about him. A loner, likes violent video games, and moves around unnoticed as he is just about the only person living on campus. He knows the victims, well at least four of them, and is a crossbow sharpshooter."

"Okay." Jenna washed her food down with coffee and nodded. "We zone in on him. Find out what he's been doing." She looked at Kane. "We could ask Kalo to cross-match our suspects with anyone serving time in the same prison as Stafford. Although that won't help us, as we can't prove Stafford sent a message to his followers through them. In fact, it could be any one of the prisoner's visitors passing on information. I was so excited we'd figured it out, but now we've hit another brick wall."

Kane shook his head. "Not necessarily. I'm convinced Bill Ripley is involved. There are too many coincidences. When we consider Jo's profile, he appears to be an unlikely suspect, but then we've proved over and over that no one serial killer fits a certain profile—they're all different. We'll lean on him some more. Maybe drag him down to the office and see if he cracks."

"Okay, we'll head out to the campus and question him again." Jenna turned the salt cellar around with her fingertips. "If he's the Bill who called Stafford, we'll have the missing link."

THIRTY-FIVE

Rowley headed into town on a hunch and drove to Alicia Palmer's house out at Fallen Rock Crescent. The local animal protection had collected her dog and discovered he wasn't angry at all, just protecting his owner's property. When he'd called to ask about the dog he was relieved to hear they'd easily find him a new home. Rowley had been sitting in the office all day chasing down leads and coming up empty. Was Alicia Palmer involved in the forest murders? She'd certainly been on the list of suspects prior to her death. This part of the investigation had been halted when Miles Nolan was discovered butchered in an alleyway.

He turned the key in the lock and peered through the open door of the small house. It smelled of wet dog and the acrid stench of dried pee. The hair on the back of his neck prickled as he stepped inside, as if Alicia were there watching him intrude on her privacy. He shook off the memory of seeing her mutilated body and, leaving the door open, searched the house. The family room was covered with trophies. It seemed she hunted everything and liked to brag about it. On every available surface she'd displayed gruesome photographs of her kills in silver frames. Disturbed by the unnecessary portrayal of carnage, he shook his head. The field-dressing of a kill was necessary, but taking selfies during the process defied logic. He hunted for the table, with any elk or deer going straight to the meat-processing plant. If he wanted sport, he fired his crossbow or guns at targets to beat a score. It seemed Alicia enjoyed the blood sport side of hunting—did she enjoying killing people as well?

The idea simmered in his mind, and although Alicia had died, he could feel her in the house. The slight smell of perfume in the bedroom, the half-filled coffee cup with TODAY WILL BE GREAT written on one side left beside the bed. The house was untidy, the dog had chewed up most of the furniture, and dishes piled up in the sink. The place would become a health hazard if they couldn't locate her next of kin and get someone to clean the place. Alicia had converted a bedroom especially for her cross-bows and she'd mounted them on the wall. He moved along them, recognizing them as her competition crossbows and quivers. A specially made chest of drawers held a variety of bolts, trackers, and fletching. A shelf held silver cups from her competition wins. The crossbows had been noted on the list from the last search, but that one had concentrated on her involvement in the forest murders, as in trophies or anything they could find to link her to the people under suspicion. Rowley had another angle and it would take someone skilled in crossbows to find the anomaly.

After checking each bow and quiver, he moved through the house, concentrating on closets large enough to hang a bow and quiver. Alicia was untidy and lived a life split in two. At work she'd be expected to maintain a sterile environment. At home, the opposite, like two sides to a coin. This information was key to his hunch. When he found a crossbow and a quiver of bolts hanging in a closet under the stairs, he wanted to punch the air. A hunting crossbow, well-worn with use, and a quiver filled with EVO-X Center Punch premium carbon arrows. Just as he hoped to find. Perhaps she made a habit of dumping her hunting gear in a closet without cleaning it. She didn't hunt for the table, so maybe didn't care if her bolts were caked with dry blood.

With care, he dropped the quiver into a large evidence bag and, using his flashlight, searched all around the closet. From what he could see, Alicia came home from hunting and left her boots, jacket, and crossbow in the same closet. He collected her boots and clothes, bagged them, and then left the house.

Rowley drove to Wolfe's office and went round back. He used his card across the scanner to gain entrance and headed for Wolfe's office. Finding the office empty, he made his way to the lab and found Wolfe with Emily bent over a microscope. He smiled at them. "We've all wondered if Alicia Palmer was involved with the forest murders. I've been thinking on it and figure I have a way of proving it." He held up the evidence bags. "Some hunters clean their bolts, others maybe wipe them. They all retrieve them. Well, everyone I know does. So I figured if she was involved, there'd be a good chance of the victim's DNA being on the bolts. Or one of them at least. I went to her house and got her quiver. These eight bolts would be what she last used. They're all EVO-X Center Punch premium carbon arrows. I grabbed her boots and jacket as well. I thought maybe there'd be some blood on them or something?"

"They should have been included in the evidence from the first search, but I guess they were looking for something to connect her to the other shooters. I'll process them and we'll see what evidence they carry. Hopefully, they won't be contaminated with animal blood." Wolfe smiled at him. "That's thinking outside the box. Jenna will be over the moon if we can link her to the murders."

Pleased, Rowley nodded. "Yeah, it was prompted by a message from Kane informing us that Alicia was a pen pal-type girlfriend to Jimmy Two Cents. It made me wonder if there was a link. I hope you find something."

"Leave it with me." Wolfe collected the evidence bags and took them to a bench. "I'll get at it. I'll call you the moment I get any news. Probably in the morning."

Grinning, Rowley held up his hands. "Call Jenna. Tomorrow I'm rostered off and I'm going hunting first thing in the morning. Sandy is going out and the twins are at playgroup, so we're all having a *me* day."

"Out hunting alone when there's a killer on the loose?" Emily frowned. "That's dangerous."

Rowley shook his head. "Nope, I'm going with another crossbow hunter. We chatted at the range early this morning. I went by to find out who buys EVO-X Center Punch premium carbon arrows. Seems a ton of us use them, so no joy there, and they don't keep records. I'll be fine. Catch you later." Satisfaction of a job well done filled him, as he gave them a wave and headed back to his truck.

THIRTY-SIX

A few clouds scattered lazily across a brilliant blue sky, and as the wind picked up, remnants of last year's fall blew golden leaves across Stanton on the ride to the college. The grounds, usually bursting with noise and people, appeared desolate as they drove through the main gates and onto the staff parking lot. The college spread out in all directions, the windows of its empty rooms black like rows of missing teeth in the smile of usually welcoming buildings. Only a few vehicles sat bunched together like sheep at one end, as if trying to avoid the dry sandy soil blowing across the blacktop. A shiver trickled down Jenna's back, and although she'd never admit it, interviewing Jimmy Two Cents had unsettled her. She slid out of the truck and checked her weapon. She caught Kane's concerned expression and her stomach flip-flopped. Kane rarely showed emotion. It was an inbuilt mechanism but since they'd married he sometimes dropped his guard for just a second. Could they be knocking on the door of a brutal murderer? What would Ripley do if cornered? She turned to Kane. "Ripley is an unknown quantity. We'll need to be on our guard for the unexpected."

"He's one man." Kane shrugged. "We're armed. He'd need a grenade or AK-47 to take us down." He grinned at her. "Why so worried?"

Serious, Jenna stared at him. "You look worried. You never look worried. Now I'm worried."

"Me? Concerned about a kid?" Kane stared up at the sky and then back to her. "You watched me take down five men without any problems."

Jenna frowned. "Yeah, but you're black and blue. If the vest hadn't taken the shot, you might be dead. I know how much that hurts, but you just wave it off like it doesn't matter."

"That's because it doesn't impede me." He shrugged. "Yeah, it hurt at the time, but I still fired my weapon with accuracy. I'm not losing my edge, Jenna. I'll retire if that happens. Like I said, he'd need to have an explosive device to take me down and I check for all possibilities before I walk into a situation." He sighed. "Truth is, I was thinking about Duke and the puppies you want to see. I'm concerned he might be jealous. It's difficult introducing a puppy into a house with an old dog. Duke is kinda territorial. Even with Zorro around, he tends to lean against my leg as if needing reassurance. I don't think he's forgotten his past owner."

Relieved, Jenna nodded. "I'd still like to go and see the pups. We don't have to take one."

"Exactly." Kane indicated with his chin toward the college. "We'll bypass the office. I don't want them to warn him we're on our way."

"If we decide to bring Ripley in for questioning, we'll need a cruiser. We should have asked Jo and Carter to follow us."

"Oh, dang, I forgot to tell you." Kane looked abashed. "The enhancements I worked on with Wolfe and Carter over winter included a Perspex screen." He leaned into the Beast and flicked a switch. "It slides up when we need it. I got the idea from a limo privacy screen, and we managed to get one made for the Beast." He shrugged. "I can't imagine how it slipped my mind. I guess I was focused on something else."

Shaking her head, Jenna stared at him. "You will tell me when you make it fly, right, or I'll figure we're sailing right out there to certain death."

"I'm sure you'd notice the rotor blades?" Kane closed the door and stared at her, his expression serious. "They're kinda big, sit on the roof, and spin around some." He twirled his fingers to demonstrate. "I considered it but I figured the blades might decapitate one of us if we forgot they were up there."

As usual, seeing her troubled, Kane had used his dark humor to lighten the mood. She wondered how many people would find his jokes as hilarious as she did. He managed to deliver them with a straight face and then stare at her dead serious. She chuckled. "So that's a no then?"

"Yeah. For now, anyway." He flicked his gaze to the back seat. "I sure miss not having Duke along, but he does love Zorro's company and they both deserve a day to themselves."

They headed through the building, their footsteps echoing, and empty dark rooms emphasized the fact that no one else was there. As they reached the courtyard and made their way through the cloisters, goosebumps rose on Jenna's arms. Why did Bill Ripley want to remain on campus during spring break? When she'd called the office earlier, the receptionist had informed her that only three students remained. The other two being roommates in a different section of the campus. Ripley obviously hadn't made any friends during his first semester, and although many camps had been running over spring break, he had decided to remain in his room. The campus didn't offer any catering and anyone remaining behind would literally have to fend for themselves for meals. It was safe, as the usual security team were on duty, as were the office staff.

They took the stairs and searched the corridors for the room number Carter had given them. Unlike the description of loud video games, Jo and Carter had mentioned from their visit that not a sound came from Bill Ripley's room. Jenna stood to one side of the door and Kane to the other. Heart beating as Kane checked the door surrounds for wires, she waited for him to give a clear signal and then rapped on the door. No movement or footsteps came from behind the door and after repeated loud knocking, she looked at Kane and shrugged. "It looks like he's out. Do we know what vehicle he drives?"

"Nope, but the parking lot is empty." Kane shrugged. "Maybe he went out for a meal?"

Disappointed, Jenna stared at her feet for a few seconds, debating what to do next. "I guess we'll head back to town. I'll do a search on his vehicle and we'll cruise past the local diners. We might just be lucky."

"Okay, but I think we're chasing our tails." Kane followed her down the steps. "He doesn't have family, right? For now, this is his only home. Where would he go?" He took her hand and squeezed. "I think we should drop by the administration office and ask them to watch out for him. Ask them to call when he gets back and then we'll head out and talk to him."

Sighing Jenna nodded. "That works for me. We've got a ton of work to do at the office."

The receptionist was very forthcoming. She informed Jenna that he rarely went out, and when he did, he'd return carrying grocery bags. Most of the rooms had a bar refrigerator, coffee machine, and a toaster at least. Some of the students had a microwave. It wasn't beyond reason that he cooked in his room.

"Did you happen to see him leave today?" Kane leaned casually on the counter.

"I did indeed." The receptionist beamed at him. "He was carrying a crossbow and the thing that carries his arrows. He left about half an hour before you arrived. If you'd have dropped by and mentioned who you were looking for, I could have saved you some time."

"Okay, thanks." Kane looked at Jenna and raised one eyebrow. "I doubt he'd go hunting alone, I figure we try the crossbow range."

Eager to get going, Jenna thanked the receptionist and they headed back to the Beast. It was a short drive to the range and there was a surprising amount of people testing their skills. This time they went to the office to discover if Ripley had signed in and asked where he might be. They were directed to an area and walked along a narrow pathway behind the shooters. They found him some ways away, returning from collecting his bolts. As they approached, he stood staring at them. Straightening, Jenna walked up to him. "Bill Ripley?"

"First the FBI and now the sheriff." Ripley eyed them with suspicion. "What's on your mind?"

Jenna lifted her chin and stared him straight in the eyes. "We have reason to believe you were involved with the murder of three people in Stanton Forest near the Devil's Punch Bowl on Sunday last."

When the color drained from his face, Jenna reached for her cuffs. She required information, but anything he said needed to be recorded. "I'm holding you for questioning over the murders of Leo Kelly, Zoe Ward, and Ash Rogers."

"If you figure I killed all of them, you're crazy." Ripley turned as if to run and Kane clamped a hand on his arm.

"You're coming with us." Kane spun him around and Jenna cuffed him. "We can do this the hard way or the easy way." He took the crossbow from him and slung the quiver over his shoulder. "What's it going to be?"

"Okay, but don't damage my crossbow. I use it for competition and it cost a fortune." Ripley shook his head. "This is crazy, you know. You can't have anything on me."

It was an unusual statement for someone they'd detained, and Jenna exchanged a meaningful glance with Kane. Did Ripley know they didn't have any evidence against him? Everything they had was circumstantial. The shooters in the forest had been so clean, the attack was almost surgical. She had so many questions to ask him but held her tongue. At this stage of the investigation, everything had to be precise. Anything he said would only be hearsay and she couldn't risk losing a conviction for her impatience.

Once back at the office, they secured Bill Ripley in interview room one before going to the conference room to bring the other members of the team up to speed. Jenna looked around the expectant faces and listened with interest at Rowley's theory. In their absence everyone had been hard at work. "It will sure tie up a few loose ends if we can place Alicia Palmer in the team of shooters. Good work." She smiled at Rowley. "You sure deserve your personal day tomorrow." She stood. "I'll go down and interview him now. I'm anticipating he'll ask for a lawyer." She looked at Rio. "You'd better have one on standby or we'll be here all night. I believe Sam Cross is available for pro bono representation this week. I doubt Ripley can afford a lawyer."

"I'm on it." Rio stood and turned to her. "Can I have a word with you and Kane?"

"Sure." Kane stood and opened the door.

Jenna followed them into the corridor. "What's the problem?"

"Nothing really, but the press has gotten hold of the shooting involving Dave and wanted a statement. I told them that after pursuing a group of kidnappers, Deputy Kane came under fire. After taking a round in his vest, he returned fire, taking down five armed men. He was highly commended by the mayor and the DA for his bravery." Rio cleared his throat. "The mayor called when the initial news story broke and asked me to extend his thanks. He wanted to give you a medal. I'm not sure how you feel about that, so I left it hanging. I managed to side-step who was kidnapped. I said it would be too traumatic to name them."

Shaking her head, Jenna smiled at him. "Thanks, Rio. The press never ceases to amaze me. They're like dogs chasing a bone." She turned to Kane. "You good with this?"

"I really don't need the publicity, but as the town grows it's going to be inevitable." He shrugged. "Thanks, Zac."

Jenna stepped back through the door into her office. "I'm heading down to interview Ripley."

"I sure would like to sit in." Carter looked up from a laptop on the table. "I've been scanning Alicia Palmer's social media for the last few hours, and she sure loves hunting. All her images are about her kills and there's some pictures of a dog. I went through her list of friends but didn't find any family members. Most of the people on the list are from all over the world. In fact, I didn't find one friend from Black Rock Falls."

Jenna nodded. "So she was a loner. Maybe that's what pushed her into writing to Jimmy Two Cents. She was lonely and he enjoyed talking about hunting, the bloodier the better, no doubt."

"I'd like to observe, if that's okay?" Jo stood. "This guy seems so gothic and out of touch with the real world. It's as if he's living inside a video game. Did you notice the way he speaks, like he's a tough guy? He seems so angry."

"Maybe it's a defense mechanism." Kane shrugged. "It's getting late. We should get at it. Sam Cross doesn't enjoy being dragged out after six."

Jenna gathered a statement book and pen from the desk. She waved at the door. "I'll follow you down."

She turned to Jo. "This anger, it's unusual, isn't it? I mean if this is a psychopathic serial killer, we usually see cooperation and self-assurance. Ripley is hostile and smart-mouthed."

"See how he shapes up in the interview." Jo headed for the door. "Do you want me to throw him the odd question?"

Jenna smiled. "Be my guest."

THIRTY-SEVEN

Ripley gave Jenna a belligerent stare as they all filed into the interview room. Jenna switched on the recording device, gave the date and time, name of the suspect, and everyone present introduced themselves. She sat down opposite Ripley and placed the statement book on the table. "We would like to ask you some questions about a murder that occurred in Stanton Forest near the Devil's Punch Bowl on Sunday. Deputy Kane will read you your rights."

She waited for Kane to finish and looked at Ripley. "Do you wish to wave your right to an attorney?"

"No." Ripley's mouth curled at the corners. "Seems to me, it doesn't matter if you're rich or poor, Sam Cross or one of the other lawyers will be here."

"I'll go see if I can chase him down. Deputy Kane leaving the interview." Kane stood and left the room.

Usually when criminals requested a lawyer they'd sit and say nothing until their representation arrived, but as Jenna and the others headed for the door to wait outside, it seemed that Ripley had changed his mind. She looked at him. "Is there something you want to say before I stop the recording, Mr. Ripley?"

"How does all this work?" Ripley leaned forward on the table and took sips from a bottle of water.

Interested, Jenna sat down. "Do you mean the way we run the interview?"

"Nope." Ripley shook his head. "I mean if I did know something and didn't tell you, what would happen to me?"

"You'd be an accessory before the fact." Carter stared down at him. "Which makes you as guilty as the killer."

"I see." Ripley rubbed his chin thoughtfully. "I guess I need to talk this through with my lawyer."

When Jenna stepped into the corridor, Kane was coming down the stairs with Sam Cross. Samuel J. Cross, attorney at law, had become a prominent member of Black Rock Falls since arriving a few years previously and often didn't see eye to eye with Jenna. She gave him a cordial smile. "Bill Ripley is a college freshman, just eighteen years old, with no family members." She handed him the information on the murder. "We have reason to believe he's involved."

"Likely a good reason if you have detained him for questioning." Cross read the document and raised both eyebrows. "This hasn't made the press. How did you keep it quiet?"

"We try to keep murders under wraps for as long as possible to give us time to catch the bad guys." Kane leaned against the wall with his arms folded across his chest. "We know there's more than one person involved in this crime due to the evidence we found on scene. This kid is young enough to be influenced by someone. I'm sure a deal could be done to lessen his sentence if it gave us information on the others involved."

"I'll see what I can do." Cross looked at them all in one sweeping gaze. "I'm not sure I want you all in the room at the same time with my client. I don't want him intimidated by you into making a statement."

Pushing both hands through her hair, Jenna stared at him. "Very well but it will have to be me and Kane. As the arresting officers, we will be conducting the interview."

When Sam Cross entered the interview room, Jenna turned to Carter and Jo. "When we interview him, I'll turn on the intercom so you can listen. If we use our coms, you'll be able to feed me questions. Alternatively, if Sam Cross agrees, we can change places, but knowing him as I do, he won't give an inch."

"I'll go and get the coms." Carter headed for the stairs.

Twenty minutes later, the buzzer on the door sounded, indicating that Cross had finished speaking to his client. Jenna led the way inside and sat down. "Is your client willing to speak to us?"

"Yeah, but he is under advisement not to say anything to incriminate himself." Cross lifted his gaze from his legal pad and frowned. "From the information you have given me, you don't have enough evidence against my client to keep him in custody. Unless you have something pertinent to the case to question him about, I can't see the reason for this interview."

As usual, Sam Cross' attitude made her hackles rise. "If we'd collected enough information to charge him with murder, it would be in front of a judge now. The only way we can get information is by speaking to your client. If he is as innocent as you profess, then he can walk free from here and we'll never bother him again."

"Okay." Cross turned to Ripley. "Answer the questions truthfully but remember my instructions."

After starting the recorder and the videotape, Jenna glanced down at her notes. "Were you in the vicinity of the Devil's Punch Bowl on Sunday last?"

"No." Ripley's fists clenched and unclenched on the table before him.

Jenna waited for him to continue but he said nothing. "Do you know Leo Kelly, Zoe Ward, or Ash Rogers?"

"Yeah, you know I do, so what?" Ripley stared at her. "We went to the same high school and took some of the same lessons. They weren't what you might call friends."

"Today we spoke to you on the crossbow range." Kane leaned back in his seat taking a casual pose. "I was told by the range manager that you are one of the top six in the current competition. Do you meet socially with any of the other shooters?"

"Socially? As in going out? Nope." Ripley narrowed his gaze. "I see them at the range. They are my competition, so of course I know them. I'm on a team with Alicia and Jesse Davis. At the moment, we're leading the competition. Although all three of us are in different events, we get sponsorship from Guns and Ammo as a team." He sighed. "Geoff Bannister, Carl Harper, and Lonnie Barlow are our main competition. I know many of the other shooters. We chat sometimes or nod to each other, but I don't have a strong friendship with any of them."

"So, Jesse Davis was lying when he told us the three of you go hunting?" Kane drummed his fingers on the table. "He actually said Alicia was never happier than when she was up to her elbows in blood."

"Yeah, we went out once or twice, but I have only two hunting bows. They have a multitude of bows." Ripley shrugged. "Bows get damaged in the forest just by carrying them around. For me it's not worth the risk."

Jenna had waited to ask one of the most important questions. It was a wild guess but acting as if she knew that Ripley had been calling Jimmy Two Cents, it might just get reaction. "But you do have a strong relationship with James Earl Stafford. From his incoming phone records, you call him at least twice a month and you're listed as one of his pen pals."

The reaction was instant, Ripley threw himself back in his seat, eyes wide with shock. "He told you it was me?"

"I think that's enough on that subject, Sheriff Alton." Cross laid one hand on Ripley's arm and stared at her. "I can't imagine what his relationship with a prison inmate has to do with this case."

Snorting, Jenna shook her head. "It has everything to do with this case, Mr. Cross." She turned her attention back to Ripley. "I know you discuss hunting, but you were really planning murders, weren't you?" She looked at Sam Cross. "Stafford has a code. He gets his followers to call or visit him and everything he says anyone listening would assume they were discussing hunting, but he's really planning a murder. He recruits people to murder in his stead. It's been done before. We just had to discover how he was doing it."

"That's not enough evidence to charge my client." Cross shrugged. "The DA won't proceed with a prosecution. Your evidence doesn't hold water."

As information filled Jenna's ear, she glanced at Kane. From his expression he had heard the same information. She turned back to Sam Cross. "I'm sure I don't have to inform your client that Alicia Palmer was also a friend of Stafford. She started as a pen pal and graduated to visiting him at the prison. She was found murdered, and on searching her house, we recovered cross bow bolts containing human DNA. A piece of material found at the Devil's Punch Bowl murder scene matched her jacket. I will be holding your client in custody until the results are in. I will also be seeking a search warrant for his room at the college and will be taking his bow and quiver into evidence for scientific analysis."

"You don't have probable cause." Cross was making hurried notes.

"Yeah, we do." Kane leaned forward. "One, he is a friend of Alicia Palmer, who we have reason to believe has used her crossbow on a human. Secondly, he admits to going hunting with her, and thirdly, they are both involved with Stafford. As the murders follow his MO to the letter, we have more than enough probable cause to get a search warrant and hold him pending further investigation. I will be arranging for him to be taken to county."

"I'll be interested to see this evidence." Cross stood and looked at Ripley. "If you're innocent, you have nothing to worry about. Sheriff Alton won't manufacture evidence against you. Right now, all you can do is wait. I'll be reviewing the evidence if and when it arrives and be in touch. Do you have anyone I need to contact?"

"Nope." Ripley shook his head as if resigned to his fate. "Just get me out as soon as possible."

"I'll do my best." Cross looked at Jenna. "I expect you to feed my client. He will have missed dinner by the time he arrives at county."

Jenna nodded. "That's a given. Innocent until proven guilty." She stopped the recording. "Mr. Ripley, Deputy Kane will take you down to the cells and arrange transport to county. It's more comfortable down there and I'll have dinner sent down for you. Any allergies I should be aware of?"

"Nope." Ripley was subdued as if all the life had been drained out of him. "I want a bloody steak and fries and a soda."

Jenna waited for Kane to escort him out and turned to Sam Cross. "Alicia Palmer was brutally murdered. It was as if someone really hated her. From what I've heard about her, she was a dominant person. I am concerned about what influence she had over Ripley."

"I appreciate you giving me that information." Cross gathered his things and headed for the door. "If it's true, it won't help him. If he was involved in the first murders with Alicia Palmer, he could have easily murdered her to keep her quiet. I'm sure you've considered that scenario because I don't see you hauling in the third member of the crossbow team. Why is that?"

Tucking the statement pad under one arm, Jenna nodded. "He is on our list of suspects with the members of the other team. They all move in the same circles. They also cross over to hunt with each other. The only time they're on separate teams is when they compete. We know this to be true as all of them, apart from Ripley, admitted hunting together at one time or another. They also admitted to hunting with many of the members of the crossbow club, but at this time we're just concentrating on sharpshooters, as the murder in the forest was very accurate."

"It will be interesting to follow your investigation." Cross stood to one side as Jenna used her card to access the door.

Outside, Kane waited for her with Jo and Carter. She smiled at them. "I was surprised he admitted to knowing Stafford. I'm sure Ripley is involved. Now we need to concentrate on finding the third shooter. I figure it has to be one of the four remaining suspects and not one from a lesser team. Two come to mind. The way Bannister acted concerns me, and Barlow was seen in the area. I figure we shake them down again and see what falls out."

"Right now, the third shooter believes he is in the clear." Jo folded her arms and leaned against the wall. "Whichever one it is will be feeling confident he's gotten away with murder. He knows Alicia is dead and for sure as hell he won't be contacting Ripley. He'll be too smart for that."

Jenna nodded. "What do you suggest?"

"Go over the interview notes again and see if we missed anything and then we hit them again tomorrow, same as before. At work." Jo straightened. "Maybe tell them Ripley is in custody and singing like a bird. Then see how they react."

Jenna smiled. "That works for me."

THIRTY-EIGHT

FRIDAY

Taking a personal day during an investigation was pure luxury and the guilty feeling deep down inside Rowley refused to abate. He sat on the family room floor playing with twins Vannah and Cooper as Sandy cleared the breakfast dishes. He looked at his children and sighed. "You sure you don't want me to come to playgroup with you? It sounds like fun."

"You work long hours every day, and during cases, seven days a week without a break." Sandy came to the door, staring at him and shaking her head. "If Jenna rosters off her deputies, it's to keep you all fresh. You know darn well the moment she has the killer in her sights, she'll call you in for backup."

Giving each of his twins a hug before getting to his feet, Rowley nodded. "Yeah, I know she will. I'd better take the satellite phone with me. I just feel guilty for enjoy myself when everyone else is hard at it."

"Stop tearing yourself apart, Jake. Jenna will be fine. Don't forget she has Jo and Carter helping out. You said yourself that it was quiet in town. If there hadn't been a murder, you'd all be sitting around twiddling your thumbs." Sandy put her arms around him. "Go and bag a few turkeys. It's been some time since we've been able to fill the freezer."

Reluctant to tear himself away from her, Rowley collected his crossbow and quiver. "Okay, I'll see what I can do."

"I think you should take this in the truck with you." Sandy handed him his service belt and weapon. "I know you figure you can take anything down with that crossbow, but you should have a backup weapon just in case something happens."

Rowley lifted up the leg of his jeans to display an ankle strap holster. "I never leave home without it." He smiled at her and took his service belt. "I'll lock it in the truck, just in case Jenna calls me for backup."

"Where are you meeting your friend?" Sandy walked into the kitchen to grab his backpack. "I've packed enough food for two." She followed him to the front door, down the steps, and to his truck.

"On Stanton in the forest warden's parking lot." Rowley smiled. "He called the forest warden yesterday to get the open areas. Apparently, there's a mess of turkeys in the forest on the west side of the ravine."

"Okay, stay safe." She pushed up the rim of his Stetson to kiss him. "I'll see you when you get back."

He dumped his gear into the back seat and climbed behind the wheel. Moments later, he hit the highway. The wind whistled through the open window, sharp and cold but invigorating. He sucked in lungfuls of mountain air, and the excitement of going hunting sizzled through him.

Twenty minutes later, he turned into the forest warden's parking lot. Surprised to see so many vehicles, he found a space and collected his gear. He'd pulled on his backpack and had his crossbow in hand when he heard a familiar voice. "Ah, there you are. Sorry I'm late."

"I'm early." His friend grinned. "Do you know your way to the hanging bridge over the ravine? I noticed most of the other hunters are heading to zone three. We'll have zone two to ourselves, even though it is farther away."

Rowley had been involved in searching that area many a time, chasing down serial killers and finding mutilated bodies. A shiver went down his spine but he shrugged it off. Nothing was going to spoil his day. "Yeah, I know the way and I'm glad we're hunting alone."

He'd worn his special orange hunting jacket. The liquid Kevlar-lined armless jacket had been a gift from Wolfe. His friend never ceased to amaze him with the strange inventions he devised for their safety. He didn't know where he managed to get some of the equipment but thought it better not to ask, knowing that both he and Kane had been in the military. Wolfe had insisted the jacket would withstand a bullet or arrow but wouldn't turn him into a superhero. He smiled at the memory and pulled up the zipper against the cool mountain breeze. He glanced at his friend. "Ready?"

"Lead the way." His friend waved him toward the trail.

Their boots crunched on the dry brown pine needles as they headed through the dense forest. Rowley followed the swirling river for a time, disturbing a white-tail doe drinking her fill on the riverbank. Her dark brown eyes blinked at him for a few seconds before she turned tail and bounced into the forest. He rarely hunted deer and never killed a deer or elk cow. It didn't seem right somehow. In the distance he noticed the orange flashes of hunters as they moved in different directions through the tall endless pines. The forest renewed itself each year and after the melt bright green patches of new growth abounded. Sandy always came to his mind when he walked past wildflowers scattered among the green tufts of grass. She loved to collect wildflowers in the forest, but bringing the twins anywhere where cats and bears prowled was never going to happen. He stopped walking and leaned his crossbow against a tree to take a drink bottle from his backpack. His friend was usually talkative. Most times he couldn't shut him up, especially when it came to hunting. They'd been out many a time to fill their freezers for the winter. "You're quiet. Something on your mind?"

"Nope. Just enjoying the solitude." His friend took a deep breath. "I've been hunting with friends who never stop talking. It's like they want to frighten the game away with their chatter." He pointed ahead. "There's the bridge. Man, I haven't been this far up the mountain for years. My pa brought me here. I must have been five, taught me how to field-dress an elk. I figure the smell stays with you forever."

Raising his eyebrows, Rowley stared at him. "At five years old? Really? Did you have nightmares?"

"Me? No." His friend flashed him a wide grin. "I've always loved hunting."

Sure he wouldn't be taking his son hunting at five, Rowley replaced his drink bottle and shrugged into his backpack and picked up his crossbow. "I guess by now you've seen it all. I was raised on a cattle ranch and would have thought processing murder scenes would be a breeze, but I spewed most times. I'm better now. After watching Sandy deliver the twins and changing diapers, I don't spew so much."

"What's the sheriff like?" His friend sipped water from an aluminum flask. "She's a real babe. Ever made a move on her?"

Astounded by his friend's question, Rowley held up his left hand. "I'm married and so is she."

"I know you're married, but it was just you and her for a time." His friend chuckled. "Don't tell me you didn't think about it."

Shaking his head, Rowley stared at him. "First, she's probably eight years older than me, and secondly, she's my boss. She may look all sweet and innocent but she's one tough lady. She never backs down and fights like a lioness. Trust me, I've seen her in action." He lifted his chin. "I never once looked at her in that way. She's more like my sister."

"Oh, I hit a nerve." His friend walked ahead of him along the trail to the rope bridge. "Shame she's married. I wonder why she didn't take her husband's name? Is he an old guy? I never see her with anyone but her partner out on patrol."

Amused Rowley snorted. "The big guy?"

"Yeah." They'd reached the flattened-out section before the bridge and his friend was breathing heavily.

It had been a steep climb but Rowley's daily visits to the dojo before work kept him in top shape. He stood beside him staring at the bridge. "That's Dave Kane, her husband. Unless you want to die a horrific death, don't go there. He's kinda protective of her."

Rowley moved closer to the beginning of the bridge and peered down the ravine to the rushing water fed by the waterfall. The old rope bridge had been there for as long as he could remember. It looked rickety and swung gently in the breeze. The slats had many repairs. The gray squares nailed over cracked planks to strengthen them resembled a random line of Band-Aids. He glanced at the sign that warned not to cross if the bridge was damaged and to contact a number to report it. Turning to look at his friend, Rowley smiled. "The turkeys are on the other side, right?"

"Yeah." His friend had removed his backpack and was rummaging through it. "I'll need my gloves. That rope looks nasty."

Nodding, Rowley pulled a pair from his pockets. A habit of carrying them on his person came from years as a deputy. He never knew when he might walk into a crime scene and leather gloves were better than none at all. He pulled them on but his friend was still wasting time. He sighed. "If that's a delay tactic to make me go first and test if the bridge is safe, it worked." He smiled at him. "I don't have a problem with heights."

After attaching his crossbow to his backpack, he took hold of both sides of the top of the rope bridge and stepped out. The bridge swung almost nauseously back and forth, back and forth, like a ship battling the waves. He took his time, stepping carefully from one rung to the next and sliding his hands along the top rope. By the time he made it to the center the wind tore at his clothes and whipped his Stetson from his head. He watched in dismay as it spun on the air before landing crown up in the swirling water below and surfing down the river. Underfoot moss covered each of the slats in a lacy green design sparkling with diamonds of water drifting from the waterfall with each gust of wind. He looked up ahead of him. It seemed such a long way to the other side. The bridge dipped in the middle, making the climb upward on the slippery slats difficult. He stopped to take a breath and turned to look over one shoulder at the sound of chopping. In horror, he gaped at his friend chopping madly at the ropes.

In a heart-stopping slide, the slats beneath his feet vanished as one side of the bridge gave way. Hanging by one hand, Rowley stared at the man he'd once called a friend. He was grinning at him like a demented monkey and waving the ax as if planning to cut through the other rope. Fear gripped him as his fingers threatened to slip and send him to an agonizing death, crushed on the rocks or drowned in the river. Anger and sorrow at never seeing Sandy and the twins again flashed into his mind. She'd always worried a serial killer would murder him. Maybe she'd been right.

THIRTY-NINE

Tendons and muscles tearing under his weight, Rowley swung like a pendulum, sucking in deep breaths. Terror gripped him and his heart threatened to tear from his chest as he looked down at his dangling feet. The bridge had opened up like a candy wrapper and, arm shaking with effort, he swung his feet onto the wooden edge of the bridge. The moment his boots hit the slippery wooden slats, he stretched out his other hand and grasped the rope. Gasping with effort, he took his weight on his legs, easing the pain from his shoulder. Shocked and confused, he clung to the bridge, resting his arms. If he wanted to survive, he'd need to climb. Dragging in deep breaths to keep his nerve, he stared across the ravine at his friend's wild expression.

Why did his friend want to kill him? He'd made many friends at the crossbow club and didn't compete, so he found it hard to believe he'd be a threat to anyone. Hair soaked from the persistent spray from the waterfall, he blinked away the rivulets of water streaming down his face and raised his voice over the roar of water. "Why are you doing this?"

"You should have fallen to your death." His friend spoke to him through cupped hands. "You couldn't make it easy for me, could you?" He turned to look behind him, searching the forest as if making sure no one was around.

Fighting rising panic, Rowley sucked in deep breaths. Kane had taught him many techniques for remaining calm and he swallowed his fear. Concentrating on his situation, finding a solution, and setting a goal would calm his terror. Kane insisted it was the key to survival. Sandy and the twins' faces filled his head. He gritted his teeth against the pain. *I must get home to my family.* Unless his so-called friend intended to cut through the other side of the rope bridge, it might be possible for him to climb hand over hand along the attached side of the rope to the other side. Brushing the water from his eyes on one sleeve, Rowley stared at the man for some moments, trying to determine his next move. Without warning, his feet slipped on the wet mossy planks and he clung on for dear life, feet hanging over the ravine. His heart picked up, racing in his chest. Right now escape seemed impossible. As he dragged his legs back onto the plank, his friend was watching him closely, ax swinging from one hand.

Fighting rising panic, Rowley glared at him. If his friend cut the remaining rope, he'd send him swinging to the other side of the ravine to crash to his death against the rocks. Trying to keep calm, he turned his head and scanned the area about halfway down the side of the ravine. It might be the best place to land. The area was well-covered with tangled vegetation and not a sheer rockface like some of the ravines in the area. If he looped the rope around both arms and rode the bridge like a swing, the chances of survival would be slim. Bounce off and he'd die on the rocks or drown in the river. He tightened his grip, determined to survive.

The answer came in seconds as the sun caught the glint of the metal ax head. Fighting waves of panic, Rowley braced himself as his friend attacked the rope. He watched in horror as the rope frayed. A twanging sound came across the noise of the falls as it snapped and leapt into the air before falling into the ravine. Legs flying out behind him, he swung in a giant loop, rushing toward the edge of the ravine at breakneck speed. He'd planned his move, and heart in his mouth, he let go with one hand, and as the bridge hit the side in a bone-shattering thump, he wrapped one arm around a sapling and slid off the bridge. The torn wooden structure bounced away from the edge. Seconds later it slammed into his back. In the shock of impact, he lost his grip with one hand and slipped down the sapling. Desperately grasping at wet foliage, he slid and slithered back to his perch. Behind him, wooden slats rained down into the ravine to be carried away on the bubbling river. Someone must have been watching over him, as his boots slid into footholds. Panting, he hung there with the remnants of the bridge behind him.

Teeth chattering with shock, Rowley looked left and right. Above him the ravine bulged out, making climbing impossible. To his left, a narrow ledge maybe ten yards away. Gathering his courage, he moved step by step, gripping the small bushes and other vegetation growing along the side of the ravine. His fingers trembled as he tested each bush. Without warning one came away by the roots, sending loose soil tumbling down the side of the ravine. He cried out as pain shot through his injured shoulder. Legs wiggling like a dying spider over the ravine, he dug deep and dragged up his aching body. He wrapped his other hand around a sturdy sapling and in one last push slid onto the ledge. Trembling with exhaustion, he dragged off his backpack and grabbed a bottle of water. After drinking it down, he pushed the backpack and crossbow to one side. Totally exhausted, he rolled onto his back just as a crossbow bolt bounced off the rock where his head had been. The elation at making it this far melted like snow in summer. Now the jerk was trying to shoot him.

The distance and wind factor would make accuracy difficult, but it wouldn't take his friend long to adjust his aim. Determined not to make it easy for him. He wriggled into the shadow against the side of the ledge and pressed himself into the vegetation. Water dripped onto him and an icy chill from the soaked rock seeped through his jeans. His hand trembled as he searched his pocket for his phone. He needed help but wanted so much to call Sandy. Swallowing the grief of never seeing her again, he gritted his teeth, determined to get back to her. He had two people on speed dial, Sandy and Kane. He hit Kane's number and didn't move as bolts slammed into the ground around him. As Kane answered, a bolt smashed into his arm just above the elbow. He choked back a sob as unbearable pain shot through him. "Kane, just listen. I'm under fire. On the west side of the rope bridge at the top of Bear Peak Falls. Jesse is trying to kill me. I've been hit in the arm. I'm stuck on a ledge below the bridge. He's on the opposite side firing his crossbow."

"Stay on the line." Kane was explaining the situation to Jenna. *"It's Jenna. We're on our way. You said, Jesse? Your friend Jesse Davis? Did you have a fight?"*

He could hear running footsteps, Kane issuing orders. Rio responding. More footsteps, doors slamming, and finally the distinct sound of the Beast's engine roaring. He only needed to survive another hour. He shook his head at the absurdity. That wasn't possible but he refused to go easy and wiggled backward, getting his head deeper into the vegetation and using his backpack as cover. His right side was exposed and his right arm useless. At least, he wouldn't bleed to death. The bolt had passed through muscle and protruded out the other side. He could only make out a slight trickle of blood, but from the agony, it had chipped the bone on the way through. More bolts zipped past him. How many more could Jesse be carrying? Surely, he'd run out soon. "No fight, Jenna. I figure he's the third member of the kill squad and I'm next on the list. Go figure, I thought he was a friend."

"Hang in there. We're heading for the chopper." Jenna sounded out of breath. *"Keep talking to me, Jake."*

Before he could reply, a bolt slammed into his calf and he couldn't bite back a cry. Jesse was using him for target practice. Trembling in agony, he gripped the phone closer to his ear. He so wanted to speak to Sandy one last time, but he'd never put her through the trauma of hearing him die. Dizziness gripped him and his vision blurred. His injuries weren't fatal, perhaps he was going into shock.

"Talk to me, Jake." Jenna's voice came in his ear. *"Is he still shooting?"*

Taking a deep breath, he pushed out words through chattering teeth. "Yeah, his backpack must be filled with bolts. His shots are getting closer. I've taken one in the arm, and one in the leg. It's only a matter of time before he hits a vital organ, Jenna. If I don't make it, tell Sandy I love her."

FORTY

Heart pounding, Jenna took the stairs to the roof of the medical examiner's building two at a time. With the phone pressed to her ear, she'd listened with horror at Rowley's desperate situation. In front of her, Kane and Wolfe ran up the steps, arms filled with gear. On the roof Carter was making final preparations for takeoff. The four of them would be going in the chopper. Jo and Rio would be heading to the forest warden's parking lot. She figured Jessie Davis would eventually return to his vehicle in hope of escaping. She burst from the dim stairwell out into the brilliant sunshine and, suddenly dazzled by the light, paused for a few seconds to get her bearings. Blinking, she hurried to the FBI chopper. "We're boarding the chopper now. I won't be able to hear you, but don't worry. We've taken your coordinates from your phone. Hang in there."

"Copy." Rowley's voice sounded weak as he disconnected.

Strapped in, she turned to look at Kane and adjusted her headphones. He was wearing his combat face. Jenna touched his arm. "He is still alive. We'll get to him on time."

"I mean to." Kane checked his harness and pulled on gloves. His determined expression eased some of Jenna's concern.

"Carter, swing over the shooter's position. If he's still there, I'll need to disable him."

"Copy that." Carter took the chopper high into the air, and moments later they were flying over the tops of pine trees.

The distinct rock formation known as Bear Peak stood out before them, dark against the brilliant blue sky. Jenna couldn't make out the falls and the ravine. Beside her, Kane stood and, taking his rifle, stretched out on the floor of the chopper beside the open door. The chopper descended slowly, the wind from the propellers swirling the pines in all directions. The chopper waved back and forth in the wind, sliding Kane perilously close to the open door. She made out Rowley's orange hunting jacket on a ledge halfway down the ravine and turned to scan the opposite side, searching for any movement.

"I see him." Kane was using the scope on his sniper rifle to search the opposite side of the ravine. "Hold it as still as you can."

The shot rang out, loud even with the headphones, and just inside the tree line, a man carrying a crossbow dropped to his knees. Incredulous that Kane had managed to make the shot, Jenna turned back to him. "He's down." The man crawled forward and dragged himself up using a tree. "You didn't kill him. He's mobile."

"I didn't intend to kill him. Shoulder, through and through." Kane got to his feet, laid his rifle across the seat. *"He won't be shooting that crossbow for a time and I figured we needed answers."*

"Hang on, folks, I'll take her back up." Carter's voice came through her headset. *I'll need to drop you down onto that ledge from above. The wind gusts are strong here, so you'll need to be careful."*

"Copy." Kane attached his harness to the rope winch. *"I'm ready. Let's do this."*

Jenna stood and stepped into a harness to assist Wolfe with

the rescue stretcher. Her heart picked up a beat as wind whistled inside the cabin. The chopper swayed back and forth until it evened out high above the ravine. Trying not to show her fear as Kane dropped over the edge and grabbed the spinning stretcher, Jenna held her breath as he rode it down. She moved to the open door and clipped her safety harness onto the bar. Taking a deep breath, she leaned out to watch his descent. Gusts of wind twisted and turned him, swinging him back and forth like a pendulum. Every second, his momentum threatened to smash him against the side of the ravine.

Concerned about the severe bruising he'd suffered from the bullet hitting his vest, Jenna chewed on her bottom lip. Kane wouldn't be at full strength. No matter how many times he'd protested all was well, she'd seen him flinch in pain lifting the equipment. Beside her, Wolfe was watching the drop from the open door and making sure the lines ran freely.

"He'll be okay." Wolfe flicked her a glance. "He's functioned well with bullet wounds, Jenna. As long as he's not losing too much blood, he can block out the pain. Like all of us, he can bleed out, but that bruise won't slow him down."

Surprised, Jenna stared at him. "How did you know what I was thinking?"

"You show it in your eyes." Wolfe leaned out of the chopper door, peering below. "It's something you need to work on. If I can see it, so can he. I've told you before if you want to keep him safe, don't become his Achilles heel." He kept his attention on Kane below, but his voice was coming loud and clear through the headphones.

"Yeah." Carter's voice flowed into her ears. *"I've never known him to run slap-bang into a situation like he did when those guys kidnapped you. No backup. If he wasn't wearing the liquid Kevlar vest, you'd be a widow."*

Annoyed and glad Kane couldn't hear the conversation, Jenna snorted. "That wasn't my fault. Trust me, I didn't have time to look at him. He's been like that since the day we met. It's not the first time he's put his body on the line to save me. It's what he does, but yeah, I'll try and avoid looking at him before a mission. I don't need him worrying about me." She hadn't taken her eyes off Kane. "Even if watching him risk his life makes me sick to my stomach."

Below, Kane swung and twirled in the wind, caught in great gusts of moisture from the falls. Jenna could see the slickness of the rope. The chopper climbed higher, sending Kane rushing toward the edge of the ravine. Transfixed, Jenna stared, helpless to do anything as he descended closer to the swirling river. One mistake and he'd smash into the rocks. Terrifying minutes dragged by, before Kane came alongside the ledge and, hanging in midair, slid the stretcher onto the narrow ledge. The wind howled around him, preventing his attempts to get Rowley onto it. There just wasn't enough room. Rowley tried to cooperate with Kane, but it was obvious he couldn't move. When Kane looked up at Wolfe and gave a hand signal, Wolfe replied with a thumbs-up. "What's happening?"

"Rowley is critical. Kane will have to use force to get him onto the stretcher. It's gonna hurt."

Sick to the stomach, Jenna white-knuckled the bar as Kane planted his feet on the ravine wall. His feet slipped on the soaking moss-covered rocks and he took a few seconds to regain his balance before trying again. Jenna held her breath as he grabbed Rowley and rolled him toward the rock face. He swiftly shoved the stretcher alongside him. After pausing a few seconds, as if speaking to Rowley, he took hold of his injured arm and leg. In one swift movement, he dragged him toward him, lost his footing, and dropped. Caught in the harness, he swung and twisted wildly. Petrified for his safety, Jenna bit down hard on her bottom lip, too terrified to speak. Shaking his head, Kane dragged himself back to the ledge and gripped the stretcher. On the ledge, Jenna could make out Rowley's contorted face as Kane slid him into place. After securing him, he signaled to Wolfe. Heart in her mouth, Jenna stared as they dangled over the ravine. Moments later Wolfe flipped the switch and the pulley spun into action, winding in the rope. As they ascended, Kane gripped the stretcher in an effort to keep it from spinning. She could see him talking to Rowley as they climbed steadily back to the chopper.

Jenna kneeled and clung to the bar beside the door, ready to help Wolfe pull the stretcher inside. The moment it slid across the floor, Kane tumbled in beside it, rolling on his back and breathing heavily. Wolfe slid the door shut. Crawling to look at Rowley, Jenna bit back a gasp. Five crossbow bolts were embedded in his body. Two in his arm, two in his leg, and one in his hip, all along the right side. He was sheet white and groaning in agony. In seconds, Wolfe was beside him examining him. He gave him a shot and Rowley's eyes fluttered shut. "Is he going to be okay?"

"Carter, call the hospital. Tell them to get a theater ready. We need an orthopedic surgeon, stat." Wolfe looked at Jenna. "He'll live, but he's banged up. We won't know to what extent until they do X-rays. There may be bone as well as soft tissue damage. You'll need to call Sandy and his folks. He'll be in surgery for hours."

The next moment Kane was beside her, lifting her to her feet. He unclipped her harness and pushed her into a seat. When he dropped into the seat beside her and pulled on his earphones, she smiled at him. "I'm glad Jake had you down there saving him." She took his hand and squeezed. "I don't know anyone else who could have gotten him off that ledge."

"Me either." Carter's voice filled her ears. "There was no way down from above. You were his only chance, Dave."

"I figure we make a good team." Kane grinned. "Maybe we should think about joining search and rescue."

Jenna glared at him. "Over my dead body."

"*Nah.*" Carter chuckled. "*We have enough danger to occupy our lives. In any case, we're always here if needed.*"

"*You're so easy to tease, Jenna.*" Kane squeezed her hand. "*Do you honestly believe I'd give up being your deputy? It's never gonna happen.*"

FORTY-ONE

As the FBI chopper passed overhead, heading in the direction of the hospital, Rio and Jo slid into the bushes along the trail. They'd taken up a position adjacent to the forest warden's parking lot where they could keep Jesse Davis' vehicle in sight. They'd waited for some time, surrounded by damp leaves and the smell of animal urine, picking insects from their exposed skin. A couple of hunters had walked by without noticing them, and confident that Davis wouldn't see them on his way back to his truck, Rio had relaxed to wait him out. When a hunched-over a man wearing a hunting jacket and carrying a crossbow came cautiously along the trail, pausing every few steps to peer between the trees to the parking lot, it didn't take them long to recognize Davis. They waited until he was adjacent to them, and Rio stepped out of the bushes. Jo closed in behind, holding her Glock in both hands and aiming center mass. "You're injured." Rio indicated toward Davis' shoulder. "Hunting accident?"

"It's nothing. Don't worry about it. Anyway, I can take myself to the hospital." Startled, Davis' eyes widened as Rio drew his weapon. His Adam's apple moved up and down as he swallowed hard before darting a look over one shoulder at Jo. "Why have you drawn down on me and what's the FBI doing in the forest on a Friday morning? I haven't done anything wrong."

"We're looking for you, Mr. Davis. I figure you've been having a fine old time in the mountains." Jo shrugged, holding her weapon as steady as a rock. "It's come to our attention that you were using Deputy Rowley as target practice out near Bear Peak. You see, Jake isn't just a deputy, he's a friend, and Deputy Rio here doesn't take too kindly to people roughing up his friends. You're sure lucky I'm here to ensure your safety. You come along quietly now and we'll have someone take a look at your shoulder."

To Rio's surprise, Davis lashed out at him with his bow, knocking his weapon from his hand. Lunging forward, Davis pushed Jo to one side and tried to make a break for it. Reacting on instinct, Rio took chase, reaching him in seconds. He grabbed him by the arm and spun him around to face him. As Davis shaped up to fight, Rio aimed a punch to his kidney and Davis bent over, groaning in agony. The next second, Jo came up behind them and pressed the muzzle of her weapon to Davis' temple.

"Move again. Go on, I dare you." Jo ground the weapon into his flesh. "You lowlife piece of garbage. Just give me an excuse."

As Davis wilted before him, Rio straightened. This man was a typical coward. As he took a step closer, Davis shied away as if avoiding another blow. He looked at Jo and smiled. "Nice work." He retrieved his weapon and held it on Davis.

"You won't let her kill me." Davis looked at him wild-eyed.

"Oh, please do." Jo moved closer. "You're still armed, Davis. It would be a righteous kill."

"Much as I'd like to see her splatter your brains, unfortunately I have a sworn duty of care to take you to the ER and I like to do things by the book." He smiled. "The book also tells me I can shoot you as a suspected felon if you aim that crossbow at us again. Drop it."

"By the book, huh? You won't shoot me in cold blood." Davis' eyes shifted from side to side and his hand tightened on his crossbow. "You can't, can you? I know the law."

Rio indicated with his chin toward Jo. "She will. Drop the crossbow. Are you carrying any other weapons?"

"Go to hell." Davis spat on the floor. "I didn't do nothing."

"Drop your weapon." Jo's eyes flashed with anger. "It's over. Are you too darn stupid to understand? Do you want me to spell it out for you? Drop it now, before I take out your kneecaps, and right now nothing would make me happier."

To his surprise, Davis complied. He leaned the crossbow against a tree and indicated to a hunting knife in his belt. Rio holstered his weapon and moved closer. The man's rank sweat mixed with the odor of stale blood filled his nostrils. "FYI Agent Wells wants to take you down, so don't try anything stupid." He gloved up and patted him down, removing the knife and dropping it into an evidence bag he carried in his pocket.

"Now what?" Davis looked belligerent but there was fear in his eyes. "You gonna say I ran, so she can take my head off?"

So they'd made the right impression. Sometimes a little intimidation worked wonders with men like him, but Rio understood him too. The first chance Davis got he'd try to kill him. He snorted. "I'm tempted."

"Deputy Rio will read you your rights and we're taking you to the sheriff's office for questioning." Jo moved closer. "Deputy Rowley was a friend of yours. Why did you try to kill him?"

"That's a crock of lies. He walked into my line of fire, is all." Davis shrugged and then smothered a moan and grasped his shoulder. "Shit happens." Sweat beaded on his forehead. "I'm in pain here. I need to get to the ER." He stared at Jo. "I didn't shoot Jake."

"Okay, fine. That's not what he's saying, and as your

crossbow bolts are embedded in him, I'm sure our medical examiner will be able to extract your DNA from them." Jo shook her head slowly. "Out of interest, who shot you? That isn't a crossbow injury."

"I have no idea." Davis straightened. "Some maniac. I'm wearing orange, it's plain to see. I figure someone shot me on purpose."

Rio read him his rights and cuffed him. As they escorted Davis to the cruiser, his phone rang. Tossing his phone to Jo, Rio settled Davis in the back seat. They stood some ways from the cruiser as Jo put the phone on speaker, and they listened together. It was Jenna. Anger spiked when she explained Rowley's condition. Jo's eyes narrowed as she stared at Davis. "We'll take Davis to the ER. Once he's cleaned up. We'll take him back to the office. How long will you be?"

"They've taken Rowley into surgery. Sandy and his folks are on the way. Wolfe is going in to observe and he'll give us an update ASAP. We'll be leaving here soon. It will be hours before we know and I want to interview Davis. Have you read him his rights?"

Rubbing the back of his neck, Rio moved closer to Jo. "Yeah, but he's denying everything. Do you want me to ask him if he wants a lawyer."

"It would save time. Don't discuss the case with him until we get him into the interview room." Jenna's footsteps came through the speaker. *"I want everything recorded. He's not sliding through the net. He must be our third shooter and I want to know what motivated the group of them to go around killing people. Was Jimmy Two Cents the instigator? We need to know."*

Nodding, Rio took back the phone. "Copy. We'll get him patched up and back to the office." He disconnected and looked at Jo. "I went through this guy's background and so did Kalo. What did we miss? He had a privileged upbringing, raised on a cattle ranch, which he now owns. What could possibly turn him into a serial killer?"

"I guess we're going to find out." Jo shrugged. "Why is a psychopath like a book?"

Rio smiled. "I dunno."

"They both have a story to tell and can be fact or fiction." Jo smiled at him. "I mean to discover everything I can about Jesse Davis. He doesn't like authority figures, which makes me believe his story goes way back to his childhood."

FORTY-TWO

Everyone was dead on their feet by the time they'd gotten back to the office. Jenna had ordered a ton of takeout from Aunt Betty's Café and Wendy had delivered it. Everyone needed to eat and she wanted to touch base with her team before she moved onto Jesse Davis. At the moment, he was spending time in the interview room speaking with Sam Cross. She dragged off her gear and stowed it in the lockers. After washing her face and hands, she composed herself. Seeing Jake Rowley, face ashen with bolts protruding from his young body, was one thing. Explaining what had happened to Sandy had been terrible. It was Sandy's worst nightmare and when she'd arrived at the hospital surrounded by her family, Jenna had hugged her. "I'm so sorry this has happened."

"He was so excited to go hunting." Sandy had wiped away tears. "Wolfe called me before he went into surgery, he said to stay positive but the bolt in his thigh might be a problem. If that can be removed without causing more damage, he'll make a full recovery. Thank the Lord, Wolfe gave him the liquid Kevlar hunting vest. One of those bolts in his torso could have killed him outright."

When Jenna called Rio and discovered they had Davis in custody, she'd headed back to the office with Kane and Carter via the ME's roof. Smothering a yawn, she made her weary way to the conference room and, grabbing a cup of coffee and something to eat, dropped into a chair. She listened to Rio and Jo about the arrest of Jesse Davis. "So, he was playing the passive side. That's not what I expected. I didn't believe we were dealing with a psychopath, but looking back at his interview, he was very confident and sure of himself. I've seen them change in a split second but the concern I have is that these murders didn't seem like the work of a serial killer." She looked at Jo and then to Kane. "You both have insights into a serial killer's mind. Doesn't this behavior sound almost cultlike? I can't get it out of my head that Jimmy Two Cents has some hold over these people. I'm sure Bill Ripley is one of the three in the forest murders. If Alicia Palmer was involved, and DNA from one of the victims from the forest murders is on her crossbow bolts, we'll know for sure. Emily will call the moment the results are through."

"It sure looks that way to me." Kane brushed crumbs from his fingers. "They had too much information about his crimes. He's involved but how he had so much hold over three people is mind-blowing. I mean you can't hypnotize someone to kill. I'd like to know how he did it."

"Likely coercive persuasion." Jo sipped her coffee and looked at him over the rim of her cup before replacing it on the table. "There are many ways of what we used to call brainwashing people." She glanced at Carter. "I'm sure you and Carter suffered loud noises, deprivation of liberty, and other methods used to condition special forces. That is one type of conditioning out of an entire list. I could go on all day explaining, but looking at our three probable killers, I'd say Jimmy Two Cents first read their letters to determine suitable candidates. He obviously knows how to manipulate people. Over time, he established control over the subjects' social environment by isolating them or selecting loners. They'd be the most vulnerable. He'd know they don't have a support team or family to go to, so they became dependent on his friendship and approval."

Intrigued, Jenna listened with interest. "So how did he make them kill for him?"

"Obviously, when they showed interest, he rewarded them by sending details of his murders to them via another prisoner, by word of mouth most likely." Jo sighed. "As he works in the library, slipping notes inside books would be easy. He'd give his contacts inside rewards, as we've already discussed." She turned her cup around with her fingertips. "In his case, he'd promote social isolation, so he would have influenced the forming of the crossbow team members. He'd likely selected the three of them a long time ago. Don't forget he has years to plan ahead. He has little else to do inside jail. So he'd keep this group as isolated as possible. They all knew about each other and most likely competed for Jimmy Two Cents' admiration. The control comes with a rewards and punishment system. They'd be expected to complete a task to his satisfaction. Remember they are all reliant on him now, so if he refuses to speak to them, they would be devastated and want to do more to please him next time. Hence the teamwork killing the kids in the forest. I'd say, he punished the person who used two shots to kill Leo Kelly. To gain his favor, that person was asked to kill Alicia. As one of the group, this would be an ultimate test of devotion. Next, the random unrelated murder of Miles Nolan. Now he has his puppet killer." She shrugged. "Which one is it? Bill Ripley or Jesse Davis?"

Blowing out a breath, Jenna stared at her. "So even after Davis tried to murder Rowley, the leader might be Ripley? I'm sure glad we locked him up." She glanced at the clock. "Although, if we don't come up with some solid evidence against him in the next twelve hours, he's going to walk."

"If Davis hadn't attacked Rowley, we'd be out reinterviewing the suspects again." Kane shook his head slowly. "I'd never figured Jesse Davis for a killer. He doesn't seem the type to be under some type of mind control. He's social, goes hunting with different people, runs a successful ranch with many employees. He doesn't fit the profile you've explained, Jo."

"I've thought about that too." Jo stood and went to the counter to refill her cup. "I don't believe Alicia Palmer or Bill Ripley are psychopaths. They fall into the mind control profile, but as Jenna suggested, we need to consider that Jesse Davis is a psychopath. Untriggered until he met Jimmy Two Cents. Profile him as one and he ticks all the boxes."

Jenna's phone chimed. It was Emily Wolfe. Jenna put the phone on speaker and raised a hand to stop the conversation. "Hi, Em, what have you got for me?"

"The results on Alicia Palmer's crossbow bolts came back. We discovered human blood and tissue on one of them and ran a cross-match on the forest victims. We got a match. There is no doubt the bolt killed Ash Rogers, one of the forest murder victims. All the bolts were examined for trace evidence. The only other DNA we discovered was from Alicia Palmer. Her prints were also all over the crossbow and bolts." Emily paused. *"I ran a test on Jesse Davis' hunting knife, as it was the same type that killed Alicia Palmer. I found human blood traces. Norrell blood-typed the sample as type AB negative. The same as Alicia Palmer. We're running it through the DNA sequencer now. AB negative is quite rare, so the chances his knife killed her is high without the DNA evidence. We're running tests on Bill Ripley's bolts as well. I'll call you the moment any information comes through."*

Punching the air, Jenna grinned at her team. "That's awesome, thanks, Em." She disconnected. "We have ammunition for our interview." She looked at Kane. "We are so gonna nail this guy."

FORTY-THREE

Jenna walked into the interview room, made all the necessary preliminaries before the interview started, and then looked at Sam Cross. She had given him the DNA results and other damning evidence. "Has your client agreed to speak to us?"

"I've mentioned to my client that as he can't escape the charge of attempted murder of a law enforcement officer, it would be in his best interests to cooperate in the hope of a deal for leniency." Cross leaned back in his chair, for once looking defeated.

Encouraged by the news, Jenna nodded. "I'll speak to you about the murders in the order they occurred. The three kids in the forest, why did you murder them?"

"I didn't murder them all." Davis stared at Kane. "Why did you shoot me? You knew darn well you had the FBI and a deputy waiting for me to return to my truck."

"You were aiming at Deputy Rowley. You're lucky I wasn't aiming for your heart or head." Kane leaned back in the chair and blew out a breath. "Stop avoiding the questions. We know Alicia Palmer was involved. She neglected to clean her bolts.

Who killed her? Was it you? You do know we have Bill Ripley in custody? Was it him?"

"So many questions." Davis ignored Kane and stared at Jenna. "I get a deal if I talk, right?"

Shrugging, Jenna tapped her pen on the table. "I'll inform the DA you cooperated. Any deal will be his decision. I can't give you promises, but if you come clean, I'll do what I can." She flipped open her statement book. Ripley hadn't said a word, but she had Davis right where she wanted him. She needed to make him believe they knew everything that had occurred. "We have DNA proof that Alicia killed one of the victims in the forest and we already have a detailed statement about your involvement from Ripley. He sung like a canary, but we'd like to have both sides to the story on the record."

"Three at once was neat, wasn't it? That was Bill's idea. Did he tell you that? Ah, you are so hard to read, Sheriff." Davis clasped his hands on the table. "He'd known those kids since grade school and they dissed him at a party at the end of semester. Zoe called him a geek freak and the other two pushed him around some. He wrote to Jimmy asking him how he should deal with them. When I called Jimmy, he suggested we go hunting together. He insisted we take Alicia along for the experience. So we did."

Jenna listened intently "How did he instruct you? Did he have a code?"

"Yeah, he'd refer to people as animals, and how to kill them. Other stuff, using the coins under the eyes to freak out you guys, came from other people. Strangers most times. They just dropped by and told me stuff and I passed it on to the others." Davis' lips curled up at the corners. "He's a genius."

"Did you kill Alicia?" Kane leaned forward.

"Yeah, I had to. Alicia spewed all the way back to the range. She wanted out." Jesse Davis pulled a face of disgust. "She called Jimmy and told him she wouldn't go see him again. She hated him for making her prove her loyalty to him. He used to call her his little bear. He told me to take her down and make her pay."

"How did he relay that instruction to you?" Kane's attention was riveted on him.

"He told me to go and hunt bear and make it messy. I did what he wanted." Jesse smiled as if he was telling them he just washed his socks. Not a care in the world. No empathy and zip emotion.

"Just like that?" Kane stared at him. "She was your friend."

"I don't have friends. I have acquaintances." Davis shrugged. "It was her fault. She didn't need to go apeshit and yell at Jimmy. He was as mad as hell and she had to pay. We all have to pay in the end, right?"

Needing more information, Jenna cleared her throat. "How did you know when Zoe, Leo, and Ash would be in the forest?"

"Bill." Davis smiled. "He overheard them planning to go fishing and what time. We just holed up and waited for them to arrive. After, when the feds went to see him, I told him to lay low for a time. I wanted to handle the kills myself anyway. I didn't like sharing."

Jenna glanced at Sam Cross, but he just nodded at her to continue. "So, you decided to kill Miles Nolan. Did you have a reason or was it a thrill kill? What had he ever done to you?"

"Not me. I didn't choose him." Davis shrugged and then winced and rubbed the bandage on his shoulder. "Jimmy had a beef with his pa because he refused to give Jimmy a loan. He works at the bank in town. Jimmy wanted him gutted and left to die. I guess, payback is a bitch." He stared directly at Kane. "Before you ask. Killing him was a rush but it meant nothing. Just like when you shot me. You know the feeling, right? No remorse."

After seeing Kane's hackles rising, Jenna gave him a meaningful glance and returned to her notes. "How did you find

Nolan? Nobody knew he'd be in the alleyway at that time of night."

"Ah, that was freaky." Davis stared into space as if reliving the moment. "I had a choice, him or his little brother. The kid brother was difficult. He didn't go out alone after dark. Miles, well, I was driving along Stanton deciding how to get to one of them and noticed someone climbing out a window of his house. It was like fate, you know. Nolan ran along the sidewalk just as I drove past. I stopped and watched him. He headed down an alleyway, so I drove around the block and walked back. I figured he was cutting through, using the alleyways to get somewhere." He smiled. "I walked straight up to him and gutted him. He didn't see it coming." He wet his lips as if savoring the memory. "He just wouldn't die, so I stabbed him in the heart. I didn't want anyone walking by and him telling them who'd cut him. Jimmy wanted me to field-dress a young buck and leave him lie. He loved the story when I told him." He sniggered and wiped the end of his nose. "That was when Jimmy suggested I go pig hunting. He hates cops. I thought about you or the female fed but there was no way I could get either of you alone. When Jake Rowley mentioned he had Friday free, I couldn't believe my luck. It was like... I needed a cop and he just walked up and volunteered. It was perfect. I suggested we go hunting. I didn't have a beef with Jake. I just needed to kill a pig, is all. He was convenient." He opened his hands as far as the cuffs would allow. "You know the rest."

Shaking her head, Jenna stared at him. She had all the proof she needed to take him down and Bill Ripley. A DNA match from Bill Ripley's bolts would seal his fate. "Why did you kill for James Earl Stafford? What hold did he have over you?"

"No hold." Davis gave her a long hard stare. "He's my pa. I wanted to make him proud."

EPILOGUE

SUNDAY, THE FOLLOWING WEEK

It had been another busy week, tying up loose ends in the murder case. Bill Ripley's bolts had traces of Zoe Ward's DNA, and after being confronted by the information and Davis' confession, Ripley made a deal to give evidence against his friend and Jimmy Two Cents. It seemed that Jimmy Two Cents would be losing his inmate trustee privileges and be charged with his involvement in the crimes.

To everyone's relief, Rowley was home from a week stay in the hospital. He would be remaining at home for five weeks to recover before he started physical therapy. To make sure he was mentally okay, Jenna had asked Jo to go and see him, to have a talk about what had happened rather than send him for a psych test. She'd reported back that, in her opinion, he hadn't suffered mentally during his ordeal and mentioned how well Kane had prepared him for the situation. Kane being Kane had hired Rowley a ranch hand for six months to help out. The young man was looking for work between rodeos, so it worked out fine for everyone.

Sunday at home was a luxury Jenna enjoyed. It was their time together. They went riding or just lazed around watching

TV, but this time, Jenna sat beside Kane as they roared up the highway to visit the res and their good friend Atohi Blackhawk. The talk of puppies was a hot topic and they weighed the pros and cons of taking one home. When they arrived at the res and made their way to Blackhawk's cabin, Jenna noticed a boy sitting on the steps playing with a toy truck. She bent to smile at him. "Hello, I'm Jenna. Is Atohi at home?"

The boy looked up at her and his golden eyes startled her. It was like looking into the eyes of an eagle.

"He'll be along soon. He said you'd be coming." The little boy slipped his hand into hers and smiled. "Are you my mommy?"

Before she could reply, Blackhawk walked onto the stoop. She smiled at him. "Morning. It's good to see you again."

Beside her Duke went into his happy dance at seeing Blackhawk. The dog's entire back half wiggled and his thick tail windmilled with excitement. When Blackhawk bent to pat him, Duke licked his cheek, something she'd only ever seen him do to Kane.

"Are you my daddy?" The little boy looked up at Kane and grinned. "You are big and strong like a bear. I think you must belong to me. I am big and strong."

"You are indeed." Kane ruffled his hair and grinned at him. "That's a fine truck you have there."

"This is Tauri." Blackhawk looked straight at Jenna and his dark brown eyes twinkled as if he was carrying a secret. "His eyes are remarkable, don't you agree? His name means 'young eagle.' He has only recently arrived and is staying with me." He indicated to an outbuilding. "The pups are in the barn."

The small hand was warm and dry against her palm as Tauri led her to the barn. His hair was dark brown with streaks of gold like sunlight through a forest. The child mesmerized her and she caught Kane staring at him. She wondered why he'd asked about his parents but didn't like to ask Blackhawk. It wasn't her place to pry. As they stepped inside the barn, the smell of fresh straw, horses, and puppies greeted her. She moved closer and, in a rush of wet noses and wiggling fat bodies, the puppies rushed to the edge of the stall. The mother, still heavy with milk, stood and looked up at her and yawned. Jenna lifted up Tauri so he could see. "Oh, they are beautiful."

"Will the bitch see Duke as a threat?" Kane picked up Duke and let him see the puppies.

"Nope." Blackhawk smiled. "They are good friends. Before you decide on a pup, come inside, I would like to talk with you. I have fresh coffee brewing."

Concerned something might be wrong, Jenna nodded. "Sure." She followed Blackhawk back to the house.

Inside, Blackhawk's mother smiled at them and hurried out the door, taking Tauri with her. Jenna sat at the kitchen table as Blackhawk poured coffee. She exchanged a glance with Kane, who shrugged. She hoped all was well. "Is something wrong?"

"Not exactly." Blackhawk sat at the table and met her gaze. "It's Tauri. He doesn't want to be here. He says we're not his people, but it's obvious he carries our blood. He has a mysterious background and was delivered here by a social worker as his last hope. He has no parents and has been tossed from one foster home to the other since birth. He looks six but is only four. He can use a computer, and videocall on a smartphone. He is way ahead of any child I've ever seen. He insists his parents are coming here today." He indicated to a calendar on the refrigerator with days crossed out. "He started that when he arrived." He sighed. "This morning he packed his backpack and has been sitting on the steps watching the road."

"Where did he come from?" Kane frowned. "What's his background?"

"His mother identified as white. She gave birth at home and died shortly after. She had no ID and was buried as a Jane Doe." Atohi frowned. "No one claimed him. It took them four years to discover the mother owned artifacts from our tribe, but we don't know of her family. Her line is untraceable but a neighbor said she wore a silver bangle many years old and went by the name of Laura. After the birth, she must have known she was dying and laid the bangle in his crib. It had the name Tauri engraved inside and that is what they called him. When they came to us, they made it clear, we take him or he faces a life in foster care. His father is unknown to us, but we used his DNA to conduct a search. We have discovered a name, her father was in the military, and I understand Wolfe has connections and perhaps Carter. You might be able to convince them to help us find his family?"

Jenna nodded. "Of course, we'll help. What information do you have?"

"Only one name on a family tree database but our search ended there. It is a very distant relative." Atohi slid a piece of paper across the table. "Annie Parkes. This lady was searching for her family tree. She opened an account in DC and then vanished. I found an obituary for her last week. She was our only hope. The boy refuses to settle here or accept us as his family."

Shocked, Jenna stared at Kane, who stood and walked out of the room. The name scrawled on the scrap of paper was the name of Kane's wife who'd died in a car bombing along with his unborn son. There could be no doubt. Blackhawk had listed her parents and grandparents.

"Oh, I have upset you." Blackhawk covered her hand. "It was not my intention." He glanced at the door. "Dave is acting strange too. Do you know this woman?"

Jenna shook her head. "Me? No. I've never met her." She swallowed the shock. She needed to speak to Kane. "Dave might have but he was injured in a gunfight last week. He probably just needs to stretch his legs. I'll go talk to him."

When she walked outside. Kane was sitting with Tauri and

then he picked him up and showed him the Beast. When he was through, he placed the little boy into Blackhawk's mother's arms and walked toward the barn with Jenna. She looked at his face. His expression was a mixture of confusion and joy. "Talk to me, Dave."

"Annie's folks are dead. I'm her only living next of kin. There's no one else, Jenna." Kane rested his hands on her shoulders. "That boy is the only living part of her left on this earth. It may be from a hundred years ago, who knows, but with all the woo-woo you believe in, don't you think that the planets aligned or something to bring us here today to meet that child?"

Jenna swallowed hard. "You want to adopt him? You're not saying this because you figure he'll replace the son Annie was carrying, are you?"

"No, not at all." Kane pushed a hand through his hair and then cupped her cheek. "I know you want our baby but maybe someone up there has given us a compromise. That little boy needs a home and we desperately want a child. We'd need to foster him first and go through the hoops before they'll allow us to adopt him, but being law enforcement officers I think we'll be okay. We also have Atohi to assist us regarding his cultural heritage. I'm sure he'll want to be involved." He gave her a long look. "Just think about it, okay? No pressure." He turned and walked away.

Jenna stood leaning against the stall, with the puppies snuffling behind her. She'd come for a puppy and was now contemplating adopting a son. She shook her head. *Contemplating* was the word. Usually so decisive, she stared out the door as Kane disappeared inside the house. She walked across the dusty yard and took the steps. A small hand slipped into her own and she held it gently and looked into intelligent eagle eyes. Her heart swelled as if she'd made an unbreakable connection. "I guess we'd better go inside."

In the kitchen, she nodded to Kane and he leaned forward

and kissed her. She sat at the kitchen table pulling Tauri onto her lap. The little boy leaned into her as if he belonged. She bent to smell his hair. The scents of sunshine and the forest filled her nostrils. She looked at Blackhawk, whose eyes danced with happiness, and smiled. "I think Tauri belongs to us."

A LETTER FROM D.K. HOOD

Dear Reader,

Thank you so much for choosing my novel and coming with me on another of Kane and Alton's thrilling cases in *Their Wicked Games*.

If you'd like to keep up to date with all my latest releases, just sign up at the website link below.

www.bookouture.com/dk-hood

I'm often asked how I come up with the storylines in my books. The truth is, I don't really know. If I get an idea, I write it down in a notebook, and an entire story can come from one sentence I scribbled down five years ago. The thrilling/frightening parts are often challenging. I go through my mind thinking what would scare me the most or what terrible situation I might face and how would I cope. The serial killers come from watching and researching the real deal. Parts of each of them came from knowledge I gained along the way, mixed up into a cocktail of despicable human.

I know readers love my characters and I love them too, and developing their stories along the way has been very enjoyable... even if I have to ruffle their feathers sometimes.

If you enjoyed *Their Wicked Games*, I would be very grateful if you could leave a review and recommend my book to your friends and family. I really enjoy hearing from readers, so feel free to ask me questions at any time. You can get in touch on my Facebook page or Twitter or through my blog.

Thank you so much for your support.

D.K. Hood

http://www.dkhood.com
dkhood-author.blogspot.com.au

facebook.com/dkhoodauthor
twitter.com/DKHood_Author

ACKNOWLEDGEMENTS

Many people work in the background to publish my books, so many thanks to Team Bookouture.

Thank you to Susan Sanchez Purvis, Barbara Stamper, Tara McPherson, Marj Ward, Christopher Wills, Tara Hanley Stapledon, Joanne Hurley, and Chelle Brown for their ongoing support and friendship.

3-24
cmw

Made in the USA
Monee, IL
09 June 2023

35522367R00149